ONE FOOT IN THE GRAVE

A Lenny Moss Mystery

By Timothy Sheard

HARDBALL PRESS

THE REVIEWERS PRAISE LENNY MOSS!

This Won't Hurt A Bit
"Things get off to a macabre start...when a student at a Philadelphia teaching hospital identifies the cadaver she is dissecting in anatomy class as a medical resident she once slept with. Although hospital administrators are relieved when a troublesome laundry worker is charged with the murder, outraged staff members go to their union representative, a scrappy custodian named Lenny Moss, and ask him to find the real killer. Since there's no merit to the case against the laundry worker to begin with, Lenny is just wasting his time. But Sheard ...makes sure that readers do not waste theirs. His intimate view of Lenny's world is a gentle eyeopener into the way a large institution looks from a workingman's perspective." —*New York Times*

Some Cuts Never Heal
"This well-plotted page-turner is guaranteed to scare the bejesus out of anyone anticipating a hospital stay anytime in the near future." —*Publishers Weekly*

"Sheard provides...polished prose and elements of warmth and humor. Strongly recommended for most mystery collections." —*Library Journal*

A Race Against Death
"While most shop stewards do not get involved in murder mysteries, they solve tough problems at work every day. Now they can look up to a fictional role model—Super Steward Lenny Moss." —*Public Employee Press*

"Timothy Sheard provides a delightful hospital investigative tale that grips readers from the moment that Dr. Singh and his team apply CPR, but fail." —*Mysteries Galore*

Slim To None
"In Slim TO None, you won't be the only reader to say 'Yes, Lenny should have an action figure in his likeness!'" —**Sue Doro, *Pride and a Paycheck***

A fast-paced mystery with more than enough twists and turns to keep you turning the page! —**Grace Edwards, author of the *Mali Anderson Mysteries*.**

No Place To Be Sick
"Does such a wonderful job of showing workers uniting to fight for justice that...unions have used Sheard's books for steward training. Find out if Lenny & his friends win their battle in this roller coaster of a story." —***Union Communications***

"There's enough suspense, fear and chills running up and down your spine to make you keep on reading it in one fell swoop. Watch your back if you're alone in the house!" —***Pride & A Paycheck***

Someone Has To Die
"The setting, characters and dialogue are so realistic, you feel as though you have walked down the halls of James Madison Hospital and met the folks who work there... This is a book about working people who..draw deep down on a reserve of strength and intelligence tha enables them to stay afloat amidst a rising tide of social and economic waves of adversity." —**Bill Hohflied, *Labor Press***

"Lenny does it again! Another corpse. Another murderer. Another management's cruel calamity of ignorance. But this time, add some incredible union organizing to cheer about. Then give Brother Moss and his friends a shot of decent bourbon for keeping us on the edge of a certain hospital death bed." —***Pride & A Paycheck***

Published by Hard Ball Press.
Information available at: www.hardballpress.com
ISBN: 978-1-7328088-3-6
Cover art by Patty Henderson
www.boulevardphotografica.yolasite.com.
Exterior and interior book design by D. Bass

Library of Congress Cataloging-in-Publication Data
Sheard, Timothy
One Foot In The Grave: A Lenny Moss Mystery/Timothy
Sheard
      1. Philadelphia (PA) 2. Hospitals. 3. Lenny Moss.

For Wanda, Diana, Felix and Francesca

I ain't got it right yet, but I'm working on it,
That counts for something.
—Chris Sheard

Nurse Catherine Feekin felt the kick inside her belly and smiled. Placing a hand on her humpy belly, through the powder blue scrub suit she felt the little one stirring.

"I knew it was a boy even before they did the ultrasound, the way he was kicking up a storm inside me," Catherine said as Mimi, the nurse on the day shift took a seat beside her at the nursing station.

"I dunno, my daughter kept me awake many a night," said Mimi. "She is kind of a tomboy, though, truth be told."

"Lord a' mighty, what a night we had. Four admissions, two transfers from the ICU and an MIA. I don't know how my poor feet held up these twelve hours, and us working short every night!"

"Oh, jeez, who went missing?" said Mimi. "Was it old Mister Pruitt, he's been cursing the doctors, demanding they discharge him even though his leg wound is still purulent as all get out and his blood sugars are off the chart."

"No, it was Missus Price. Security found her in bed with a stroke patient on Seven North. The supervisor went ballistic when she found out, like it was my fault an Alzheimer's patient went and eloped. I'd asked for an aide for a one-to-one to watch her, but the nursing office said they didn't have anyone they could spare."

Covering the GPS communication unit that was suspended around her neck, Mimi dropped her voice to a whisper to prevent the dispatcher from hearing. "Same old bull crap from Mother Burgess. We're down six nurses and they won't even give us an extra aide." She pulled out a blank sheet of paper and clicked her ballpoint pen, ready for report.

"Miss Barry even threatened me with mandatory overtime. I told her I was dead on my feet, how could I stay over until noon?"

"That is crazy," said Mimi. "Did you refuse?"

"I couldn't. The last nurse who refused mandatory O-T was fired for abandoning her patients. In the end they decided to just leave you short, like always."

Turning the page of her notebook to begin report, the night nurse opened her mouth to speak, hesitated, closed her mouth. Mimi could see the fear in Catherine's eyes. "What is it, Cath? What's wrong?"

Catherine struggled to hold back her tears. "I walked the dog before coming to work tonight."

"Okay..."

Catherine fought to hold back her tears. "Since the Zika outbreak, Louis has been walking her, he doesn't want me to risk getting bit. But he had a job interview, and it ran so late and the dog was crying..."

"But you don't have to get bit, Catherine, you have insect repellant, don't you?"

"That's just it," said Catherine, her voice quavering. "I was in such a hurry, I had to get to work. I ran out with the dog without spraying on the repellant. I didn't get more than a block when the mosquitos started biting. I had to wait for Ginger to do her business, and by the time I got back I was covered with mosquito bites!"

"Oh, Cath. Maybe they weren't carrying the virus. It's not like every mosquito is infected."

"Hey, it could be worse, right? You're well into your third trimester, there shouldn't be any danger of congenital defects now."

"That's not what Doctor Auginello says. He says the virus can affect the brain development even after the baby is born!"

Catherine resumed her report, but when before she could finish, she broke down crying once more. Mimi did her best to comfort her friend.

"Why don't you go to the ER, they could give you an anti-viral medication. That should give you some protection, shouldn't it?"

Catherine wiped her eyes. "The drug is contraindicated in pregnant women, remember the in-service? I can't take it." She put her notebook in her purse and slowly rose from the chair. "God, I wish I didn't need this job. Louis was laid off again, we really need the paycheck."

As the exhausted night nurse waddled off to the lounge to change her shoes and fetch her purse, Mimi remembered one of the many conversations she'd had with her co-workers about the RN's at James Madison needing a union. There had been sharp words, always with the hated GPS units switched off or placed in a drawer so the dispatcher couldn't hear.

The unit hanging from a lanyard around her neck suddenly squawked: "Patient in seven-ten requires assistance!"

"Okay!" Mimi answered. Under her breath she mumbled, "God forbid he'd tell me what kind of assistance."

Laying her report down on the station, she wrote an addendum on the bottom in large capital letters. TALK TO LENNY. Then she took a deep breath and headed to room 710.

Lenny Moss cursed under his breath as he plunged his mop into a bucket of soapy water. He was an ordinary looking man, not very tall, with black-rimmed glasses poised on a large nose, bushy eyebrows and a bald spot on the back of his head that his wife insisted was growing larger by the day. Not a handsome man, but a man with a kind face and eyes that could switch in an instant from impish to furious.

He ran the mop over the old, cracked marble floor in broad strokes, washing away a night's worth of spills and stains. It wasn't the work he had to do this morning that was annoying Lenny, although the day's extra assignment was reason enough to curse his housekeeping supervisor, Mr. Childress. It was the boss's unwillingness to supply him and his co-workers with bleach that had gotten under his skin.

Bleach. Sure, it could take out some of the color if he mixed too strong a solution and he splashed any on the furniture. But bleach was the best cleaning solution for killing viruses, and since the first hot, muggy days of a Philadelphia summer arrived, viruses were on everybody's mind.

Especially, Zika virus.

Setting out the yellow CAUTION WET FLOOR sign in the hallway, he stood a moment leaning on the mop handle as a troupe of doctors and medical students ambled down the hall toward him. The Attending physician was telling his team something, they were all watching him and not paying much attention to what was going on around them.

"Watch the wet floor!" Lenny called as the team approached him.

"Good morning, Lenny," said Dr. Auginello, chief of the Infectious Disease Division. "How is housekeeping this morning?"

"Crappy. Mister Childress doesn't want to release a gallon of bleach for me. He says we're 'degrading the environment' with it."

Dr. Auginello scowled. Turning to his team, he asked, "What is the most effective measure for preventing transmission of virus from patient to patient?"

"Good hand hygiene," said a young resident.

"Wearing a mask, gown, and gloves," offered a med student.

"All good precautions to be sure," said Auginello. "But the most effective preventive strategy is to continually clean horizontal surfaces. And why is that?"

The resident and student pondered the question, not sure where to take the discussion.

"When a patient sneezes. Or coughs. Or talks, they release clouds of droplets. And in those droplets are suspended millions of microorganisms. Once the droplets fall onto horizontal surfaces, we touch them with our hands and transfer them to our skin. So continuous cleaning of the environment with a strong antiseptic solution remains the most effective procedure for preventing horizontal transmission, and bleach is the most effective solution for killing virus."

When the medical student asked why the hospital wouldn't use the best product, Auginello said. "A strong bleach solution can be irritating to the skin and nasal passages, some patients complained about it. Patient relations is very sensitive to customer satisfaction surveys, our reimbursement depends on good scores."

Auginello promised Lenny he would see what he could do about securing some bleach. Then he led his team to the next patient on their rounds.

***

Roy Reading opened the rear doors of the ambulance

while his partner inside the van released the brake on the stretcher. Together the EMTs lowered the stretcher to the ground and began wheeling the patient up the long ramp to the Emergency Room entrance. A large stop sign on the door announced: FOR ANY SIGNS OF CNS INFECTION, STOP AT THE TRIAGE TENT. Under the direction of the Infectious Disease Division, the ER had stationed a tent just outside the entrance. There, a pair of nurses assessed anyone seeking admission to the ER with signs of encephalitis or paralysis, since the new strain of the virus, dubbed "Zika II," was showing a more aggressive infection of the nervous system.

Roy stepped into the tent and greeted the nurses. "Hey, guys, you keeping busy?"

"Is the Pope Jewish?" said the first nurse, who was cleaning the head of her stethoscope with an alcohol pad. "What ya got for us today, Roy, a nice clean stroke patient, maybe?"

"She's a frequent flyer. Asthma exacerbation. Her EKG shows some right heart strain, but nothing acute. Seems she ran out of her oral meds and her inhaler wasn't providing relief."

"Okay," said the second nurse. "No fever, chills, no itching mosquito bites?"

"Nope, she's clean, I checked her arms and legs. No bites."

"All right, you can take her in."

With a snappy salute Roy returned to his partner. Together they wheeled the patient through the automatic doors and into the busy Emergency Room. All the bays were full, with several overflow patients waiting on stretchers or in wheelchairs in the hallways. A tech with a phlebotomy tray was drawing blood on a patient while nodding his head to orders a doctor was calling out to him from across the hallway.

Delivering the paperwork to the clerk, who managed a smile for him despite her harried station, Roy and his partner transferred the patient to a hospital stretcher. A nurse took a brief report while the clerk printed out the admission sheet and an identification label for the wrist band. The nurse listened to the patient's breath sounds, determined that the patient was not yet in status asthmaticus—a life-threatening condition—and called to the tech to set up an inhaler.

"We'll get you sorted out in a squeak," she told the patient. "Just breathe slowly and let the medication help you. Okay?"

As the out-of-breath woman gave the nurse a thumbs up sign, the tech placed the inhaler over the patient's face and turned up the oxygen flow, releasing a medicated mist. The patient closed her eyes and lay back, waiting for relief.

Roy was standing outside a bay filling out his EMT report when he heard the familiar voice of a female physician coming from behind a curtain. The voice was asking the patient about his level of energy.

"Do you have trouble getting up and going in the morning? Do you drag yourself through the day?"

The patient behind the curtain confirmed he didn't have the energy he used to enjoy. He napped every day. Some days, he napped twice, it was very worrisome.

The female physician, apparently speaking to a student or intern, asked if he had ordered a thyroid panel and cortico-steroid study. Told that the lab work was pending, the doctor told the patient they would wait on whether to get a CAT scan until the results of the blood work were back.

Roy stepped away from the bay just as the doctor pulled the curtain back. Moving to the far side of the nursing station, he looked back to see the physician leading two assistants to a computer station, where one of them entered more orders as the female doctor watched. She was a handsome woman, with long dark hair tied up in a bun, revealing a round face that produced dimples when she smiled.

"Well," Roy mumbled to himself, "looks like Doctor Austin is an Attending now."

He joined his partner, who had thrown a clean sheet over their stretcher and was ready to answer another call.

"What are you smiling about?" said his partner.

"Oh, it's nothing. I just saw an old friend, she's made Attending. I haven't talked to her in years."

"Old girlfriend, huh? Guess you missed your chance to marry a doctor."

"Yeah, guess I did." Roy glanced back at the woman who had turned his heart to stone, then he followed his partner out the door thinking of different ways that he could hurt her.

3

Lenny had finished mopping the hallway when he saw Mimi coming toward him pushing her medication cart. The nurse did not look happy.

"Hey, Mimi, what's up, you look kinda down."

"I'm worried about Catherine, one of the night nurses."

"The one who replaced Anna Louisa?"

"Yes, that's her. She's pregnant and she got bit by a bunch of mosquitoes last night. She's scared big time that she was exposed to the virus and it will harm her baby, and on top of that, she had to care for a Zika patient."

"It's un-fricking believable. Our health and safety officer filed a complaint with the administration over the same issue. We don't want our pregnant workers caring for those patients."

"My, Lord, what a summer to be pregnant!" said Mimi. Taking hold of her medication cart along, she asked what time was Lenny taking his break.

"Nine-thirty, like always," he said.

Mimi held her hands out as if holding a needle and thread and pantomimed sewing a few stitches. Lenny glanced at the GPS unit hanging from the nurse's neck— the despised device that enabled a dispatcher to overhear anything that Mimi said. He understood she couldn't ask him out loud if he was taking his break in the sewing room, a favorite spot among several of the service workers.

"Uh, yeah, nine-thirty," Lenny confirmed, wondering what the nurse wanted to talk about. He hoped she wasn't in trouble. Without a union, the nurses were at the mercy of Mother Burgess, the Director of Nursing. Lenny remembered defending Anna Louisa, even though the nurse wasn't in the union, when she was accused of causing the wrongful death of a patient. That had been a dicey experience, one he had no wish to repeat, given all the issues he had to deal with defending his own union members.

Mimi winked at him and pushed her cart on down the hall, satisfied that Lenny understood she would be joining him for coffee in the basement. She stepped into the room of the Alzheimer's patient, who would not remember what Mimi did, and sent a text message to two of her nursing colleagues: MEET IN SEWING ROOM IN BASEMENT 9:30. IMPORTANT. Then she gave the Alzheimer's patient a dose of strawberry-flavored liquid medication and gently wiped her chin.

***

Donning a disposable yellow isolation gown outside room 712, Dr. Auginello said to his resident, "Tell me the history, Clive."

The resident, a short, chubby fellow with a Fu Manchu mustache and long hair tied in a knot, listed the patient's history of gout and diabetes, on an oral glycoside and a once-a-week injectable. The patient had previously been treated for one episode of bronchitis requiring long-term antibiotic therapy.

"Why was he admitted?" Auginello asked. "Most Zika cases are treated in the clinic."

The resident listed the patient's complaints of severe headache, dizziness, malaise, and difficulty walking. He worked for the city pruning trees and was not diligent about spraying his exposed skin with insect repellant.

"Zika may be the most likely etiologic agent, but a good diagnostician has to always consider other unlikely causes," he said, tying the string of the isolation gown around his waist. "I take it you found signs of mosquito bites?"

"Yes. He has multiple lesions that he scratched and are now erythematous."

"And he was admitted for possible Guillain barre syndrome?" The resident affirmed, the admitting doctor was worried about an ascending paralysis or some atypical form of encephalitis.

As Auginello pulled a TB mask from a box on the cart, the resident asked why the patient was on respiratory isolation. The ID Attending told him that the virus, dubbed Zika II, had undergone a surprising genetic shift. "The virus seems to have acquired new virulence factors that enable it to adhere to epithelial cells in the airway and lungs," he said, donning the mask.

Asked how that was possible, Auginello explained that the research was in the early stages. It's known that viruses and bacteria can share genetic factors that increase their virulence and increase their resistance to antibiotics. Our own DNA is permanently altered after a bacterial infection. We don't know how that effects our long-term health, only that you acquire new genetic markers directly from the infecting pathogen.

Auginello took a dollop of alcohol gel from a wall dispenser and rubbed it into his hands and wrists. "Now, the Aides mosquito feeds on wild birds as well as mammals, and we know that wild birds are reservoirs for a number of viruses, including influenza. Did the Zika virus mix with a flu virus? We just don't know, but we are isolating Zika patients with neurologic symptoms because those are the cases that have yielded virus in their sputum, not just in blood, semen and vaginal secretions."

The ID Fellow pointed out that only two cases of confirmed person-to-person transmission had been reported. Auginello responded that the demand to isolate Zika cases was coming from the hospital staff, especially from nurses to dietary aides.

"Their demand may be based more on fear than on good science," Auginello added. "But by the same token, if the virus continues to show an affinity for the pulmonary system, we don't want to confirm the transmission from hospital employees who acquired the infection."

Auginello knocked on the patient's door and led his team into the room, where they found a middle-aged man dressed in red pajamas sitting up in bed reading the Wall Street Journal. The man lowered the paper, saw the masked and gowned figures approaching, and said, "You fellows ought to rob banks, they'd never identify you with those outfits on."

Auginello reached out and shook the patient's hand. "That would be too risky an occupation for me, I'll stick with medicine, thanks." He explained they were the Infectious Disease team asked to consult on the case.

"I was tested for that nasty virus, but nobody wants to tell me anything."

"The initial test was positive," said the Attending. "You showed signs of neurological impairment, so we think it's best to keep an eye on you for a couple of days until we know how the disease will progress."

Taking a Q-tip from his lab coat, Auginello broke the wooden end off, leaving a sharp point, and asked the patient to close his eyes.

"Tell me if you feel sharp or dull," he said. The doctor poked the bottom of the patient's foot with the sharp tip of the stick.

"Uh, sharp, I think," said the patient. "No, dull."

Auginello switched to the soft cotton tip on the other end.

"Uh, dull, I think..."

The doctor poked the patient's calf.

"Sharp. Definitely sharp."

"Good." Auginello instructed the resident to note in the consultation sheet the level at which the patient's sensation became normal. He told the patient he would look in on him in the late afternoon, then led his team out of the room.

"Is it an ascending paralysis?" asked the medical student.

"Not necessarily," said Auginello, pulling off his mask and gown. "The patient is diabetic. Diabetes can cause peripheral nerve damage, resulting in loss of sensation in the feet. We will have to wait and see if the sensory deficit progresses up the legs."

With the team in tow heading toward the next case, Auginello reminded them, "When you hear the sound of hoofbeats, don't always think of horses." Punching the down button on the elevator, he added, "Or coconuts," referencing one of his favorite Monty Python movies.

4

Lenny knocked three times on the door to the sewing room and stepped inside, where he found his friend Moose Maddox seated beside Moose's wife, Birdie. Birdie was patching an old fitted sheet on her big industrial sewing machine.

"Yo, Lenny, I got your text, what's goin' on?" said Moose. A big man who had boxed when he was young, Moose had given up his boxing gloves for a pen and pencil, drawing hilarious caricatures of the bosses. And Lenny.

"Hey, Moose. Birdie." Lenny opened a battered metal folding chair and settled into the seat. He set his cup of coffee on the floor beside him and pulled a jelly donut from a paper bag. Taking a sizable bite from the donut, he said, "Mimi wants to talk to us, it looks like this Zika outbreak is freaking a lot of the nurses out."

"It ain't only the nurses that's freaking out," said Birdie, holding up the sheet to examine her stitches. She decided they were strong enough to put the sheet back into service, knowing the hospital was skimping on buying new linens. "I'm afraid t' go outside my house and come to work."

"The dietary workers are scared shitless," said Moose. "'Specially when they got to bring a paper tray in to one of the isolation rooms. They're scared they're gonna get the bug."

"I know," said Lenny, sipping his coffee. "The ID doc gave us that in-service about how to use the PPE's correctly. As long as we wear the protective gear, we should be safe."

"I don't think it's right," Moose said. "Our people aren't used to puttin' those masks and gowns on and off. Not like the nurses and aides. They the ones should be taking the trays into the isolation room, not us dietary workers."

"We tried to argue that with the risk management people,

but they wouldn't buy it. They pointed out that if the dietary department forces nursing to take the trays into the isolation rooms, it increases their risk of contracting the disease. I have to agree. We can't unload our risk by putting it onto another worker."

Moose grumbled but conceded Lenny's point. "You know what I can never figure, though?" Lenny had no idea. "How come you don't dunk your donut in the coffee? It was made to be dunked. Dunking is it's destiny."

"Destiny? What are you, some new age donut worshipper or something? I don't dunk my donut because I take my coffee black with no sugar. If I dunked, it would sweeten the coffee."

Moose looked at his wife and shook his head. "Purist," he mumbled.

Lenny was about to take another bite of his donut when he heard a gentle knock on the door.

"C'mon in!" Birdie called.

The door opened a crack. Mimi peeked in, saw Lenny and the others and opened the door wider, revealing two more nurses standing behind her.

"Okay if we all join you?" she asked.

"The more the merrier," said Birdie. She pulled three more folding chairs out and set them out for the nurses. As the nurses settled into their seats, Mimi introduced her friends, Agnes Sedley and Myung Kim.

"Are you sure the dispatcher can't hear what we say down here?" said Agnes. She was a middle-aged woman with thinning hair and a pale complexion that Mimi worried could be anemia but had never been able to get Agnes to talk about.

"The GPS units don't receive a signal in the basement," Lenny said. "They haven't installed the relay units, I guess because there's no patient care units down here."

Agnes tried calling the dispatcher. There was no reply. Provisionally assured, she turned to Mimi and said, "You called for this meeting, you start."

Mimi explained that the nurses had a long list of grievances that Miss Burgess had been ignoring for years: staffing shortages, mandatory overtime, the hated GPS units they were forced to wear around their neck as long as they were on duty, and those were just for starters.

"We're not even allowed to take the units off when we go to the toilet!" said Agnes. "It's very unfair!"

Mimi added that the dispatcher could tell if the nurse was doing number one or number two by the sounds they picked up.

"That's a clear invasion of privacy," said Lenny. "It borders on a Peeping Tom situation."

"That's just what we've been telling Mother Burgess!" said Mimi. "Not to mention that most of the dispatchers are men. They probably get off on listening to us pass urine, they sit in these little booths where nobody can see what they're doing with their hands."

"That is g'ross in the extreme," said Birdie. "I sure as hell wouldn't put up with some strange man listening to what I did on the toilet!"

"That's just it, we don't have anyone to speak for us," said Agnes. "We don't have a union, or even a professional association."

Miss Kim, petite and shy, looked up from her lap and added in a quiet voice that the hospital had a 'nursing best practice' committee that was supposed to recommend new and improved methods for delivering care, but whenever they brought up issues of staff safety or rights, they were told to take that to Human Resources.

"Human resources do not listen to us," Kim said. "I think they are the inhuman resources."

Mimi said, "We complained to H-R when a single mother was forced to stay over eight hours. Her daughter had to be picked up from the after-school program and she didn't have any family to take care of the child. But Human Resources told her if she refused to stay she would be terminated, and the Nursing Board would charge her with abandoning her patient. That could mean taking away her license!"

"But the worst part of it," said Agnes, "the hottest, most emotional issue is assigning a pregnant nurse to care for a patient on isolation for the Zika virus. I don't care what the CDC or the DOH says about there's no danger if we follow infection control procedures. I mean come on, they can't assign the patient to a girl who's not pregnant? How hard would that be? It is totally unfair."

Lenny told Mimi they had just been discussing whether a worker had the right to avoid a risky assignment if it meant putting another worker at risk. But given the special risk to the baby for this particular kind of isolation, he agreed, the pregnant worker should get a pass.

"So, what do we have to do to join the union?" said Mimi, gripping the hated GPS unit that she wanted to rip from her neck and toss in the trash.

Lenny looked at Moose, who leaned forward. "The first thing you got to do is understand, the bosses aren't gonna be too happy with what you're tryin' to do. You got to be careful who you talk to and where you say it."

"Could they fire us for organizing?" asked Mimi. "I really need this job."

"You have protections under the labor laws," Lenny said. "But I have to admit, the hospital would try and get around them, they could make up some fake charges they say have nothing to do with the union drive."

"We take a big chance," said Miss Kim.

"There are risks, sure, but without the union everyone is at risk, you can be fired for all sorts of bullshit charges. With the union, you'll be protected by the contract."

Moose added: "Some of the nurses won't like the idea being in the same union as us service workers. You would be in a separate division, with your own bargaining unit and your own union representatives, but you'd be expected to support us when we had a labor dispute, just as we would support you."

"I don't like the sound of that," said Agnes. "If we refuse to go to work when you are on strike, we could be charged with abandoning our patients. That would mean good-bye license."

"The union would inform the hospital before the walk-out, that would protect you from charges."

"And give them time to bring in temporary nurses that they hire and replace us all," said Agnes, the color in her cheeks rising.

Mimi looked at her two friends. "I know it's dangerous as all get out. But you know there's no other way we can get the hospital to get rid of these disgusting GPS units." She waited while Agnes and Kim looked at each other. "Well, are you girls in?"

"Hell, yes, sign me up!" said Miss Kim, surprising Mimi with her language.

Agnes hesitated. As much as she hated how the nursing office was treating her and the other nurses, she was not sure she wanted to be in a union with the service workers, she was a professional, they were all non-professionals.

After a moment of silence, Agnes said, "I don't know, I'm just not sure the nurses will accept joining the same union as the people we supervise. I mean, we don't always get along, you know?"

"Well then we'll just have to convince them," said Mimi, a look of stubborn conviction on her face. "Let's get real here, things can't get any worse than they are already."

"I wish that was true," said Lenny, "but as my dad used to tell me, things can always get worse. And they usually do."

5

Regis Devoe ran a powerful spray of water over the stainless steel autopsy table, flushing the body fluids and bits of tissue into the drain. A neat line of specimen containers sat in a Zip-loc bag with a large, red BIOHAZARD label on the front.

"I'll run the specimens over to the lab soon as I finish cleaning up," he said.

Dr. Leslie Fingers, James Madison's chief pathologist, signaled that was fine, no rush, there were no more postmortems scheduled. So far.

Glancing back at the young morgue assistant, the physician smiled to remember his doubts about hiring the hot-headed young man. Regis had been in trouble with his supervisor multiple times when he asked to transfer from the laundry to the pathology department, making the pathologist wary of hiring him. But when Lenny Moss recommended Regis for the position, Fingers took a chance, knowing Lenny did not give recommendations lightly.

"Oh, uh, Regis," said the doctor.

"Yeah, doc?"

"Have you thought any more about my proposal?"

Regis turned off the water and set the spray handle in its holder. "Yeah, I've been giving it a lotta thought. I'm interested, don't get me wrong, I'm just not sure I want to go back to school, school was never my thing."

"You will do quite well, I'm sure. But you need to let me know by the end of the week, registration closes next Wednesday."

"Okay, doc, thanks."

After seeing that the autopsy suite was clean and ready for

another case, Regis dropped the specimens in a little wheeled cart and headed for the labs. He was sorely tempted to take up the doctor's offer. After all, when was anyone ever again going to offer to pay his tuition to go to school for two years to become a pathology technician? It would mean better pay, something hard to turn down. If only he was sure he could stick with it and pass all those damn exams.

At the lab he handed the specimens to a tech and signed his name in the log book.

"What you got for us today, Re'ege?" asked the tech.

"Brain tissue, spinal cord and lymph nodes," said Regis.

Reading the label on the first specimens, the tech said, "Didn't you get the date of birth wrong? It looks like the patient was only..."

"Yeah, I know, he was one day old. It was a premie, died in the nik-u."

"Sweet mother of god," said the tech, gently putting the specimen down on her marble table.

"It's the first time I ever saw Doc Fingers tear up at autopsy."

****

As he stepped up to the Admissions Desk, Dr. Auginello tried to put on a smile for the woman seated there. The clerk had one phone line on hold and was telling someone on the other that she was doing the best she could, the ER was already boarding twelve admitted patients, where was she supposed to put them if she gave the neurology clinic a bed?

Finishing with her calls, she looked up at Dr. Auginello, one of her favorite doctors. "What can I do for you today, doctor? Just please don't ask me to pull a rabbit out of a hat!"

"Thanks, Molly, rabbits won't help me much right now. I'm just checking on how many isolation rooms are currently available."

"They're all full up. And we have a bunch more on isola-

24

tion with HEPA filters. Let's see, how many are there?"

Molly called up a program on her computer screen and went in descending order from the eighth floor down to the ER on the first. All of the isolation patients were designated by a red colored room number and red name.

"We've got seven additional rooms used for isolation with the HEPA filters. You know they're playing havoc with our admissions, I've had to shut down the second bed in a bunch of the double rooms, all the single rooms are occupied. Utilization is giving me hell for taking the second beds out of service."

Auginello looked over Molly's shoulder at the screen. "I have an idea," he said "Why don't we put two confirmed Zika cases in the same double room? That will expand the coverage for the HEPA filters."

Molly's face tightened. "You sure we can get away with that? I was told Zika cases have to all go in single rooms."

"In ordinary circumstances, that's true, but the DOH has declared an emergency outbreak situation, we can bend the rules a bit."

Molly trusted the Infectious Disease doctor, it was her boss that she didn't have any faith in. "Okay, I'll do it, but it's gonna be your head on the block if the DOH throws a hissy fit."

"I will fall on my sword for you, Molly, thank you."

As the busy physician hurried out of the department, Molly watched him go. Knowing he was married, Molly muttered, "Some girls get all the luck."

Unaware of the Admission clerk's romantic thoughts, Dr. Auginello hurried to the Chief Medical Officer's suite, afraid that when they ran out of HEPA filters—and they would run out in a matter of days—the hospital would have no place to accommodate additional Zika cases. He was sure there would be more cases.

A lot more.

***

Mimi stood outside Mr. Havers' room with a little paper cup of pills in her hand. As she opened the isolation cart to pull out the protective gear, the housekeeper came out of the room wearing a yellow isolation gown and mask.

"Yo, Mimi, you want I should give the pills for you?" said Mary.

"That's gracious of you to offer, but I really have to be the one administering them." The nurse pointed at the GPS unit hanging from her neck.

Mary said, "That's okay, I understand. It's just I already had three children, my birthing days are over, and you young enough to have a bunch more..."

After looking up and down the hall to be sure no one was watching, Mimi set the cup of pills on the top of the isolation cart. Leaning in to Mary, she whispered, "Be sure to check his name on the wrist badge, just to be sure: Havers."

With a wink Mary picked up the cup of pills and slipped back into the room, while the nurse stepped away from the door. Even though the patient was in a room with a HEPA filter that was supposed to scrub the air, Mimi thought she would be safer with a negative pressure room that sucked air into the room, not out, whenever the door was opened.

God bless Little Mary, she thought. God save us from this awful pestilence.

6

At lunch time Lenny caught up with Moose, who was passing out the trays from the big wheeled meal cart.

"Aren't you kinda late with the trays?" asked Lenny.

"Puttin' on the gowns and masks for all these isolation patients is slowin' us dietary people down. I've been telling my supervisor that we need more time for the trays, but he says there are only twenty-four hours in a day, he can't make it twenty-five."

"A philosopher for a boss, who would've thunk it," said Lenny. "Wish I could give you a hand."

Moose shrugged his broad shoulders. "You can pick up the dirty trays after lunch and throw them in the cart, that'll save me a heap o' time."

"Will do."

Moose took a big dollop of alcohol gel from a wall dispenser, rubbed it into his hands and grabbed another tray. "You think the nurses are really gonna sign up with the union? A lot of 'em think they're better than us service workers. I expect they'll be trying for an all RN Union, don't you think?"

"Some of the nurses feel that way, sure, but the more the bosses screw them over, the more they're going to see we're all in the same boat. We sink or swim together."

"Maybe so. But I'm not too sure everyone in our union is gonna be happy about it, either." Moose put on a mask, gown and gloves and carried the tray into an isolation room while Lenny stood outside the room waiting for his friend to come out.

"Moose, if the nurses join our union it'll give us more punch at the negotiating table. And if it comes to a strike vote..."

"Don't count your eggs before they're scrambled," said Moose. "Nurses goin' on strike, that's not gonna happen. Not the ones I run into."

Lenny reminded his friend about the fears of Catherine, the pregnant night nurse who may have been exposed to the Zika virus. He pointed out that their union was fighting the same issue for their pregnant members. Moose agreed in theory, but he kept his doubts that even an epidemic like this one could erase the years of antagonism between the RNs and the aides and clerks and even the custodians they bossed around.

Just then Little Mary hurried up to the meal cart. "Lenny, how come you ain't helping Moose with the trays?"

"C'mon, Mary, if Childress hears about me giving out trays it's grounds for suspension."

"Huh. Looks like you need a woman to show you how to man up." She grabbed a pair of trays and carried them into a room.

Lenny looked at Moose, who chuckled as he pulled two more trays out of the cart. "You know you can't argue with Little Mary, I gave up tryin' a long time ago."

***

Seeing through the open door that the Chief Medical Officer was seated at his desk, Dr. Auginello walked past the secretary, who stopped speaking on the phone in mid-sentence to call out that Dr. Slocum was in a meeting. Auginello ignored her, Slocum was always in a meeting.

"Jeffrey," the ID physician said, "the situation with the patients on isolation is getting more dire. We've run out of isolation rooms and will soon be out of HEPA filters."

Slocum closed the computer program he had been running, leaned back in his big leather chair and folded his hands on top of the desk.

"I am keenly aware of the bed situation, Michael, I receive updates twice a day. I am doing all that I can to accommodate the admissions, but there are limits on my resources. Do we even have to isolate the Zika cases?"

"If they have neurologic signs, I'm afraid so, Zika II is proving significantly more aggressive than last year's strain." He leaned in over the desk. "I asked for more rooms to be converted to negative pressure six months before the mosquito season began, but Engineering kept telling me they didn't have approval for the work. What is it going to take, an exposure of one of our employees? A deformed baby born from a hospital-acquired infection?"

"You're being overly dramatic. Our isolation cases are meeting all CDC and DOH guidelines."

Auginello felt a wave of anger pass through him. He knew that yelling would not get him anywhere, but reasoning hadn't helped any, either. There was only one other avenue open to him: one that he hated to take, it would bring an avalanche of ill will down on him and on his department. He could take the heat, the situation was worth it, but damaging the Infectious Disease Division was a risk he was reluctant to take.

"Jeffrey, I don't want to notify the Department of Health that we are failing to meet the standard of care for Zika cases. I don't like the idea any better than you do. But if you can't provide me with more negative pressure rooms, I will have no other choice."

The CMO told Auginello he was free to tell anybody he wanted, the HEPA filters were sufficient for droplet isolation. Slocum said he was under no requirement to retrofit more rooms, especially when it would take them out of service during the construction, and that would lower the hospital's available bed count by converting double rooms to single ones.

Before turning to leave, Auginello reminded the CMO he

had recommended a weak bleach solution for housekeeping to use in the rooms of Zika patients. Slocum replied the smell was irritating to the patients and the solution damaged the furniture.

"As long as Housekeeping keeps the bleach to a one-to-twenty solution, there shouldn't be any damage to the furniture. And the odor dissipates within minutes, they can tolerate it for that long."

"We'll discuss it at the monthly Infection Control meeting. I don't want any bleach triggering an asthma attack."

Auginello left unhappy, unsatisfied and unsure of what to do next, but he was damned sure he had to do something.

***

As he dropped his time card into the Housekeeping time clock to punch out, Lenny smiled, as he often did, remembering the day Regis Devoe poured glue into the machine in protest of the eight-minute rule. That was the rule stating that a worker who punched in more than eight minutes after the official start time of the shift would be considered late and subject to disciplinary action. A third infraction within a calendar year could bring permanent dismissal. When Regis destroyed the time clock with the glue, for a week the housekeeping staff had to sign in and out on a ledger, which offered a few opportunities for the latecomers to fudge the time. A small victory, now a legend among the workers.

Meeting his wife Patience in the lobby, he walked with her out to the employee parking lot. Lenny waved to Sandy, an old security guard who was stationed at the little guard house overlooking the lot. Sandy ambled over. "I see your man ain't got rid of that old car yet," he said, tapping on the roof.

"He promised last year he would trade it in on a newer car, but Lenny's all talk, no action." She poked her husband in the ribs, who winced a little too much.

"Maybe I'll go check out some used cars this weekend, I've got to change the oil and wash and wax the old beast, anyway."

"Too bad you can't keep 'er," said Sandy, "she's a classic."

As Lenny turned the key, the big V8 coughed and roared into life, sending a cloud of blue smoke out of the exhaust pipes. In a few seconds the exhaust cleared and the engine purred.

With a wave to his friend, Lenny pulled out onto Germantown Ave and headed home. Along the way, Patience suggested they pick up a pizza and salad, she didn't feel like cooking. "Good idea," said Lenny as she took out her cell phone. "Be sure to get pepperoni."

"No pepperoni! I'm ordering spinach, mushroom and red peppers. We're eating healthy!"

Lenny grumbled that Malcolm loved pepperoni, but Patience insisted the boy learn to eat healthy food the way Takia did. Lenny knew it was useless to protest when Patience was ordering dinner.

7

Biting off a big piece of pizza, Malcolm said, "Lenny, we all gone get sick with the Zika?"

"Are we all going to get sick," his mother corrected him. "I won't have you use that street talk in this house."

"O-kay," said Malcolm, who at nine years felt he was old enough to choose his own way of talking. After all, Patience never corrected his eleven-year-old sister Takia, and she made all kinds of mistakes when she talked. "Are we?" he asked again.

Lenny told him as long as they used the bug spray and wore long sleeve shirts and long pants outdoors, they would be fine.

"I hate that spray. When I rub my eyes it burns 'em something terrible!" said Malcolm.

"Then don't rub your eyes," said Patience. "You carry that handkerchief I gave you and use that. Okay?"

Malcolm promised, though he was pretty sure he would forget at least once when he was outdoors playing with his mates.

Takia said she didn't like the bug spray their mother sprayed all over them before they left for school either. "It smells yucky," she complained. "I don't want to smell like a wet dog when I'm at school!"

Patience told her she was not putting her children at risk of getting the virus, too many children were already home sick from it.

"We could stay home!" said Malcolm, the look of hope on his face fading before his mother's stern countenance.

After dinner Takia washed the dishes, since Malcolm had set the table, chores Patience made sure they carried out properly. Once she had made sure Malcolm was working on his homework, a task he protested in vain every night of the week, Patience asked Lenny if he was going out with the block captain tonight.

"Yeah, I promised Desmond I'd go door to door with him, check on the seniors."

"Can I come with you?" Malcolm asked.

"You have to finish your homework!" Patience said. "Besides, I don't want you outside once the sun starts to go down, that's when the mosquitoes come out. The same goes for you, Lenny."

Lenny agreed not be out late. As he stepped out onto the front door, Patience followed him with a can of mosquito repellant.

"Here, hold out your bare arms." She sent a heavy spray over his arms. "Hold out your hands." She sprayed more onto his hands, telling Lenny to rub it on his face and neck.

As he reached for the porch door, Patience sent a last spray to the back of his head, focusing on the bald spot there. She turned back to the house and gave Malcolm a wink. The child opened his mouth to try one more plea, but when he saw the stern look on his mother's face, he shut his mouth and trudged with heavy feet up the stairs to finish his school work.

Out on the sidewalk Lenny met Desmond, the block captain, who carried a clipboard and flyers. They looked over the list of seniors, noting there were six households occupied by elderly retirees. "We have enough surplus paint for the weekend, but we're short of brushes and rollers," said Desmond.

"Yeah," said Lenny, "the hardware shops and the paint stores were okay giving us their rusted, outdated cans of paint, but they didn't want to part with anything they could sell."

"Some of the neighbors will lend us brushes s'long as we promise to clean them and get them back in good condition.

We can use our block fund to buy the rollers."

They stepped up to the first house on the list of seniors and knocked on the door, the doorbell being long out of order. A high-pitched voice from inside asked who was at the door.

"It's Dez and Lenny, Missus Filtcher. We're here for the block club."

They heard a shuffling step coming toward the door, then the sound of two locks turning and a chain being released. The door opened slowly.

"Hello, boys. What brings you out of an evening like this?"

Desmond explained they were collecting names and addresses of seniors on the block who needed their porch painted.

"Come in, come in. No sense leaving the door open and let those nasty skeeters in." She ushered them into the living room and told them to be seated. The room was dark, the shades all lowered and one dim light on. Noting the old woman did not have the air conditioning unit on, Lenny assumed she was saving on the PECO bill. A box fan on the floor in the corner provided scant relief from the heat and humidity.

"Would you like some lemonade? I have a fresh pitcher chilling in the fridge."

Declining the offer, Desmond explained they had solicited free cans of paint from the local merchants. Volunteers from the block were planning on painting porches Saturday and Sunday. "We hope to paint two, maybe three porches the first weekend, then take care of a couple more the next week."

"Why, isn't that the Christian spirit, how lovely of you to offer. I have been concerned of late my house might be looking a wee bit shabby, like myself."

"You look strong to me," said Lenny.

"Bless you, child, but I'm eighty-six years old. There's not much pep in my step these days."

Desmond asked Mrs. Filtcher if any of her screens had

holes in them. "You don't want mosquitoes coming in through openings," he said.

When the elderly woman said she believed a few of her screens were old and torn, Desmond promised to bring some screening patches when they came to paint. "We'll get them all repaired so you won't have to worry." Heading for the front door, he stopped to add, "Oh, do you have any open containers in your yard that can hold water? The Department of Health wants us to eliminate any breeding grounds for mosquitoes."

Mrs. Filtcher said she didn't have any pots or cans in the yard, but they were welcome to check just to be sure. Lenny noted the large number of books packed into a bookshelf. The shelves were made of thick, rough wood.

"You sure have a lot of books."

"Oh, these are only a little bit of my collection. My husband and I were fierce readers in our prime. I have a whole lot more upstairs in the spare bedroom."

"Excuse me for asking, Missus Filtcher, are those book shelves made of roof timbers?"

"Indeed they are. My dear husband Ronald harvested them from a house that was torn down. That was a good forty years ago if it's a day."

"They hold the weight, that's for sure."

Leaving the house, Desmond made a note to make Mrs. Filtcher's the first house to be painted. The two went on to the next house, where an elderly Russian couple lived with their grandson and his wife.

***

Roy Reading walked up the ramp of the James Madison Emergency Room and passed the security guard with a nod of his head, his EMT uniform and ID badge giving him easy access to the facility. Once inside, he made his way through the crowded room, unnoticed by the harried staff.

He watched a resident outside one of the isolation rooms remove his lab coat and hang it on an IV pole attached to the isolation cart. The young physician donned an isolation gown, mask and gloves, slid open the glass door and stepped in, closing the door and drawing the curtain around the bed for privacy.

Roy noted the bright blue-trimmed James Madison identification badge clipped to the resident's lab coat. Seeing that the ER staff were too busy and harried to notice him, Roy plucked the ID badge from the lab coat and tucked it into the wide pocket of his mast trousers. Certain he had not been seen, he walked casually back to the entrance and made his way down the long ramp, whistling a little tune, excited to think how surprised Dr. Rachel Austin was going to be when he gave her a token of his esteem.

Everything in the world seemed bright and beautiful.

***

After completing his rounds of the block with Desmond, Lenny returned home, where he washed up and put on his pajamas. Stepping into the bedroom, he saw that Patience was rubbing lotion into her foot and ankle. "My skin gets so dry!" she said.

"Here, let me rub them." He squeezed a dollop of lotion into his hand and gently rubbed it into the sole of her foot, admiring, as he had for many years, the rich cocoa color of her skin. Then he applied a smaller amount to her ankle.

"You know what surprised me about you when we were first together?" she said.

"No, what?"

"Your hands are calloused and rough from all the chemicals and all the work that you do, but when you put lotion on my feet, you are always very gentle."

"Just another part of a good union steward's skill set," he said.

"You better not be rubbing some other woman's foot, it'll be the last thing you touch."

Lenny smiled and kissed his wife, knowing she didn't really worry about him straying from the nest. His faults might be many, but looking at another woman for love was something that never entered his mind, he was so thankful to be loved by this beautiful, passionate woman.

Before turning off his cell phone for the night, he checked one last time for messages. Sure enough, Mimi had sent him a text: she and Miss Kim had found five more nurses who wanted to learn about the union, could they come over the following night after dinner?

After running it by Patience, who was all for bringing the RNs into the union, Lenny texted back that would be okay, they could come by at 8 pm after finishing their twelve-hour shift.

"I'll pick up extra coffee and some cookies on the way home from work tomorrow," Patience said.

Lenny kissed her good-night, plumped his pillow, stuck his feet out from beneath the sheet to air them, and inside of ten seconds was fast asleep.

Patience looked down at her sleeping husband, marveling at his ability to instantly go to sleep. She always found the night a challenge to relax. Thinking about the mosquitos that may have bit Lenny, she thought about how she did not have to worry about the virus, since she could not get pregnant, thanks in all likelihood to that butcher who operated on her. That mean there would never be a little Lenny Moss, possibly because of what that racist butcher did to her years ago. The thought made Patience sad, not for herself, but for her husband. He never complained about the loss, that wasn't his way, but she was sure it hurt him in a place he never spoke about.

Closing her eyes, she began counting sheep, then switched to kiwi birds, the thought of those funny, flightless creatures always made her smile. Malcolm had written a report about them for school and wanted to raise some in the back yard. Patience had to explain they were an endangered species that lived in New Zealand, which was very, very far away.

She finally fell asleep thinking of mother birds nesting with their eggs.

***

Sitting up in the rocking chair her husband had found in a used furniture shop, Catherine could not help but worry about losing her job at the hospital. Hours before she had called the nursing supervisor to say she wasn't coming in to work that night, she felt kind of punk. She did not tell the supervisor it was just too scary. Her husband Louis hadn't objected, even though, out of work and only able to pick up occasional jobs with a local delivery service, he was worried about their finances.

"Maybe you could start your maternity leave early," he said.

"God, if only I could. But I would need a note from my doctor saying I was at risk going to work. Besides, they don't pay for the leave, you have to use your sick days and vacation time."

"That's okay, use your time. Use it all. My mom would take us in if you couldn't work and we lost the apartment."

Catherine didn't like the idea of giving up their little one bedroom in Manyunk, it was cozy and clean. Plus, Louis' mom smoked, that would be bad for the baby.

She felt her baby turn and kick inside her. If she had been exposed to the virus and the baby was born with any defects, she didn't think she would be able to handle it. Not when it was all her fault.

***

In his small studio apartment above a dollar store, Roy dissolved exactly one teaspoon of arsenic, purchased online (how simple to pose as a researcher!) in 4 tablespoons of boiling water. Once the ocher-colored powder was dissolved, he poured it into a mug and swirled the liquid around, coating the entire surface, then he swirled the liquid in the bottom of the mug until the water evaporated away. Satisfied, he filled the mug with fresh coffee.

Sniffing the poisoned cup, he detected no unusual odor. Roy poured a fresh, hot coffee into a second mug. He dipped a teaspoon into the ordinary brew and dropped it slowly onto his tongue. Swirling the liquid around in his mouth, he studied the flavor, noting its bitterness. Bitter was good, it would mask the taste of the poison.

Roy dropped a teaspoon of the tainted coffee onto his tongue and rolled it around his mouth. It was more bitter than the first, but not strongly so. Not enough, he believed, to cause someone to wonder what was wrong with it. And with enough sugar, the bitterness would be missed completely.

Spitting out the poisoned liquid, he decided that coffee was the optimal vehicle for carrying poison. Besides, his victim probably added milk and sugar anyway.

Now all he had to do was confirm that the good Dr. Austin had a coffee machine in her office. If not, no worries, he was confident he could find some other way of delivering the poison.

8

As Lenny dipped a rag in a bucket of cleaning solution he grumbled to Little Mary, "It's fricking outrageous. I'm going to file a health and safety grievance if the hospital doesn't supply us with more resources, and I don't just mean gowns and gloves, I'm talking about hiring more housekeeping staff to take on the extra cleaning we have to do."

He was cleaning a discharge bed, lifting the mattress to wipe the bed frame and platform beneath, since sometimes blood or other bodily secretions ran over the mattress and soiled the structure beneath.

Mary wiped down the bedside cabinet and table. "We sure can't beat back this Zika outbreak if we don't get more help. How're we supposed to keep everything germ free? We got patients coughing and throwing up and god knows what else. It's too much, Lenny. You file that grievance, I wanna be at the hearing when they try to tell us to work harder, work smarter. Like we stupid. Like we don't work our asses off every day."

The bed and furniture cleaned, they put fresh linen over the mattress, after which Lenny mopped the floor, cursing that he still didn't have bleach to add to the soapy solution.

Mimi stepped into the room to ask when it would be ready, she had an admission waiting to come up. "Give the floor ten minutes to dry," he said. Mimi went to the nursing station to tell the ER when they could send up the patient.

Following her, Lenny asked how the pregnant night nurse who may have been exposed to the Zika virus was doing. "Catherine called out sick last night. Can't say as I blame her, we have three patients on isolation, she was bound to be assigned to one of them, if not more."

Lenny agreed, there was no escaping care of a Zika patient. "I see you put two patients on isolation in the same room. You sure that's kosher?"

"Yeah, Doctor Auginello said it was okay on account of the DOH proclaimed a public health emergency. I just hope we don't run out of PPEs, the night shift had to reuse their isolation gowns and masks, Central Supply said they were running low on supplies."

"I know, we're fighting for supplies, too," said Lenny. "My fricking supervisor still won't release a gallon of bleach to put in my cleaning solution."

"I love the smell of bleach when you clean, it tells me you're killing all those bugs."

"I can think of something else I'd like to kill," said Lenny.

As he stepped away, Mimi grabbed his arm. Pointing at her watch, Mimi drew an imaginary number 9 on her palm. Lenny understood, the nurse would be coming to his house at 9 pm that night to learn about the union. Then Mimi drew a 6 and pointed at the big RN letters on her ID badge. Lenny winked, knowing Mimi would be bringing 5 more nurses with her.

The nurse hurried off with her medication cart, whispering a short prayer under her breath.

**

Roy Reardon walked through the Seven South ward wearing a dress shirt and tie, neatly pressed trousers and a crisp white lab coat, looking every bit like a young physician in training. He sported a new black shoulder bag that was stuffed with folders, medical journals and a textbook.

With a hospital ID proclaiming him to be a House Officer PGY I, complete with photograph carefully superimposed on the original intern's image, Roy passed among the patients and hospital personnel with cool confidence. He reviewed in his mind the two goals for the day: steal someone's password so he could access laboratory information, and leave Dr. Rachel Austin a little token of his admiration. A gift for all she meant to him.

He spied a surgery team standing outside a patient's room. The senior physician, a big florid-faced fellow with large hands, was explaining an emergency surgical procedure for compartment syndrome. Roy stood at the back of the group, noting their occupation and rank by the titles on their ID badges. There was a clinical pharmacist, a Physician Assistant, Medical students and residents, a staff nurse and even a dietitian: a comprehensive team.

The chief was just finishing explaining how to identify compartment syndrome early enough that surgical intervention would save the limb, when a resident hit the start button on one of the portable computers in anticipation of entering new orders. Roy stepped over to stand behind the resident, rejoicing in his luck that the young doctor was quite short.

As the surgical resident typed in his name and password, Roy committed the letters and numbers to memory. The senior physician called out lab work to be ordered, a cue to Roy to step unnoticed from the group. When Mimi, who was caring for the patient, saw Roy take out a pocket notebook and scribble down a note, she thought, *now that's a conscientious resident, taking notes on Dr. McDonough. I wish they all paid that much attention.*

***

Dr. Rachel Austin stood outside Mr. Havers' room with her Hospitalist team looking over the latest lab results on the portable computer as the intern reported his physical findings from the morning.

"So, no sign of an ascending paralysis?" she asked. The intern confirmed, the neurological exam was unchanged.

"That's good news." Austin held up the EKG and studied it. "I see evidence of right heart strain. See that?" She showed the students and intern the classic changes.

As she donned an isolation gown, Austin told the intern to order a cardiology consult. Adjusting the mask to ensure a snug fit, she stepped into the room, her garbed team following behind.

"Good morning, Mister Havers. My, you have some lovely red pajamas. I'm going to have to look for a pair for myself."

Havers told her he had a bathrobe in the closet that was deep purple, "in honor of Prince, God rest his soul. It's too warm in this place to wear. Can't they get the air conditioning to work in this place?"

Austin promised to speak to the charge nurse about the room temperature.

"I have good news for you. We were worried you might be experiencing a rare type of paralysis called Guillain-Barre syndrome, but I think we can rule that out."

"That's great. When can I get out of here, I have a business to run?"

"I noticed a little abnormality on your cardiogram. I put in a consult to cardiology. I am okay with you going home as far as my service is concerned, but I'd like you to wait to see if cardiology wants to run any more tests. Okay?"

Havers shrugged. He knew better than to argue with his physician.

Leading her team out of the room, Austin removed her isolation gear, then took a healthy dollop of alcohol gel from the wall dispenser and rubbed it over her hands and wrists. As she held her hands out to dry, she saw Mimi coming down the hall with her medication cart.

"Good morning Doctor Austin," said the nurse. "How is Mister Havers?"

Dr. Austin told her she was ready to send the patient home, pending a cardiology consultation.

"Admitting will be happy, they have a passel of patients waiting to come up from the ER. I just hope it's not another isolation case, we're running out of gowns and masks!"

Mimi went to the nursing station to page cardiology and find out how soon they could see Mr. Havers. She spotted that conscientious intern who had been taking notes on rounds standing at the station reviewing a chart, now with a mask over his nose and mouth.

She thought, *Hmm, I hope he's not wearing that mask because he's immune-compromised. Probably he's just cautious. You never know who's going to cough a bunch of virus into the air and expose you.*

***

Walking away from the Seven-South nursing station where he had confirmed Dr. Austin was making patient rounds, Roy made his way downstairs to the Hospitalist Office on the first floor, discarding the surgical mask as he walked. He stopped at the secretary's desk. "Good morning," he said, flashing a broad smile illuminated by bright white teeth. "I have those articles Doctor Austin asked me to copy for her. Okay if I leave them on her desk?"

"Sure, it's the third door on the right. The door's open."

"Thank you, that's very considerate of you."

The secretary, young and single, liked Roy's handsome face and warm smile. She read the name on his hospital ID. "Doctor Nathan Baumann. Are you a Fellow?"

"Do I look that old?" When the secretary tried to apologize, he shushed her. "No, I took it as a compliment. I'm just a lowly intern trying to please my Attending." He read her name tag. "Shu... Shu-vaun, is that how you say it?"

"Very good, Doctor. It's Irish, but I guess you knew that already. My grandmother was from Galway. She—"

Brnnng!

The ringing phone interrupted her. As the secretary turned her attention to the voice on the phone, making notes on a scratch pad, Roy walked quietly down the hall toward Austin's office, noting a table in an alcove with a coffee machine. All the offices were empty, the Hospitalists no doubt busy in clinic or making rounds.

Dropping a folder with journal articles on Austin's desk, he spotted a framed picture of a little girl with Austin's arm around her. On a filing cabinet was a coffee mug with the image of the same child on it next to a bowl with packets of artificial sweetener and powdered milk. He was confident that anyone who drank coffee with artificial sweeteners and powdered milk would never pick up an unusual taste in her coffee.

From his lab coat pocket Roy removed a small syringe with a plastic cap on the tip in place of a needle. Removing the cap, he squirted the liquid into the coffee mug, then picked it up and swirled the liquid around, coating the sides of the mug. Satisfied, for he had practiced this maneuver several times, he set the mug back down on the tray, confident the last bit of liquid would evaporate before the doctor returned to her office.

As he left the office, Roy wished the secretary a good day, addressing the young woman by name. He had long mastered the art of flattery, knowing how such remarks endeared him to stupid people who never realized they were being played for fools.

Passing through the main entrance of the hospital and walking down the broad marble steps, he decided to celebrate his cunning and courage with a visit to his favorite masseuse, a petite girl from Thailand. A lewd smile formed on his lips as he thought about the best part of the session, when he would be massaging her.

9

Whenever he saw Carlton approaching him on the ward, Lenny braced for trouble, since his friend had a knack for getting into it and calling on his shop steward to get him out.

"Yo, Lenny, how's it goin'?"

"Hey, Carlton. I'm okay, just busy as shit."

"You want some fresh deer meat? I got thirty pounds of prime cuts in my freezer, give you a real good price."

"Are you still hunting deer in Fairmount Park? I thought you gave that up after your run-in with the police."

"I'm doin' it for the *trees,* bro. The fricking deer chew the tender bark off the young saplings, kill the trees. S'long as the city won't bring back the wolf, somebody's gotta cull the herd, know what I mean?"

"Bring back the wolf. That would go over real big with the mothers walking their kids through the park."

"I'm just sayin'. Any-hoo, what's with the nurses, they really gonna join our union? The pro-fessionals hanging with us slobs in the lower depths? I don't see it happening."

"'Lower depths'? Have you been reading Russian novels or something?"

"Read it in a movie review. Hey, you gotta hear this idea of mine, it just popped into my head all of a sudden, it's fricking brilliant!"

"Okay, what have you cooked up this time?"

"This one's about the Zika outbreak. You know the virus is spread by mosquitoes, right?"

"Yeah..."

"But did you know that the mosquito tracks you through the smell of your breath? Every time you exhale, the smell from your breath spreads out through the air. The bug homes in on it and finds you...through your breath!"

"That's very interesting, Carlton. What's your brilliant idea?"

"Well, I was out last night in the little park across the street from my house in Manyunk."

"Hunting?"

"No, drinking, there's no deer in that park. We were slapping away the mosquitoes, and I saw that some people weren't slapping their arms or legs or neck." Carlton had a twinkle in his eye as he paused for dramatic effect. "You know why they weren't slapping away mosquitoes?"

"No, but it sounds like I don't have a choice, you're gonna tell me anyway."

"It's on account of some people don't naturally attract mosquitoes, and the reason mosquitoes don't go after them is..."

"Their breath," said Lenny.

"Bingo! So my idea is to experiment with different kinds of breath fresheners, see if any of them keep the 'skeeters away. Sweet, huh?"

Lenny put a hand lightly on his friend's shoulder. "Carlton, I gotta tell ya, you've come up with some goofy ideas in the past. Like the lining of a bra you sewed into a hoodie to form a cup so a hard-of-hearing senior wouldn't have to cup his hand behind his ear to hear somebody talking to them."

"That still has a lot of promise," said Carlton.

"But *this* idea sounds truly promising. You want me to run it by Doctor Auginello, the Zika infection is his responsibility."

"Yeah, that'd be great, thanks. Thanks for believing in me. I just hope I can help people escape this terrible plague."

***

After taking report from the ID Fellow who had covered the night consultations, Dr. Auginello hurried to the Engineering

Department. Walking past a cubbyhole where two men with rolled up sleeves were studying blueprints, he approached Katchi's cubby. His friend was staring into his computer screen with headphones over his ears, which meant he was listening to music while simultaneously typing a message on the computer and reading a document on his desk. The physician never understood how the fellow could concentrate on so many things at once. Katchi was the ultimate multi-tasker.

Auginello tapped the young engineer on the shoulder. Katchi turned his head, saw Auginello and smiled like it was Christmas morning.

Removing the headphones, which leaked hip hop music out into the enclosed space, Katchi reached out a hand offering to shake the doctor's, then quickly withdrew it with a laugh.

"Oops. Sorry, Mike, I forgot, no handshaking in the hospital. Right?" He rubbed his finger under his nose and held up his hand, referencing the multitude of micro-organisms he would pass to another by shaking hands after touching that bacteria-rich reservoir.

"The World Health Organization banned hand shaking among their members years ago," said Auginello. "So did the British and the Irish national health services. I wish to hell the DOH would get on board."

Auginello pulled over a rolling chair and sat down. "So, we're out of negative pressure rooms and using HEPA filters. What the hell are we going to do?"

"Don't tell me, I looked over the bed situation as soon as I came in, which was at, like, five-thirty. If the admissions for Zika cases continues at the same rate, I project we'll be out of HEPA filters by the weekend. Monday at the latest."

"You really should go for a Masters in Public Health, Katchi, you're a natural."

Rubbing his bald head, Katchi ignored the doctor's suggestion, one that Auginello had been proposing for years. "What the hell can we do, you asked. Good question. The CFO hasn't approved a purchase order to convert more inpatient rooms to negative pressure, so that ain't gonna happen. I have an order in for ten more HEPA filters, but every facility in the Delaware Valley put in the same requisition, the wholesalers can't supply them fast enough."

"I know," said Auginello, "the companies doubled the price of the filters at the start of the outbreak, the bastards know how to work the market to their advantage." He stretched out his long legs and poked his tongue into his cheek. "I could put the ER on diversion, that would stop the ambulance cases. But it wouldn't have any effect on the walk-ins, that's where we're getting most of our Zika cases."

Katchi smiled a little boy's smile, like he'd gotten out of having to do his homework and was still going to pass. "You know Mike, the State only requires a positive smoke test to certify a room is negative pressure."

"Yeah, so...?"

"So that means we don't have to install the pressure manometers that read the degree of negative pressure in the room. We don't even have to install hospital grade variable speed fans in the window!"

"Are you telling me all we have to do is stick some cheap fan from Home Depot in the window, seal the space around it and call it a certified negative pressure room?"

Katchi slapped his knee and chuckled. "That's right! I could go to the Dollar Plus store on Germantown Ave and buy up a dozen window fans. The ones with the sliding curtains on the sides will fit the old sashes perfectly!"

"Sure, sure, I know the ones you mean, I have one in the guest room at my house."

Katchi watched as the implications of his proposal sank in. "Mike, you realize this is going to create a big brouhaha when the Chief Medical Officer finds out. He's going to worry we'll be cited by the DOH for noncompliance, not to mention the hospital's certification with NASH."

"Screw the hospital standards association," said the physician. "This is a public health emergency, those pinheads wouldn't know a Zika virus from a case of syphilis. I'll handle the fallout with Slocum, how soon can you get the fans?"

"I'll need approval from my boss, but he's so fed up with the complaints coming in to our department, he'll be happy we've come up with such a simple, low cost solution." Katchi leaned in closer to his friend. "The Chief Engineer knows the CFO is one cheap son of a bitch. When he hears my department just saved him thousands of dollars..."

"Hundreds of thousands, given the cost of retrofitting all those rooms."

"Plus the monster loss of inpatient bed revenue during the room renovations..."

Auginello held out his hand. Katchi looked at it, puzzled at first. Then he took his friend's hand and gave it a strong shake. Katchi would purchase the fans today, he and Auginello would put the plan into effect, and they would be heroes or villains together.

10

Mimi saw the Cardiology resident filling out the consultation form for Mr. Havers. She leaned over his shoulder to try and read his handwriting, always a challenge. "You going to okay Mister Havers' discharge today?" she asked him. "That's up to the Attending, I just do the exam. He's going to need an echocardiogram first."

"An echo should be easy enough, it's totally noninvasive." "Yeah, I'll ask the chief tech to add it to her schedule. They're pretty busy in the department, I don't know they can do it today."

"Oh my god, doctor, this is a Zika case and we have two pregnant nurses on staff. Can't you pul-eeze order the echo STAT? I can send him home as soon as the test is done."

The cardiology resident clicked his ballpoint pen, stuck it into his lab coat pocket and promised to do what he could. "Anything for the nurses, Mimi, you know that."

"Thanks, doc! I won't forget you!"

Mimi hurried to put the order for the echocardiogram in the computer, being sure to flag it as a STAT order. She prayed they would perform the test before the end of their shift, that would mean one less Zika patient to worry about.

***

After the lunch trays were passed out, Mimi got a call from cardiology asking her to send Mr. Havers down to their department for the echocardiogram. "Lord, lord," Mimi replied, "didn't you read the request, it says he's on respiratory isolation for Zika?"

The secretary in cardiology apologized for missing the isolation status, saying she'd get back to Mimi as soon as she could.

"Wait! Don't hang up, I need the patient discharged today and the echo is the only thing holding up his going home. Can't you send a tech with the portable machine?" She listened to a long moment of silence. "Hello? Are you still there?"

"Yes, I'm still here. I'm going to have to run this through the department administrator, I'll get back to you."

"But—"

Click.

Mimi heard the sound of the dial tone, the secretary having hung up on her.

"Jesus Lord have mercy," Mimi muttered, not caring that the dispatcher could be hearing her take the Lord's name in vain. She figured all the dispatchers were devil worshippers anyway. Anybody who listened to a nurse taking a wee was no Christian, of that Mimi was certain.

**

Having given her team instructions for the rest of the day, including research questions for the students to pursue, Dr. Austin hurried to the cafeteria, where she picked up her favorite soup, Cow Heal, along with a salad, and made her way to her office, grateful for a few moments of peace. She placed the soup and salad on her desk, picked up her favorite coffee mug with the picture of her sweet daughter on it and went to the coffee machine in the hall. Austin set it to brew a single cup. With a lusty hum the machine heated the water, delivering a hot, aromatic brew into her mug.

Austin sprinkled sweetener and artificial milk into her coffee and gave it a quick stir. With a wink at the picture on the mug, she blew over the hot coffee and took a first sip, as welcome as the first draw on a glass of fine wine. Or whiskey.

The coffee tasted a bit bitter. Austin wondered if the office manager had changed the brand of coffee. She added more sweetener and took another sip. Definitely better.

With student reviews scheduled in less than an hour, she looked over the literature summaries she had requested. The student with the scruffy beard, a former electrical engineer, had organized his research clearly and succinctly. Nothing like a trained scientist to wade through research papers and find the key issue.

The secretary knocked on the open door and stuck her head in. "Doctor Austin, one of your residents stopped by to drop off some articles you asked for. They're on your desk."

"Okay, thanks, Siobhan, I'll look at them later."

Austin did not recall asking any of the House staff to reprint medical journal articles. Well, maybe one of them was taking initiative, that would be a welcome change. She took a spoonful of the soup, thick and flavorful, and munched on the salad. The mug of coffee was tasting better, and she had never needed the boost from the caffeine more.

***

Mimi was returning from her lunch break when she saw Katchi coming down the hall carrying a cardboard box and a work bag. Curious, she followed the engineer into an empty room with a HEPA filter standing in the corner, the next admission due to arrive soon.

"Whatcha got there?" Mimi asked.

"Hey, Mimi, how's it going? Looks like you've got your hands full with these isolation patients."

"You can say that again. Seems like all we do is put on a gown and mask, take off a gown and mask." She read the logo on the box: DELUXE BREEZEWAY WINDOW FAN. "You're installing a fan?"

"That's exactly what I'm doing. I'm going to make this a

temporary negative pressure room, we won't have to use the HEPA filter."

"Just what we need, more isolation patients, thanks a lot."

"Hey, don't shoot the messenger, I'm just trying to patch the holes and keep the ocean at bay."

"I understand, it's not your fault we're all working like dogs."

At that moment Dr. Auginello passed the room with his ID team. Seeing Katchi in the empty room measuring the window, he led his team into the room. Approaching his friend, the doctor said, "Did you get that thing from the dollar store?"

Katchi laughed as he ripped open the box. "Nah, I spent the big bucks, went to Home Depot." The engineer placed the fan in the opened window, spread the side curtains until they met the side walls, and lowered the window until it filled the groove along the top of the fan. "There isn't much that silicone caulk and a roll of duct tape can't fix!" He tilted his head and studied the setup while Auginello's team stood and watched. Katchi set the tube of caulk in the gun and ran a bead along the bottom of the fan.

With a flourish, he turned on the fan, setting it on high. He stuck a finger in his mouth to wet it, then held it in front of the fan, feeling the breeze blowing across it and out the window.

"That's it?" said Mimi. "That's all there is to it?"

"It's not rocket science, it's just simple Newtonian physics. I have to confirm the effectiveness of the fan with a smoke test, but I'm sure the window fan will suffice."

"Doctor Auginello, is that thing really kosher?" asked the resident.

"As kosher as a Hebrew frankfurter." He explained that while a consumer-grade window fan was not a permanent solution to the need for more negative pressure rooms, during the current public health emergency they would make do until the hospital had remodeled additional rooms.

Finished caulking and taping up the window, the grinning engineer shooed everyone out of the room. He slowly closed the door, examining the alignment and the space at the bottom. With a wink at Auginello, the engineer plucked out a small device that resembled an e-cigarette. "I've been trying to kick the habit for years, but somehow..."

Pointing the device at the bottom of the door, he pressed a plunger, sending a long stream of smoke out of the tip. The smoke was sucked into the narrow free space at the bottom of the door.

"Bulls-eye!" he exclaimed.

"Better crack the door, just to be certain," said Auginello.

Katchi opened the door a crack and released more smoke. The plume raced merrily through the narrow opening.

Auginello nodded his head. "All right, you can tell Admitting we have a new negative pressure room on line, they can admit to it any time."

Mimi swore softly underneath her breath not loud enough for the dispatcher to hear. "Just what I need, more respiratory cases."

"Sorry to have to bring you more Zika cases, Mimi," Auginello said.

"That's okay, I know we have to care for them. I just wish we could keep from assigning a pregnant nurse to the room, it's not right!"

"I'm going to bring it up at the Infection Control meeting again. I proposed guidelines for exempting pregnant staff from caring for these patients, but Miss Burgess won't accept them, and the Chief Medical Officer agrees with her."

"Those are two peas in a pea pod," said Mimi. "Good luck trying to get Doctor Slocum from bucking her."

Auginello winked at her and continued on his rounds, leaving Mimi to take report from the ER on the new admission: a woman who tested positive for Zika.

Katchi carried the now unneeded HEPA filter out of the room along with the empty cardboard box. At the service elevator he pressed the down button, still chuckling about the hundreds of thousands of dollars his boss would be able to report the Engineering Department had saved, and imagining the look of shock on the face of Slocum, the Chief Medical Officer, when he heard what they were using to create a negative pressure room.

The shit was definitely going to hit the fan.

11

After going through case reviews with the medical students, a vital part of their education, Dr. Austin decided to look in on Mr. Havers one more time before completing paperwork in the office. As she donned the yellow isolation gown, she felt a wave of nausea erupt in her gut and rise to her throat, bringing the taste of bile to her mouth. She gripped the edge of the isolation cart, feeling woozy.

"Are you okay, Doctor Austin?" asked Mimi, who was dispensing her 2 pm meds.

"I feel a little weak," said Austin, who knew Mimi and respected her dedication to the patients.

"You look kind of pale, maybe you should sit down."

Mimi spotted an empty wheelchair in the hall, a miraculous find given the scarcity of wheelchairs, and brought it to the stricken doctor.

After sitting for a moment, Austin felt a little better. She declined Mimi's offer for the aide to wheel her down to the Emergency Room. "I'll be all right, it must have been something in the salad I had for lunch. A little Pepto-Bismol and I'll be fine."

Still a bit wobbly, the doctor got to her feet and made her way to the elevator, leaving Mimi to worry that the doctor was not nearly as healthy as she suggested.

***

By three o'clock Cardiology had not sent a portable machine to perform the echocardiogram on Mr. Havers. Nor had they agreed to test him in the department. Frustrated and angry, Mimi called down to ask what was going on.

"I'm so sorry," said the secretary. "I think the technician on duty today is a woman and she's reluctant to be exposed to the virus."

"Reluctant? Of course she's reluctant, all of us are, but we still do our job and we care for our patient! Does this mean you won't do the echo?"

"No, she didn't say she wouldn't perform the test. She just wants to get the okay from the department administrator that she can take the portable machine into the room. She's worried about contaminating the equipment."

"Equipment? Are you kidding me? You tell your technician that if she's worried about contaminating her precious machine, then I will personally wipe it down with anti-microbial wipes. This is a STAT order. That means it gets done today? O-kay?"

The secretary promised to pass on the nurse's message to the technician and hung up, leaving Mimi to curse under her breath.

Determined to get her patient discharged before Catherine came on duty at 7:30, Mimi decided she needed to call on a reliable ally. She paged Dr. Auginello.

***

In the Cardiology Department, Dr. Auginello listened patiently as the Cardiology Attending explained that their echocardiogram technician was worried she might be pregnant and was afraid of exposure to the Zika virus. The ID physician nodded his head, trying to show understanding and sympathy, while knowing the tech was trying to put the work onto somebody else.

"We have a number of pregnant women on staff who are fearful of caring for Zika cases," said Auginello. "Wherever possible we make allowances for reassigning personnel. But that doesn't change the fact we need somebody to perform the echo on Mister Havers."

"I will ask the Fellow to do it, he is well versed in the procedure."

"Well at least he won't be pregnant. He's not going to balk at going into Havers' room, is he?"

"My Fellow is totally reliable," said the Attending. "The test will be conducted sometime today."

"Well, he can wipe down the machine with antibacterial wipes when he's done," said Auginello. "That will disinfect it adequately."

Auginello left the Cardiology department, glad there was somebody there who put the patient's care ahead of his own worries. Zika was scary, to be sure, especially for a woman who might be pregnant or might become pregnant later on. The hospital needed staff who had more flexibility in their staff assignments.

And more guts.

***

After taking a double dose of Pepto-Bismol and Mylanta, Dr. Austin felt a little better, though still nauseous She told the secretary she was not feeling well and leaving the department a little early.

"Gee, Doctor Austin, I hope it's nothing serious," said Siobhan. "Did you get a chance to look at those journal articles that nice young resident dropped off?"

"No, I didn't have a chance. Who dropped off journal articles?"

"A very polite young doctor. A Doctor Baumann, I think it was."

"Funny, I don't have any Doctor Baumann on my service."

"Maybe he's on one of the consultation services."

"Probably so," said Austin.

"Well, he was very polite. I'm sure you'll recognize him when you see him again."

Austin slung her leather satchel over her shoulder, a goat-skin bag her husband had given her for Christmas, and slowly made her way to the main entrance of the hospital. Standing at the head of the broad marble steps, she felt a little wobbly and her stomach threatened to send more bile into her throat. She used the handrail, something she had never done before.

I must be getting old, she thought.

***

When Regis Devoe made his afternoon rounds delivering pathology reports for the inpatient charts, he always made Seven-South his last stop, even though it meant visiting the wards on the lower floors and then doubling back to seven. Per usual, Lenny was at the housekeeping closet hanging up his mop for the day and rinsing out his trusty bucket.

"Yo, Lenny, what's goin' on?"

"Hey, Re'ege. Same old same old. Childress still won't release bleach to us."

"You want I should bring you some from home?"

"Thanks, but he'll hear about it, you can't hide the odor." Lenny turned his bucket upside down to dry, looked once more over the room making sure it was shipshape and ready for the morning.

"You coming to the meet with the nurses at my house tonight?"

"Oh, yeah. I've been waiting for them to come around a long time." In a whisper Regis added, "You think we can get a majority of them to sign pledge cards? A lotta nurses think they better than the rest of us. Like they're closer to doctors than service workers."

"Regis, I think it won't be long before the doctors join a union. I hear James Madison has upped how much of the doctor's fee they take off the top. There's a lot of pissed off doctors in this place."

"Yeah, some of 'em gotta give up their Bentleys and settle for a Lexus."

Ignoring the wisecrack, Lenny closed the housekeeping closet and headed for the stairwell. "I hear you, Re'ege, old attitudes die hard. But there's nothing like downward mobility to change a person's loyalties. And the docs are going nowhere but down."

***

A frowning Cardiology Fellow pushed the portable echo-cardiogram machine past the nursing station. Mimi looked up from her charting, relieved that Mr. Havers was finally getting his test.

"It's the second isolation room on the left," she said, rising from her chair. "I'll show you."

She led the Fellow down the hall to Mr. Havers' room, where he parked the machine beside the isolation cart and began donning a disposable gown.

"I'll tie you up," said Mimi, standing behind the young doctor and knotting the string around his waist. When the Fellow opened his mouth to comment on her words, she told him, "Don't even try it, mister."

With a shrug, the Fellow donned a cap and mask, pulled on disposable gloves and pushed the door open. Hesitating, he said to Mimi, "You know, it's not just the pregnant women that can be injured by this virus. It can mess with a man's sperm, too."

"Then I guess you'll have to be careful and not break isolation protocol," said Mimi. Sympathetic to the doctor's fears, she was still secretly glad a man was experiencing just a little bit of the fear the nurses felt every day caring for the Zika patients.

Back at the station, Mimi caught up on her notes. She answered a STAT message on the computer from the pharmacy notifying the staff of a shortage in the anti-viral drug most commonly ordered for Zika cases. She took up one of the 3 x 5 note cards that the old fashioned Attendings still preferred over a computerized list of their inpatients and began a list of issues she wanted the nurses to bring up with Mother Burgess, once they finally had a real union representing them. Adequate medications to suppress the virus was one more in a very long list.

She looked up, surprised to see the Fellow coming back. "Finished already?" she said.

"Yeah, it's a normal echo. There's a touch of mitral regurg, but nothing requiring treatment."

"Great. Can you fill out the Consultation in the chart? Doctor Austin said if you don't need him to stay in the hospital, I can send him home."

The Fellow looked at his watch. "Yeah, all right, I'm not going home any time soon as it is." He opened the patient's chart and scratched out a quick note on the consultation form. "Hey, I was going to ask you, I saw that fan in the window. You sure that thing's kosher? It looks like something I'd pick up at Home Depot."

Suppressing a smile at how the engineer had installed another of the inexpensive fans, Mimi said, "All I know is, as long as Doctor Auginello says it meets DOH standards, it's okay with me."

Three hours later, Mimi went over her notes for the day one more time, knowing the night nurse was due to come take report in a few minutes, and glad that Catherine had the night off, she didn't even have to use a sick day. Mimi had given out all her meds, made last rounds on all the patients. There were enough PPEs to get the night shift through until morning caring for the isolation patients as long as Admitting didn't replace Mr Havers with *another* Zika case. The float housekeeper hadn't come up to clean the empty room yet, so 712 was empty.

Not that it would stay that way long, the ER was still boarding too many patients. Mimi knew that when Catherine did come back to work, she was sure to get another isolation patient. Mimi hoped Cath got a break and they gave her a TB patient. TB: a nice, safe communicable disease.

12

When the doorbell rang, Malcolm jumped up from the floor, where he'd been lying on his stomach watching television. "I got it!" he called out, racing to the door. His sister Takia rolled her eyes, thinking her little brother hopelessly immature.

Lenny followed the boy to the door, where he greeted Mimi, Agnes and Miss Kim, who were joined by three other nurses Lenny only knew by their faces, not their names. After introductions, he ushered them into the living room, where Patience had made a pot of coffee.

"Ooo, are those nachos? Did you make them, Patience?" Mimi asked.

"Yes, I did. Lenny volunteered to do it, but he wouldn't have put roasted sweet potatoes and corn on them, it would have been all meat and fake cheese."

"Velveeta isn't fake," said Lenny, "It's just a product of modern chemistry."

"I like it in mac and cheese!" Malcolm volunteered.

"That's what I'm afraid of," said Patience. She sent the children upstairs to get in their pajamas and brush their teeth, then joined the others in the now crowded living room.

Mimi looked at Lenny, who turned to Moose. "Why don't you start off, Moose, I know you have some issues about the union drive."

"Yeah, okay. Well, not issues so much as worries. I mean, we gotta be honest with each other if we're gonna make this campaign happen. There's some bad blood between some of the nurses and the rest of us service workers in the union. We got to find a way to get past that if we're gonna get the nurses to sign union cards."

"We talked about that a lot," said Mimi. "It's true, some of us RNs have misgivings about being in the same union as the ancillary staff. One nurse said she was told it was illegal to be in the same union because we supervise a lot of your people."

"The hospital's gonna make a lot of noise about that, but it's all bullshit," said Lenny. "You would be in a different division. And generally, the NLRB has ruled that, since staff nurses don't hire or fire aides or custodians or dietary workers, they are not actual supervisors, so that shouldn't be a problem."

"That could change a hundred percent under the new crew of scumbags they got in Washington," said Regis.

"We can't let those bastards stop us," said Moose. "If they throw some new legal shit at us, we fight it, like we always do."

Patience said, "I've heard a lot of complaints from the nurses over the years. Could you all maybe set them in some kind of priority? If you can put out the most important grievances, the things that every nurse wants changed, that will help you win support."

Mimi turned to Agnes, who said, "Where do I begin, there are so many ways they mistreat us. Short staffing is super important. California nurses got the state to define minimum nurse-patient ratios. We'd like to see that in a contract for sure."

"It is not fair, making us stay over when someone calls out sick," said Miss Kim. "I have a small child at home, it is very hard asking babysitter to come at the last minute."

"Her husband works the midnight shift," said Mimi. "If she has to stay from eight to twelve, he's late for work."

"They are very strict where he works, he cannot be late, not even one time. The boss has a heart of stone."

"Okay, staffing and mandatory OT, that's good," said Lenny. "What about the GPS units you have to wear?"

"*Hate them!*" all the nurses said at once, raising laughter among the group.

"I guess you can't put 'respect' into a union contract," said

Mary Jane, a petite young nurse with a bouffant hairdo and a sparkling engagement ring on her finger. "But a lot of the nursing supervisors don't respect us. And when a doctor or a technician is rude, they don't back us up!"

"We always get the blame if a patient is late being discharged or being sent for a procedure," said Agnes. "Always!"

Mimi leaned over toward Mary Jane. "You're wanting to start a family. You shouldn't have to take care of the Zika cases, that is totally unfair."

Mary Jane began to tear up at the mention of a family. "I don't want to be accused of abandoning my patient. And I feel bad for the nurse who would have to take my patient, but come on, pregnant or trying to conceive and risking exposure to that virus? It's not like I wouldn't mind caring for a TB patient. Or a scabies case, no problem. I'd quell a dozen infested patients in exchange for one Zika patient!"

Taking notes, Patience ticked off the nurses' complaints in what seemed to be their priority of resentment. The nurses all nodded their heads, agreeing it was a good start, though everyone agreed the list was actually much longer.

"So how does this thing work?" asked Mimi. "How do we get this ball rolling downhill?"

Lenny explained that first they had to be very, very circumspect about who they talked to about the union. "The bosses have snitches in my union, I'm sure the Director of Nursing has her stooges, too."

"You better believe Mother Burgess has her favorites," said Mimi. "Nurses looking to move up into the administration and get away from the bedside."

"The word is gonna get out sooner or late," said Patience. "But if you can keep them in the dark as long as possible, it will help you get enough signatures to call for a vote on the union."

Agnes was frowning. "I would like to know, and I'm sure a lot of our sister nurses would like to know, what is the union going to do for us? What do we get for giving them our dues?"

Lenny told them that without a union, each individual nurse had to bargain and argue her case alone. Since a single nurse can be easily replaced, she had no leverage. No power. But if a majority of nurses vote the union in, they can speak in one voice. And they can act as one body. "It's a whole lot harder to replace an entire staff of nurses, even on a temporary basis, than it is to replace one or two or three," he added.

"So it will take a strike to get our contract, is that what you're saying?" Agnes had a skeptical look on her face and a hard edge to her voice.

"Not necessarily," said Moose. "Yeah, we went out on strike for forty-five days to get our first contract. But we ain't had to strike since then. Although truth be told, I think the next contract is gonna be the toughest nut to crack yet."

"Which is why the service workers will support the nurses in *their* union drive," said Patience. "They know we're stronger together, it's just common sense."

Lenny cautioned the nurses that organizing for a union could put their jobs in jeopardy. Although they had some protections under the labor laws, the bosses wouldn't hesitate to come up with bogus charges in order to terminate a nurse who threatened them.

"Miss Burgess fires nurses all the time just for pissing her off," said Mimi. "If I'm gonna lose my job, might as well be for something worth fighting for."

After more discussion about keeping a low profile, Mimi and Miss Kim agreed to write up a preliminary flyer they would give to Patience and Moose to review.

Lenny suggested their next meeting should be in the union hall so they could work with the nursing division organizer. "She's sharp as a tack, we've sent our members to support her picket lines at other hospitals, you'll like her."

As the nurses thanked Lenny and Patience for hosting the meeting, Malcolm peeked down from his perch at the top of the stairs. He loved to hear Lenny and his mom leading the fight. He couldn't wait until he was old enough to walk a picket line, he bet if he cursed the bosses out loud his mom wouldn't even punish him for saying bad words.

***

Settling into his comfortable easy chair, Michael Auginello extended his long legs and settled his feet on the desk of his study. Rows of books on oak bookshelves comforted him, as did the two fingers of Scotch in his glass caressed by a single cube of ice.

The room was beginning to show its age. He wondered how long had it been since they painted. It must be since they bought the house a good eighteen years ago. No, twenty. His wife had remodeled the kitchen, living room and the master bedroom, but left his treasured study to her husband's whims. The ceiling paint was peeling from that roof leak last year. And the chimney, such a big part of the charm of the room, needed new pointing, the mortar was powdering.

Well, his wife was right, as usual, thought Auginello. On the weekend he would go to the paint store, pick up a gallon, rollers and paint brushes, the old brushes were stiff and useless, he was sure. And a mask for the mortar dust. Mike remembered how, when he had been in college studying pre-med, his dad got him to scrape and repoint a chimney in the old house. The dust had been horrendous, a possible source of emphysema he was sure, had he not used a good mask.

A painter's mask!

Could it really work? Could he actually use the tried and true painter's mask in the hospital in the event they ran out of N95 masks for the Zika cases? He would have to test one to prove the mask provided sufficient protection from small particulates, but he saw no reason why they wouldn't provide adequate protection.

Anticipating a peal of laughter from his friend Katchi in engineering when he heard the proposal, Auginello celebrated his brainstorm by pouring himself another two fingers of Scotch. He was so pleased with his idea, he opened a Churchill, clipped the end of the cigar and lit it, enjoying the sublime pleasure of a good cigar, and damn the risk of throat cancer!

***

Catherine's husband Louis was awakened by a stirring in the bed. His wife had stood up and was tip-toeing out of the room.

"Getting a snack, babe?"

"No, I'm still nauseous. I'm going to sit up awhile, you go back to sleep."

Louis lay back in bed and closed his eyes, but his worry overcame the drowsiness. With a long sigh he got out of bed, pulled on his old felt slippers and went looking for Catherine. He found her seated in the living room with the television on, but no sound.

"Don't you want to hear the show?" he asked.

"I didn't want to disturb you."

He knelt down beside her and placed a hand gently on hers. "I've got a serious worry 'bout you, baby, you have to get some food in you. For your own good, *and* the baby's."

Catherine's lips began to tremble. The tears rolled down her cheeks as she rubbed her swollen belly. "What's going to happen to my baby? What if she's got the virus?"

Louis put his arms around her. "You have to go to the clinic and get tested. You have to." He kissed her tear-streaked cheek. "Let me take you in the morning? Okay?"

"But you have to look for work."

"I can do that later." He wiped the tears from her face and looked into her eyes until she nodded her agreement.

"Good. Now, how's about I get you a nice cup of tea and toast? With lots of sugar and cream. Won't that be nice?"

"Oh-kay." Catherine turned her attention back to the tv screen. She stared at the image as silent as the muted show.

13

At 6:00 in the morning Roy Reading walked through the entrance to the Family Practice offices, dressed in his intern outfit: crisply pressed white lab coat, shirt, tie and neatly pressed slacks, a stethoscope dangling around his neck. He was confident the secretary Siobhan had not yet come on duty, the hospital secretaries kept business hours, unlike the nurses and doctors. Sure enough, the only one in the office was a tired resident, on call the night before, who was copying lab results to present on morning rounds.

Waving to the resident, who barely looked up from his computer screen, Roy made his way to Dr. Austin's office, where he again deposited a dose of the arsenic in her coffee mug with the image of the little girl on it. Glancing at the little girl's image, he found a deep satisfaction in knowing he was not only destroying the woman who had ruined his career, he was also leaving a child to grow up without her mother, a sweet bonus.

As he wiped down the outer surface of the mug with a cloth to remove any finger prints, he reminded himself once again that he should be a real resident making rounds, typing orders in the computer and hearing the nurses hang on his every word. Roy knew he would have made an excellent physician, if it hadn't been for that arrogant bitch Rachel Austin reporting him to the Dean of the Medical School. It was all a lot of crap, there had been nothing sexual about his work, he had simply been conducting a physical exam on a comatose woman on the OB service. A beautiful young woman, it turned out, with long flowing hair the nurses had tied up in a ponytail.

It had been a preeclampsia case, the woman falling into

a coma after suffering a stroke. The baby had been saved, thanks to fast work by the OB Fellow and the nurse midwife, but the mother never regained consciousness.

So why was anyone surprised he had conducted a GYN examination of the birth canal? He had often fantasized about engaging in intercourse with a pregnant woman in labor, he imagined it would be the ultimate erotic experience, her moans being doubly loud from the combination of contractions and vigorous fucking. It was never going to happen, of course, but nonetheless the fantasy drove him to heights of arousal.

Dr. Austin had come into the room and pulled the curtain back just as he was inspecting the woman's uterus and peering at the opening of the uterus — the internal os. Austin claimed to have seen him sexually abusing her, which was a lie, the physical exam of a post-partum woman always included a vaginal inspection, there was nothing unprofessional about that. Admittedly, he hadn't bothered wearing gloves. *That* had been his downfall, he couldn't really explain the lack of basic infection control protocols.

He was thrown out of the program and blacklisted from the medical schools, leading him to work as an EMT, and all the while seeing the happy, successful physicians barking orders and throwing their weight around while he received hardly any recognition at all.

Austin. It was all her fault.

Leaving the Family Practice suite, he made his way to the medical wards in search of a bottle of insulin. Roy knew that at the shift change the portable medication carts were often left unattended. And unlocked.

Halfway down the Seven-South hallway, a cart was standing, plugged into a wall outlet to recharge its battery. Not wanting to draw attention to himself, Roy called up the computer and logged in with the stolen password. That way he would look like a busy intern reviewing lab results while he surreptitiously went through the medication drawers.

It took him only a minute to find an open bottle of insulin. Normally kept in the refrigerator behind the station, the night nurse had left the bottle for the day shift, knowing they would be administering several doses after the morning lab results came in.

Roy scooped up the bottle, along with several syringes, and dropped them in his lab coat pocket. The plan was coming together beautifully. He went to the stairwell and made his way downstairs, noting he had plenty of time to change and start his shift with the ambulance service.

He hoped he would have a run to James Madison, he might get word on how poor Dr. Austin was feeling. Who knows, with a little luck, the doctor might end up in the ER: a place where Roy could roam freely without attracting anyone's attention.

***

When Catherine felt the warm flow of water running down her thighs, she knew the worst had happened; her water had broken, she was going into labor. The cramps in her abdomen felt like an electric probe striking her spinal cord. The tears streaming down her face mirrored the waters from her womb, as if something in her heart had ruptured as well.

She will be a Zika baby. I know it. I feel it. Although Catherine had no clinical reason to expect that a baby infected with the virus would cause a mother to endure a premature labor, she dreaded the coming event, expecting the worst. Perhaps the baby would die at birth, wouldn't that be better for her? Better to die than to be deformed, with no functioning cerebral cortex, no hope of developing into a laughing, running happy little girl.

She hated to call her husband at work, he'd had so much trouble finding this job, laid off for more than six months and struggling to keep a positive attitude. But if she called the ambulance company and went into the hospital alone, he would be fit to be tied. "The boss will let me off," he had assured her. "It's our first child, for goodness sake, *call me!*"

So she called Louis, who came racing back to the house in the old Corolla, 100,000 miles but still humming along. He literally threw her suitcase into the back seat and helped her into the passenger side, closing the door as gently as he could, as if slamming the door would speed up the labor and deliver the baby in the car.

"Now don't speed, we have more than enough time," Catherine told him. "I won't, I'll be careful," he told her, though he still ran a couple of yellow lights, something he never did under normal circumstances.

Parking in the Emergency Room parking lot, he led her past the tent where the nurses assessed patients for communicable diseases. The nurses gave them a thumbs up and waved her through. From there it was a quick wheelchair ride to the Labor & Delivery suite, where a chipper young nurse in hot Freely scrubs settled Catherine into a bed and strapped a monitor onto her plump round belly. The baby's rat-a-tat tat heart beat was in the normal range. The nurse tried to reassure Catherine, but the laboring mom was still frightened.

"Please, god, let it be normal," Catherine said, grabbing the nurse's hand.

"Of *course* you will have a normal baby," said the nurse. "She's just a wee bit early is all. Don't you worry, dear one, we deliver babies at thirty weeks all the time. She will do just fine."

Louis took heart at the young nurse's positive attitude, he just wished his wife would be convinced. How was she going to bond with her baby and nurse her and love her if she still feared the baby would be malformed from that cursed virus?

14

Lenny had begun his shift mad enough to kill somebody. His supervisor had pulled his housekeeping partner Little Mary to Seven North, leaving him to cover the ward alone, along with the physician offices and pulmonary function lab on the eighth floor. And still there was no bleach to disinfect the four isolation rooms.

He fired off a text to the union health and safety inspector asking him to visit James Madison today to assess the threat to the staff of working so short and without adequate supplies. Knowing that bringing a complaint by itself would not change the administration's ways, Lenny sent text messages to the most militant members of the union.

He called on clerks, dietary aides, nurse aides and pharmacy techs to join him for a delegates' meeting in the cafeteria at 9:30. Everyone understood what that meant: no more polite requests, it was time for action.

The first to reply was Moose, who texted: On it with four. That was good news. If Moose could bring four workers from dietary, it would present a strong presence.

Regis, who had worked for years in the laundry before transferring to pathology, was the second to reply: laundry for four. More good news, the laundry workers were seasoned union advocates, they would lead the charge.

Celeste, the Seven-South ward clerk, winked at Lenny when he rolled past her with his mop and bucket. She held up her hands, five fingers extended. That meant at least five ward clerks would join him, maybe more. Everyone knew the reason for the meeting, he didn't have to spell it out, they were fed up and wanted action.

His spirits lifted, Lenny attacked the black stains on the

old marble floor with a vengeance, prying thick deposits with a putty knife, then going over it with the mop. The floor would need buffing, but there was no time for that, he was covering too many areas. Besides, management had assigned buffing to the night shift. Not that they had the time, either. The facility was going down the toilet. It broke Lenny's heart.

More than that, it made him fighting mad.

***

When Miss Burgess entered the Chief Medical Officer's office and saw Joe West, the Chief of Security, standing by Dr. Slocum's desk, she knew bad news was coming. Burgess settled her ample hips into the chair across from the CMO's desk, wishing she could rest her feet on the desk, the arthritis was unbearable today.

"Margaret, Joe West has new information about the issue of your nurses organizing a union at James Madison."

"My girls may be grumbling about things, but they're never joining a union, you can take that to the bank."

West silently placed three sheets of paper on the desk in front of Burgess. Each one showed a picture of a nurse entering an elevator.

"What's this?" said the Director. "Girls going on their lunch break?"

"Each one of these nurses rode the elevator to the basement the day before yesterday at nine-thirty in the morning. The cafeteria is on the first floor, not in the basement."

"Perhaps they were picking up supplies at Central Stores."

"The sewing room is in the basement," said West. "We know that's where Lenny Moss and his followers gather to hatch their union plots."

"You saw them go into the sewing room?" asked Burgess.

"We believe they did. We installed a video camera outside the basement elevator, they all went down toward the sewing room, Central Stores is in the opposite direction."

"I didn't receive any report from the Dispatch Office that my girls were talking about any union activity. I know they have their issues, my head nurses get a bellyful every day, but still..."

"There are no transponders down there, the GPS units don't transmit from the basement," said Slocum. "*Yet.*" He reminded Burgess that Engineering had argued that installing the transponders in the basement was not cost effective, since there were no patient services there.

"Can you have them installed?" asked Burgess. "I want to hear every word my girls say down there."

"I'm working on it," said West. "But it will take some time, they need to be installed at night when no one is around to see the work. And they have to be concealed inside the ceiling."

"Get it done," said Slocum. "We need to have evidence of their conspiring against the hospital. Once we have that, we can find a reason to discharge them."

Burgess reiterated her conviction that the nurses would never vote for a union, especially not the service workers union. "That union is full of unskilled, illiterate halfwits. My girls would never be in their union. *Never.*"

Slocum reminded Miss Burgess that the nurses did have serious grievances. "Your policy of not permitting pregnant nurses or nurses trying to get pregnant from caring for the Zika patients has caused a lot of heat. Infectious Disease is supporting a policy to exempt pregnant women from assignment to those cases. Auginello carries a lot of weight in this facility."

"Let him show me a CDC guideline!" said Burgess. "Let him show me something from the Department of Health! Until he does my policy stands."

"Okay, Margaret. I just hope you don't drive the nurses into the arms of one of the unions, those creatures are always looking for suckers to sign up and hand over their dues."

"They'll just have to suck it up. You don't get to choose your patient, you take your assignment and not complain about it." Wanting to be sure that security kept a close eye on the three nurses captured on the video, Burgess turned to comment to Joe West, only to discover the security officer had silently left the room, one of his more annoying habits. West would arrive silently, say as few words as possible, and then disappear, a ghost who seemed to pass through walls.

**

Dr. Auginello found Katchi in his cubicle looking over specifications for the rooftop air conditioning system, a unit that was high risk for harboring a particularly dangerous droplet-borne bacteria that could infect patients in the wards below: Legionella. The wily physician dropped a bag on Katchi's desk.

"Check it out, you're going to like it."

Puzzled, the engineer reached in the bag, noting the Home Supply Center logo on the bag. Pulling out a box of painter's masks, Katchi held the mask up in front of his face. "You're *serious?* You really think this is gonna pass the N-95 smell test?"

"I already tested it. But I want you to sample the mask, too, so I have some backup."

"More like somebody to share your jail cell."

As Katchi pulled the mask over his face and adjusted the clip for the nose, Auginello placed a large transparent plastic headpiece over the engineer's head. The device looked like the hood that bee keepers wore. It was designed to trap scents introduced through a port.

Auginello took out an injector filled with a sweet-smelling liquid. He injected a few cc's through a port on the headpiece, filling the airspace inside with the sickly-sweet smell.

Katchi sniffed through his mask. Sniffed again. His eyes

grew wide. Pulling off the headpiece and mask, he said, "Damn, I didn't smell a thing, this mask is effing grrreat!"

"Central Stores agreed to order five cases of the mask from the Home Supply Center, they'll be delivered today." Auginello stood back and stroked his chin. "It's a pity we never put a wager on our respective proposals. You could've won with the Dollar Store window fans, and I'd have made it even with the painter's masks."

Katchi told him they should probably save their money while they still had a job, a comment Auginello heartily supported, saying, "Be not faint of heart, my friend, we must be prepared for battle."

"I'm a lover, not a fighter," said Katchi. "And I'd love to keep my job."

***

When Regis Devoe was leaving for work this morning, his wife had stood in the doorway blocking his path with that serious don't bullshit me look on her face.

"Re'ege, you gonna tell Doc Fingers you're taking that scholarship, right?"

He had already made up his mind to give the program his best shot. After all, staying with his current job that had no certification, no specialized training, how was he ever going to pay off the damned mortgage? Or trade in their ten year old Echo for something newer and roomier?

He hoisted his old black backpack over one shoulder. It was the backpack a hospital security guard had demanded he open for inspection one day when leaving work. Regis had chewed out the guard, as well as a white doctor walking out with his bag that wasn't searched, leading to a shit storm he and Salina thought they would never survive.

But he was cooler now. More in control and not getting in any fights at work. "Yeah, I'm gonna put in the papers today."

83

Salina looked into his eyes, saw he was not leading her on.

"Good. You'll do fine. Hell, you'll probably be the top of your class!" She gave him a long, sloppy kiss. "Hold onto that while you're at work," she told him.

"You know I will," he said, heading for the car and hoping the battery wasn't dead. Again.

Getting to work on time, Regis was setting up the autopsy suite for a dissection when he saw Lenny's text message on his phone. He had several pathology reports to take to the wards that day, so he told Dr. Fingers he would make his rounds early and be through in time for the first case.

"Was the HEPA filter serviced?" the pathologist asked, "We have a post-mortem on a Zika case."

Regis assured his boss the filter was in good working order. He understood that the pathologist would be joined by several doctors and medical students, they would all want to see the gross anatomical changes that the virus brought.

"I'll have the school application on your desk before I clock out," Regis added.

"Excellent." Fingers was already thinking about a college degree for his young assistant, he knew Regis was intelligent, he just needed to build up his self-confidence.

15

Mimi knew it was trouble the minute she saw Mother Burgess coming down the hall, her Assistant Director and three obsequious head nurses trailing behind her. Burgess liked to sweep through the wards so she could see for herself how "her girls" were managing during the public health emergency.

"This is one of the temporary fixes we told you about, Miss Burgess." The Seven-South Head Nurse, sporting a traditional nursing cap that she had been wearing for a hundred years ago, pointed at the room number beside the door: 712. A bright blue sign on the door read: RESPIRATORY ISOLATION – N95 MASKS REQUIRED. The sign went on to direct visitors to stop at the nursing station for instructions before entering the room.

"You say Engineering has installed a consumer-grade fan in the window and is claiming it conforms with Department of Health requirements for respiratory isolation?" said Burgess.

"Yes, ma'am, that's what they are telling us."

"I was suspicious when I learned Admitting was doubling up on isolation patients, but this is too much. Too much!" Burgess gestured to Mimi to join them. "Are you assigned to this patient, miss..."

"Missus Rogers. Yes, she is my patient."

"The isolation, is it for Zika?"

"That's right."

"Are you comfortable caring for that kind of patient without a properly certified negative pressure system installed? Hmmm?"

Mimi opened a drawer and pointed to the gowns inside. "I'm more concerned with the shortage of PPEs. We have to reuse the isolation gowns, there's never enough of them. Same thing with the N95 masks, Central Supply only sends one box up at a time. One box! It's empty in a couple of hours, and then we have to beg them for more."

Burgess turned to an assistant. "Why aren't my girls being supplied with the isolation equipment they need?"

The assistant reminded the Director that there was a city-wide shortage of isolation equipment. Central Supply was doing the best they could to purchase more supplies, but it was a challenge.

"We all must tighten our belts and utilize the resources available to us," Burgess said. "If there is one sign of a first rate nurse, it is making do with what is given her." Burgess cast a cold eye on Mimi. "That, and loyalty to the institution. Loyalty has always been the core value of professional nurses. Loyalty, Missus Rogers."

As the Director of Nursing lumbered down the hall with her retinue, Mimi worried that Mother Burgess knew of her involvement in the nurses' union drive. She couldn't see how the cantankerous old bat could know about their plans, they'd only had their first real meeting the night before at Lenny's house. But nurses were prone to gossip, and there were plenty who still felt a strong loyalty to the hospital and to the Director of Nursing.

It was becoming more and more clear to Mimi that this union drive was going to be the toughest assignment she'd ever taken on. Tougher than caring for a dying child. Or a severely burned patient. Tougher even than cleaning the body of a favorite patient, wrapping it in the body bag and sending it down to the morgue for its final appointments: the autopsy suite and the funeral home.

**

At 9:30 am, members of the service workers union brought

their coffee and donuts to a pair of tables in the corner of the cafeteria. Lenny looked up and down the table, estimating his strength. It was a good start: sixteen workers, all pissed off and ready to act.

"Okay, thanks for coming to a meeting on such short notice. We all know that with the Zika outbreak the hospital isn't getting us the supplies or staffing we need to handle all the isolation rooms. I wanted you to know I asked our union's health and safety inspector to come down and assess the situation. We'll have to see what she finds, but I think we have grounds for a complaint to the NLRB. The union is also going to file an official complaint with the Department of Health."

"Lenny, you think that's gonna get the hospital to do right by us and hire more staff?" said Little Mary. "I mean right now, the bosses have the NLRB in their pocket."

Moose said, "We all know a health and safety complaint ain't gonna get the job done. We have to talk to Human Resources, nose to nose. All of us, together. That's how we get something done."

"We're marching to Mister Freelyu's office," said Regis. "Today, twelve o'cock."

"That's right," said Lenny. "I already called and told him I was bringing delegates from all the departments to talk to him. He said he was busy, I said we were busier, we were working to keep the patients safe."

"So we're marching on his office without an appointment?" said a new worker from Central Supplies.

"That's right." Moose said with a wink and a sly grin. "We're gonna interrupt his busy schedule."

Lenny told them he wanted everyone to bring a co-worker. If somebody asks why you brought the co-worker, they should say it's a delegate in training.

"What if I'm not scheduled to take my lunch break at twelve?" said a young laundry worker.

"Tell your supervisor it's a union meeting, you have to go.

Ask another worker to switch times with you, your supervisor won't have any excuse to write you up."

Everyone agreed to meet in the main lobby at 12. From there they would walk to Human Resources and demand to see the Director, Lenny reminding everyone that under the union contract they could not hold a march inside the facility, but the first rule of organizing was, *always bring a crowd.*

***

Dr. Austin looked over her schedule on her cell phone calendar while brewing her first cup of coffee of the day. The smell of the coffee as the machine forced hot water through the grounds always improved her mood. Making a note to prepare for an upcoming meeting, she carried the cup to her office and settled into her chair. She stirred the milk and sweetener in the coffee and took a first sip. It was hot. Hot and bitter.

"I swear they changed the coffee bean in this batch," she told herself, adding a second sweetener. Taking another sip, she closed her eyes and imagined herself on a sunny beach on the Mediterranean Sea. Corfu, perhaps. Or Mikonos. She made a vow to herself to raise the issue of a long vacation with Lawrence. He was as much a workaholic as she, but this season she was determined to put their schedules together and find the time. His mother could watch their daughter, mom loved having the child all to herself, living alone as she did out in Plymouth Meeting.

Taking more of the coffee, she looked down at her legs, decided they weren't as fat as she often complained to her husband, who always replied, "You've still got the legs of Lana Turner, dear." She thought she just might indulge in a new two-piece bathing suit. When she complained about her belly, Lawrence reminded her it was the price she paid for bearing children.

Today she decided the price was worth paying, though they had yet to deal with the dreaded teenage years.

Draining the last of her cup, Austin slung her stethoscope around her neck, having tied up her hair in a bun to keep it away from the diaphragm, and stood up. As she reached for her lab coat hanging on the back of the door, she felt a wave of nausea ripple up from her gut. Her head pounded with a drum-beat headache.

The nausea was like the bout she had experienced the day before, but was worse. Much worse. Gripping her belly, she stumbled out the door and hurried toward the bathroom. "Please don't let me vomit in the department," she mumbled half aloud.

"Are you okay, Doctor Austin?" the secretary called after her.

Too sick to speak, the frightened physician ran to the bathroom door, hurried into a stall and wretched.

The fluid spewing from her mouth was black. She hoped it was from the coffee, and not from blood.

***

In the Labor & Delivery suite, Catherine was oblivious to the pain, the fear for her baby was overwhelming. When the baby's heartbeat slowed during a contraction she was sure the infant would be deformed. She was six weeks premature, which put the baby at risk even without a viral infection.

Drenched in sweat, her hair sticking to her neck and face, the tired mother closed her eyes and gave one more long push as the doctor eased the baby out into the world. The only sound was the beeping of the heart monitor.

Alarmed by the silence, Catherine opened her eyes. The doctor was cutting the umbilical cord while a nurse suctioned fluid from baby's mouth and throat. Louis, who had been holding his wife's hand, stepped over to the bassinette where the OB team was examining the newborn.

"Shouldn't she cry?" He looked down, saw the sunken chest and gray pallor of the skin. Baby was breathing rapidly, mouth open, struggling for air.

"We need to support her breathing until her lungs mature a bit," the doctor explained. "She will be crying up a storm soon enough, you needn't worry about that."

Returning to his wife, Louis took her hand in his, speaking softly. Gently. "She looks okay, Cath. I mean, she's early, sure, but I don't see any, you know, anything *bad*. Know what I mean?"

Catherine looked up at her husband, too frightened to speak. Too frightened even to ask to see her daughter before the team took baby off to the neonatal ICU.

16

Standing in front of her portable computer checking the medication time and dose for a patient, Mimi smiled to see Dr. Auginello coming down the hall with his ID team carrying a mysterious black plastic bag. As the physician reached Mimi, he reached his hand into the bag as if conducting a magic trick.

"What kind of trick are you going to pull out of your hat this time, Doctor Auginello?"

With a coy smile, the physician withdrew his hand holding a box of masks.

"Central Stores will be providing this type of mask starting tomorrow, they put in a drop shipment order today," he said. "These masks will make up for the shortage of the standard N95 mask we've been using until the outbreak is over."

Mimi took the mask and turned it over. It was thicker than the mask she'd been using. She looked more closely at the box. Suddenly her face lit up in a smile and a chuckle escaped. "Oh, Doctor Auginello, you've really done it this time. This is a painter's mask!"

"The very same. Katchi and I tested it in engineering, the mask passed with flying colors. It will trap particles as small as the N-95 mask does, you won't have to worry about viral exposure."

Mimi shook her head, amazed at the doctor's ingenuity. And guts. She had no doubt the administration would not look kindly on the substitution. But the city was facing a public health emergency, what else could they do?

"Thank you for supporting us," said Mimi. "Nobody else seems to give a damn about our risk of exposure." As the ID physician turned to go, Mimi said, "Uh, Doctor Auginello, can I ask you a question? It's about a Zika exposure."

The physician halted his troop, who gathered around the nurse.

"Of course, what's your question?"

"Well, one of the night nurses may have been exposed, she broke protocol and touched her eye with her gloved hand when she was in an isolation room with a patient."

"Hmm. Had she touched any horizontal surfaces or the patient's bare skin while she was in the room?"

Mimi admitted she didn't know, but it was at the end of a patient visit, so she supposed Catherine could have touched a contaminated surface. "Oh, and the worst part of it is, she's in her third trimester."

Auginello stuck his tongue in his cheek and thought a moment. "Your question is, what is the likelihood of a viral infection. Correct?"

"Yeah, pretty much. I was wondering if she should take the anti-viral medication, and if she did, what are the chances it would harm the fetus?"

Auginello turned to the ID Fellow. "What do you think, Dmitri. What is the greater risk to the baby, anti-viral medication or viral infection?"

"Infection is greater, to be sure," said the Fellow, a thickly built man with jet black hair and piercing dark eyes. "But the mother must be tested right away."

'The problem there is the test has a fairly high rate of false negatives," said Auginello.

"So even if it comes back negative, she still could be exposed?" asked Mimi.

"That's correct. It takes several days for her immune system to produce enough Zika antibodies for the lab to measure them. We can run a viral culture, that's a more accurate test, but it takes longer."

Mimi told him the anxiety was tearing the mother up, she was afraid the fear alone could trigger an early labor.

"Possible exposure versus definite risk of drug interaction with the fetus. It's a Hobbesian choice," said Auginello. "I would be inclined to recommend prophylaxis. If she goes into premature labor because of the anxiety, I would treat the newborn as well."

Thanking the physician, Mimi decided to call Catherine as soon as she had a break and tell her what Dr. Auginello advised, maybe it would allay her fears.

As Auginello led his team toward Seven-North to deliver another box of masks, his beeper went off. It was Dr. Slocum's office. The CMO wanted him in his office.

Now.

***

"You have created a negative pressure room using WHAT? A cheap window fan from Home Supply Center? Have you lost your ever-loving mind?" Dr. Slocum's face was red with anger as he spat out the words.

Auginello opened his mouth to answer the Chief Medical Officer when Katchi cut him off. "It was all my idea, sir. I thought it would save the hospital beaucoup dollars. It will just be while the DOH continues the public health emergency."

"And do you honestly believe they will accept those cheap fans meet DOH standards? Are you insane? They will cite us up the ass, the negative publicity will kill us!"

"Philadelphia and the entire Delaware valley is under a state of emergency," said Auginello. "We have to protect our staff from exposure. Supplies are difficult to obtain."

"More like impossible when it comes to HEPA filters and N-95 masks," said Katchi.

"You think I don't know that? And what about your doubling up isolation cases two to a room? We've never done that before."

"It's no different from a TB ward," said Auginello. "We have to be creative. With so many isolation cases coming through the ER, we have to find some way to accommodate them." Auginello slid a sheet of paper onto the CMO's desk. "This is a copy of the DOH guidelines. As you can see in the yellow highlighted area, a negative smoke test is adequate to assign a room to a negative pressure status. The use of manometers to measure the degree of negative pressure is recommended, but it's not required."

Slocum glanced at the highlighted section of text, shaking his head. "If the city cites us for this, I will have both your heads on a platter! Is that clear?"

Offering silence for an answer, Auginello and Katchi turned and left the office. Once outside in the hallway and away from the CMO's secretary, Katchi slapped his friend on the back. "You should've told him about the painter's masks. I'd love to see his face when he hears about that!"

Chuckling, Auginello told his friend he was saving that little piece of infectious disease creativity for their next run-in with Slocum, he didn't want to overload him with too many innovative ideas.

17

At exactly 12 pm, Lenny met a troop of union members in the main hospital lobby. After being sure everyone knew what the plan was, Lenny, Moose and Regis led the way down the Administrative corridor. Their footfalls made no sound as they trudged over thick carpeting. Reaching the Human Resources office, Lenny opened the door for Moose and Regis, then followed them inside, with fifteen other workers close behind.

The secretary looked with surprise at the size of the gathering. "I'm sorry, Lenny, I thought you said you wanted a delegate's meeting."

"That's what it is, these are all delegates. The union is expanding the number of representatives, we've had to file so many grievances the way James Madison has violated the contract."

"Uh, I'll see if Mister Freely can accommodate all of you."

"That's okay, the others can stand, it's not like we brought the retirees this time." Lenny was recalling the big demonstration the union had held when the new owners of the hospital had threatened to drop out of the health & welfare fund, which would have bankrupted the fund, leaving retirees with no pension, and current and retired workers without health insurance: a death sentence.

Charging into the Director's office, Lenny, Moose, Regis and Little Mary took a seat around the conference table. Without enough chairs for everyone, the rest stood against the wall.

Freely chuckled when he saw that Lenny had brought twice the number of delegates who normally met with human resources. He was familiar with the tactics Lenny and his friends often employed, and was even supportive to a degree.

Freely wanted a workforce that supported the hospital's mission, realizing that short staffing, arbitrary punishments and attacks on the union only created ill will and mistrust, to the great harm of the patients. He was all too aware of how 'disloyal' his views were in the eyes of the CEO.

"Well, gentlemen," said Freely, addressing the three senior delegates, "what are your issues today?"

Before Lenny could get a word out, Little Mary said, "How do you expect us t' keep our patients safe when you won't give us enough housekeepers and equipment to even do the ever loving *work?*"

The Director cleared his throat, but was silenced when Little Mary pointed a finger at him. "Every patient and every worker is scared t' death of this Zika virus, right? Well they goin' be mighty pissed off when they hear we don't even have the bleach that we need to kill that terrible plague, let alone hands and feet to put it to work!"

Moose added that all the other departments were unable to complete their work as well because of all the isolation patients. "Dietary can't hardly find a mask and a gown so we can bring the patient his food. And our rounds are taking half again as long with all the putting on and taking off." He added that it was a crime to force pregnant women to go into a room that had the Zika virus all over it.

Lenny said, "The bottom line is, we need more resources and staff. We need more cleaning supplies, and Childress won't even release bleach so we can wipe out the virus from patient rooms."

Freely promised to speak with the Housekeeping supervisor about providing more supplies, making a note in his tablet computer.

"What about forcing pregnant women to take care of the Zika cases?" said Little Mary. "You got to give pregnant women and women who are trying to get pregnant a pass on those cases."

The Director told them his department had no issue with selective staffing patterns, it was the department heads who were refusing the practice. "They tell me it creates a myriad of difficulties figuring out who cares for what patient."

"That's a lie," said Moose. "You hire enough workers to do the work, we can cover for each other, no problem. We'll get the work done."

"Do you want me to cancel all the summer vacations?" asked Freely. "How would your union respond to that initiative?"

Lenny pointed out that in past years the hospital hired temps to fill in or gave overtime. Now, they wouldn't approve temps *or* overtime. As for new hires to replace workers who retired or left for another reason, there were no job postings. "You're cutting back the number of workers when we need more of them to deal with the outbreak!"

As he added more notes to his file, Lenny thought the union might finally make some headway.

"I may be able to authorize some overtime for critical departments. As for hiring temps, the president has made it clear we've got to lower our costs, reimbursements are not meeting projections. You can't operate a business with more money going out than coming in."

"Same old crap," said Little Mary.

"If you want to cry poverty, show us the books," said Lenny. "Show us the numbers."

"Now, Lenny, you know the president is never going to allow the union to audit the hospital books. That's not how we do business."

"That's not how you choose to do business," said Moose. "That's how you hide the money. We know all the VPs and supervisors got big-time bonuses last year for cutting salaries by using part-time workers with no benefits."

"Yeah, and not paying overtime when they should," said Little Mary. "All you do is cut, cut, cut and fill the big shots' pockets."

"I have no say over how the administration chooses to reward our leadership. You know that, I know that. So let's talk about what we can do in the real world, shall we?"

There was a moment of silence while both sides considered their options.

"Overtime for every department directly serving patients," said Lenny.

"Agreed. I can sell that for the duration of the outbreak, but not a day later."

"Approve twenty new hires to start work and let us mentor them from the get-go on the job. That will cut down the days they're stuck in a classroom while you're paying their salaries."

"So long as the union agrees to let us shorten the contractually agreed classroom orientation hours, I'm okay ten new hires."

"Full time!" said Little Mary.

"Half full time, half part time," said Freely.

"They gotta all be full time," said Moose. "Part time won't do the job."

The Director did some quick calculations on his notepad. "I'll hire the part-timers at twenty hours a week but let them work forty."

"And they get time and a half for working over forty, or for a double shift," said Lenny.

"After twelve hours on the job, Lenny, not eight."

As several union members started to object, Freely added, "I'm still going to have to sell this to the President. I will plead your case, you have my word on that."

Lenny rose and shook Freely's hand. "Yeah, I know you don't sling a lot of bull. It's the rest of the den of thieves I have to deal with. Tell them if they refuse to hire the staff and give us the resources we need, our health and safety officer will file a petition of unsafe working conditions to the Department of Health, and the union will release a press statement saying the patients are not being protected from infections."

"You'll be going down a dangerous path if you make that statement, Lenny."

"It won't be nearly as dangerous as it is for the patients and the workers. We're not safe and the public deserves to know it. I can't predict how many more will call out sick, afraid their colds and sniffles are the first sign of a Zika infection."

Lenny didn't have to spell it out, Freely understood that the union could encourage their members to call out sick en masse, a dangerous action they all hated to do, since it would leave the patients without the support and services they needed, especially in the presence of the Zika outbreak. But if the administration refused to provide the resources they needed, there was no other way.

Lenny knew the union was playing a dangerous game. He just hoped the CEO got the message loud and clear.

18

The minute Mimi saw Dr. Austin wobbling on her feet in front of the nursing station, the nurse knew something was terribly wrong. She hoped the physician hadn't contracted Zika, it was a bad-ass infection.

"Doctor Austin, what's wrong, you don't look so good?"

Austin forced a smile, but it faded quickly. "Oh, Mimi, I've been sick to my stomach and throwing up. I feel like crap."

"Come sit in a chair, let me take your temperature."

The nurse pulled out a disposable thermometer and gently tucked it under Austin's tongue, the physician being too weary to resist. Mimi followed with a check of the doctor's pulse and respirations.

"Your pulse is kinda high, and your respirations are like thirty a minute."

Mimi read the temperature, which was just a tick over 100. "At least you don't have a fever. Do you know what's going on? Do you think it's Zika?"

Austin said she had no idea what was wrong. "I used proper isolation technique with every isolation patient I visited. And I've doused my hands in alcohol rub every chance I get. It's weird."

"Well I think you need to go to the ER and be tested, they can find out if you caught the virus in like ten seconds."

"I don't know, I have so much work to do. I have a meeting with the students, and then I have office hours..."

"All that can wait, Doctor Austin. You won't be doing anybody any good as sick as you are, not to mention if you were spreading infection around."

Austin admitted that resting on a stretcher in the ER sounded like the closest thing to heaven at that moment. She knew she was badly dehydrated from all the vomiting. A few liters of intravenous lactated ringers would definitely perk her up, whatever the hell was making her sick.

"Okay, I'll head down to—"

"Oh no you don't, doctor, I'm sending you down in a wheelchair!"

Mimi called to the nurse's aide to bring a wheelchair. Once she was settled in the chair, Dr. Austin said, "Uh, Mimi, any chance you have an extra kidney basin handy, in case..."

"Of course." Mimi retrieved the small basin used to capture vomit and placed it in Austin's lap as the aide wheeled her down the hall.

"Thank you, Mimi, you are a godsend!" called the doctor as the elevator swallowed her up.

The nurse whispered a quiet prayer for the doctor, asking god that Austin's illness not be Zika, or any other serious diagnosis.

***

In the ER a tall, baby-faced physician in pink scrubs and sporting a ponytail greeted Dr. Austin. "Wow, Doctor Austin, I never expected to see you utilizing our services. What seems to be the trouble?"

"I'm sick, Robert. I feel like death would be an improvement."

Dr. Robert Schwartz took Austin's arm, and while taking her pulse he assessed her for sweaty skin, edema and circulation to the fingers. As he listened to her list of symptoms, he noted her speech, which was clear, as well as her state of dehydration as evidenced by dry lips and tongue.

While the ER physician was assessing Austin, a tech inserted an intravenous line and drew off several vials of blood.

"Be sure to include viral studies," Schwartz said. "And the

rapid test for Zika, don't forget that."

The ER tech drawing the blood asked Dr. Austin if there was any chance she was pregnant. Austin offered a wan smile. "I wish. We were thrilled when I was able to carry our daughter to term."

As the tech opened the line for the first liter of IV fluids, Schwartz told him to run the fluid in fast, the patient was seriously dehydrated. "And don't worry about fluid overload, she has a strong heart," he added with a wink to Austin that elicited the faintest of smiles.

The tech opened the roller clamp and let the first liter run in fast, not bothering to use the IV pump. Austin settled in, already feeling relief as her thirsty cells welcomed the new fluids, rich with electrolytes and glucose.

With a weary sigh, she opened her cell phone and dialed her husband's number to tell him the bad news.

**

Punching out at the Housekeeping time clock, Lenny met his wife at the main entrance. Together they walked hand in hand across to the employee parking lot, where Sandy was stationed at the little guard tower.

"Don't you two look like a couple o' lovebirds," said the old guard. "How long now you been together?"

"I don't know," said Lenny. "Four, five years I guess."

Patience jabbed him hard in the ribcage. "Four years this September," she said. "Why can't men remember anniversaries and birthdays?" She reached for the door to the car. "I bet you don't know Takia's and Malcolm's birthdays, do you?"

"I know the month," said Lenny. "Besides, the dates are in my phone calendar, I'll check it at the start of the month. It's not like I'm going to miss them."

"It's the man's brain!" called out Sandy as the big V8

roared into life. "We ain't got room for all those details!"

Lenny pulled out onto Germantown Ave and headed for home, glad it was Friday and he had the weekend off. He was looking forward to painting a couple of their neighbor's porches.

And to not having to deal with any union issues until Monday.

***

Katchi called Dr. Auginello to tell him he had finished installing the six window fans they had agreed to. Three of them were double rooms, which meant Admitting could put two confirmed Zika cases in the same room.

"You didn't get any blowback from the DOH yet, did you Mike?"

"No, but I doubt they are aware of our do-it-yourself solution to the isolation crisis. I wouldn't worry about it."

"Yeah, I hear you. The nurses are sure glad to get the extra masks, Stores was parceling out the N95 masks like they were home plate seat tickets to a Phillies game."

Katchi asked his friend what was he planning to do next to shore up the hospital's outbreak capabilities. Auginello said he wanted to address the issue of giving pregnant and possibly pregnant women a waiver to enter the isolation rooms with Zika patients. "I'm going to press hard at Monday's Infection Control meeting. I've asked all the relevant departments to send representatives. It's time to knock some heads together."

Katchi chuckled. "I'll be there with both guns loaded to defend what we've done so far. My director is happy as a pig in mud that we've saved the hospital beaucoup dollars, even though it's only a temporary fix. Nobody wants to take the long view around here, anyway."

"It's true, the place needs a ten-year plan and they can't

see past next week."

Auginello said good-bye and hurried to meet the ID resident, who would be on call that night. The resident needed to know about the additional negative pressure rooms, and not take any guff from a supervisor who voices objections. They had to decant the ER or the backlog of patients waiting for a bed would bring sanctions and penalties from the Department of Health.

When it rains, it pours, mused Auginello. *And it's raining down shit all over.*

19

Lenny handed the report back to his union Health & Safety officer. Donnie shook the hard-charging steward's hand. "You know the shit is going to hit the fan when the hospital gets this. Are you ready for it?"

Lenny told him he and the others were long past ready for any blowback. They had put up with too much for too long. Workers were at risk every day. So were patients. They had stepped up to the plate and done the work, put in extra hours, missed break time to get the job done. It was time for the bosses to do the same.

"I don't want to see another female worker going into a room with a Zika virus," he said. "And we can't tolerate pulling a housekeeper to fill a hole they can fill with a temp or a new hire. The shit's gotta stop, Donnie."

His friend promised to file the grievance that day. The administration had five business days to respond. They both expected a reply before that time, the epidemic was driving the hospital staff to exhaustion, so there was pressure on the bosses to act.

***

Roy could not believe his luck. After finishing his tour with the ambulance service, he had driven to James Madison Hospital, parking his car several blocks away ("caution curtails calamity"). Walking through the ambulance bay doors as if he had just come in on a run, he scanned the crowded hallways, looking for one particular patient, and sure enough, there she was, in an isolation room with the glass door closed and a blue RESPIRATORY ISOLATION! sign taped to the glass.

As he moved to a place where he could observe Austin without her seeing him, he smiled, realizing by the blue sign that the ER physician was probably ruling out a Zika virus. Excellent, that was exactly what he had been aiming for, as long as they were looking for Zika they wouldn't think to test for poison. And if the bitch was pregnant, all the better, it would give her a good scare.

"Hey, Roy, you bring us a new victim?"

The ward clerk on the 3-11 shift called out to Roy from her seat behind the desk. She had one phone up to her ear and another line blinking on hold, as well as a pile of admission orders to input.

"No, Mandy, not for the ER. We brought in a direct admission. I was hoping I could scarf a cup of your coffee, got anything in the breakroom?"

"You're welcome to check it out, but I don't know anybody's had time to make a fresh pot, we're dancing on a hot frying pan around here, there's no rest for the weary."

"Yeah, I hear you. The service keeps offering me overtime, but I can't work sixteen hours a day."

Roy walked slowly to the break room, where he confirmed the coffee pot was empty. Stepping back out into the hall, this time away from where the ward clerk could see him, he grabbed a white lab coat hanging on a hook by one of the bays, then donned a surgical mask and yellow isolation gown to hide the name stitched on his EMT uniform. Now he looked for all the world like the young resident he should have been all along.

Booting up one of the portable computers, he called up the lab results for Austin. The CBC and chem panel were back; they showed signs of dehydration and stress, a classic response to arsenic poisoning. The viral studies were not back yet, they would take several days to confirm or rule out Zika.

As he stood at the portable computer screen, he watched

Austin through the glass door of the isolation room. Her eyes were closed, her breathing, slow and regular. Was she asleep? It looked that way. If so, now was the time to strike. Otherwise, he'd have to wait for her to be admitted to the ward.

He pulled the syringe filled with insulin from his mast pocket and walked cautiously to Austin's room. A quick look around: nobody looking his way. The secretary was buried in her computer screen, the techs and nurses were rushing about or ministering to their patients.

Roy opened the sliding door as quietly as he could. Austin didn't stir.

Good.

He stepped toward the bed. Reaching the IV pole with its pump regulating the intravenous infusion, he was about to connect to the port in the IV line when he heard a voice say, "Adding something special just for me?"

Austin had opened her eyes. Roy looked down at her.

"Uh, yes, Doctor Austin, your chem panel came back, your magnesium is low, I was told to add 10 M-E-Q's to the solution."

"Doctor Schwartz is the best. I always liked the way he supervises the ER. And who can't love a man who wears pink scrubs?"

Finishing with the syringe, Roy stepped to the sharps container on the wall and dropped it with a *thunk* into the bucket. As he stepped toward the door, Austin called out, "Hey, don't forget to record the additive on the IV label, you don't want somebody coming after you giving me a double dose."

"Or course, doctor, sorry."

Roy scribbled a note on the IV label, then he hurried out of the room. Satisfied that no one else had noticed his visit, he stepped to the back of the ER, where he removed his mask and gown and hung the lab coat back on the hook.

Walking past the station, the ward clerk called back. "Hey,

Roy, you get any java?"

"Nah, the pot was dry. I helped myself to a carton of milk instead."

He left through the ambulance bay, walked out along the curling entrance and made his way to his car. Once inside, he rapped his palms on the steering wheel, giddy with joy at his successful action.

"Calm nerves steady the ship," he muttered to himself. Driving down Germantown Ave, he considered collecting the many aphorisms he had created over the years. Who knows, there might be a bestseller in there for him.

As long as he didn't say anything about how easy it is to commit murder.

20

At 7:30 pm, Doctor Schwartz was standing in the middle of the ER going over their patient census one last time with his team before the night crew came on duty, when he heard a shout from one of the isolation rooms.

"Doctor! Doctor, come quick, something's wrong!" Austin's husband Lawrence had opened the sliding glass door, pulled the mask down from his face and leaned out of the room, his eyes wide with fear.

The ER physician hurried to the room, grabbing a mask from the cart as he stepped into the room. Schwartz saw that the patient's arms were quivering. Beneath the top sheet, her legs were shaking as well.

He pried open Austin's eyelids. The eyes were moving rapidly back and forth, her teeth clenched in a fierce bite while mucous dribbled from her mouth.

"She's seizing! Get me three cc's of midazolam, STAT! And an amp of glucose!"

A nurse rushed to the medication room, where she unlocked the narcotic cabinet and hurriedly drew up a syringe with the rapid-acting sedative. Running back to the room, the nurse handed the doctor the syringes. He slowly injected the medication in the IV line, then quickly followed it with a gram of glucose, standard procedure for a seizure of unknown cause. He opened the pump door, flushing the medications into the blood stream.

As the seizures abated with painful slowness, the physician asked the husband if Austin had a history of seizures.

"Never. She has never had any sort of neurologic problem." He stood in the corner of the room watching, the mask still dangling about his neck.

"What about diabetes? Is she on any medication to lower her blood glucose level?"

'No, nothing like that. Apart from her endometriosis and the hysterectomy, she's been in perfect health."

"It's unlikely the seizure was from hypoglycemia, but we'll follow her glucose levels closely to be sure." Schwartz was talking now to his team as he quickly ran through the mechanisms that can trigger a seizure. He was worried, at the top of the list were brain tumors, aneurysms and strokes.

He pulled out a pocket flashlight and shone it in Austin's eyes. The pupils reacted, though sluggishly.

"I want a STAT neurology consult," he said, turning to a resident. "And I want a lumbar puncture. Get a consent form for Mister...Austin?"

"Libretti," said the husband. "She kept her maiden name for professional reasons."

"For Mister Libretti to sign. If this is a viral meningitis, we need to determine if it's Zika." Knowing the husband was in the room and that the patient herself, though sedated, might be able to hear him, Schwartz did not want to say out loud what the other members of his team already understood: that a brain infected by the Zika virus was inevitably going to suffer permanent, critical damage.

If the patient even survived the infection.

**

As he was getting ready to go upstairs to bed, Michael Auginello heard his phone chirp three times: a STAT message, he could tell by the sound. It was Dr. Schwartz in the ER. Dialing the number, he heard an edge in his colleague's voice he hadn't heard before.

"Mike, it's Bob. Listen, Austin just threw a grand mal seizure. Her blood sugar was twenty-five after an amp of glucose. Your ID Fellow promised to come right down, but I wanted your perspective on the case."

"Of course, I'm glad you called. Have you run a sepsis panel?"

"It's pending, but the STAT lactic acid and CPR levels are high. Her diff is more consistent with a stress response than a systemic infection."

"Hmm. Has she been taking oral meds or injecting insulin for diabetes?" asked Auginello.

'That's why I called you straight up, she says she doesn't have diabetes. That she never had it. I checked her labs from Employee Health, her A-One-C was normal."

Though it was a hot summer night with the air conditioning on low, Auginello felt a chill. "Is she on any other medication that could lower her glucose level?"

"Just a statin, and she's been on that for years. She's experienced severe nausea, and she vomited in her office. Her dietary intake has been poor the last day or so, but it shouldn't lower her blood sugar that much. Certainly not after an amp of glucose."

"I agree, this is not a case of starvation. It wouldn't be pancreatitis, her glucose would be elevated, not lowered."

The two kept silent a moment, processing what they'd discussed.

"Listen, get my ID Fellow to email me all her labs, including x-rays, CAT scans, anything else you study. I'll look at them before I sack out and let you know if I come up with anything. Otherwise I'll put her first in my rounds tomorrow."

"Okay, thanks. She'll be in the ICU by then, I'm moving her if I have to push the damn stretcher up to the unit myself."

"Hey, thanks for keeping me in the loop, I've always had a soft spot for Austin, she's a thoughtful clinician and a damn fine lady."

Shutting down the phone, Auginello found himself worried about Dr. Austin's diagnosis. An infection could lower blood sugar, but in that case there would be signs in the blood work. The simplest explanation was that a nurse had mixed up her meds with someone else's, though he thought that was unlikely, the staff had strict protocols when administering any medication.

He wondered if someone else in the family was diabetic. Could Austin have been taking a wrong drug somehow? But that would mean she had been taking the wrong drug for some time, which seemed highly unlikely.

It was puzzling. But practicing medicine was often working a jigsaw puzzle with missing pieces. The one thought that filled him with dread was that sometimes the correct diagnosis wasn't made until the autopsy was complete.

**

Louis had begged Catherine to come with him to the neonatal intensive care unit to visit their baby, but she had not come. She didn't refuse outright, she simply pulled the blanket and sheet up over her head and lay in bed silent as a stone. As a corpse. Now he had two people he loved to worry about, his wife and their child on support in the NICU and oh so vulnerable. So fragile.

He stood at the isolette peering in through the plexiglass, watching the baby's flat little chest rise and fall. Her belly was big, he wondered if that was normal and made a mental note to ask the OB doctors when they were available. The intravenous line was connected through the baby's umbilical cord, rather than the usual hand or wrist or arm. He thought that odd, but the nurse had assured him it was the best way to give baby fluids and nutrition.

Asked when the baby would be able to take milk, meaning his wife's breast milk, the NICU nurse assured him it would be soon, the baby wasn't so very premature, her GI tract should soon tolerate food. Probably tomorrow they would start her on sugar water, and if the baby kept it down, they would go on to formula. Or breast milk, if mom was up to pumping it.

Louis pictured his wife on the Post-Partum ward, the sheet pulled over her head, indifferent to the world. He had no idea how he was going to convince her to nurse their precious little girl.

***

On the pediatric ward, Roy called up Austin's latest lab results on a portable computer. He was not surprised she had survived the insulin injection, the doctors in the ER weren't fools, just mediocre practitioners. They had ordered a long list of labs, none of which were for poisons. That was good news: the dimwits weren't smart enough to realize that the hand of an omnipotent agent was controlling her fate.

The clearest eyes live in shadow. Another aphorism to add to his collection.

Austin was another step closer to death, one foot in the grave already. But not too close, he was having too much fun to end the game so quickly.

21

Lenny's chest was heaving as he tried in vain to keep up with Moose on the Fairmount Park path. They had passed young couples with infants and toddlers who were enjoying the cool morning air, and a pair of seniors walking briskly with small weights in their hands as they pumped their arms. Below the trail, the Wissahickon Creek bubbled its way downward toward the Schuylkill River.

Slowing to a stagger, Lenny wiped his brow with his sleeve as he labored to take in lungfuls of air. Ahead, Moose was flying along the path, his face as in a trance. A big man, his feet seemed to barely touch the ground as he ran, as light as a deer racing through a forest.

A few moments later Moose turned around and rejoined his friend.

"Heh, heh, now don't you feel better, getting out and goin' for a good run?" said Moose.

"No. I don't know why I let you talk me into this jogging business. It's Saturday morning, I could be laying in bed with my second cup of coffee watching the news, or cartoons with Malcolm, but instead I'm out here risking my life in this mosquito-infested swamp."

Moose wiped his face and neck with a towel. "You love it and you know it. Nobody's twisting your arm to come out, ya know."

"Psychological pressure."

Once he had caught his breath, Lenny told his friend he was going to spend most of Saturday painting porches and repairing window screens for his neighbors. "Our block club collected a bunch of rusted paint cans from neighborhood shops, we're helping the seniors keep their property looking sharp."

"That's a beautiful thing to do, maybe I'll stop by, give you all a hand."

Farther along the trail, Moose again raised his doubts that the nurses would ever agree to join the same union as the service workers. Lenny admitted, there would be some who looked down their noses at the custodians, dietary aides and transporters. But Mimi and her friends had a weekend meeting set up with the nursing division organizer for their union, so it looked like they were moving ahead with the campaign.

"What about *our* people?" said Moose. "If the bosses don't give us more workers and let the pregnant women stay out o' the Zika rooms, we got to turn up the heat. I know it won't look good, the union calling for a sickout in the middle of the outbreak, but we gotta show the bosses we're not gonna take it."

"I agree, we'll take some serious heat if we organize a walkout or sickout, even if we make it clear the patients are in danger if we don't get the resources we need."

"Sometimes the best time to fight the boss is during a crisis," said Moose. "It kinda sharpens your mind."

Lenny smiled. "Did you take my copy of *The Art of War*?"

"Heh, heh. You ain't the only one strategizing for the union."

Lenny agreed, they needed to do some serious planning if they were going to call for any kind of mass action. They needed a meeting of the stewards and the most committed members, and they needed it now.

***

In the ICU, Dr. Auginello pinched the metal strip on his face mask, smiling to know it was designed for painters, not doctors, and stepped into Austin's room, the ID Fellow following behind him. He found Rachel Austin sitting up in bed sipping a tall cup of coffee, her husband seated beside her leaning in close, ready to help. Their daughter was seated on the bed beside her mother looking scared.

"I'm going to be fine, Bethany, really I will," Austin was saying to her daughter. "Michael, tell them I will be all right," she added, seeing the ID physician enter.

As Lawrence stood up and held out his hand to shake Dr. Auginello's, the ID physician held his palms together and bowed slightly. Austin chuckled. "The ID Service wants us to abandon hand shaking, dear, at least during the outbreak, it's an effective way of transmitting microorganisms from hand to hand."

"Ah, excellent idea," said her husband, who bowed to the two doctors and resumed his seat.

Auginello stood watching Austin. He noted the slight tremor in her hand as she put the coffee cup down on the overbed table, and a slow cadence in her words, as if she had to think of each word before she spoke it.

"Of course, you are on the mend, no doubt at all," said the ID physician, turning his gaze to the daughter. "The CAT scan of the head was negative, as was the abdominal. That is *very* good news, it means there was no stroke or tumor or anything bad like that causing the seizure."

"Why was mommy so sick?" asked the girl, pulling her mask away from her mouth as she talked.

"Well, sometimes the answer takes a little more time. There are a bunch of tests for infections that aren't back yet, we have to wait to see if anything grows in a culture. It's like planting a seed and waiting for it to sprout, you see what I mean?"

Bethany shrugged her shoulders. "I guess." She climbed into bed to lie beside her mother, who put her arms around the girl.

"Then there is no sign of the Zika virus?" asked Lawrence, getting up from his bedside chair to make room for Auginello.

"No, but the rapid test is not one-hundred percent accurate, it can sometimes yield a false negative, we'll have to wait for the culture. That will take two or three more days. It's best to maintain the isolation until then."

"And if that test is negative...?"

Auginello told him they never ran out of things to test for, it was best to take it one day at a time. The absence of a stroke or tumor was very good news, they should take comfort in that. Not to mention how well the patient was doing.

"And you have never taken any diabetes medication," said Auginello. "Nothing that could lower your blood sugar."

"No, I'm only on a statin for my cholesterol, vascular disease runs in my family."

"No one else in your house is on medication for diabetes?"

Austen shook her head No.

"I haven't seen any more drop in your blood sugar, so that's good news, too." Auginello poked his tongue in his cheek, musing on the information he had. "If you're able to take in sufficient fluids, we can stop the IV, you were profoundly dehydrated on admission."

"That would be the vomiting and the diarrhea," said Austin.

"Yes. You'll be on a clear liquid diet this morning."

"Yum, jello and broth. Thank god Lawrence brought me coffee. I can't get through my morning without my coffee."

Auginello promised to stop back in the afternoon, promising to monitor the lab results as they came in. Austin held her cup of coffee in two hands, wishing she could enjoy a cup from her office machine. But she didn't want to ask Lawrence to go all the way to the Family Medicine office, the brew from the hospital cafeteria was drinkable.

She knew her husband and daughter were worried about her. They had probably imagined what it could be like to have a day or a week without her: a dreadful thought, even for her. Austin took comfort in the negative scans: no cancer, no stroke. She just wished her GI tract was back to normal, even the simple cup of coffee was threatening to send her to the bathroom on the run.

***

Not long after Dr. Auginello left Austin's room, a dietary aide placed Dr. Austin's breakfast tray on the isolation cart outside her room and prepared to don a mask and gown. A young resident in a crisp lab coat and understated tie stepped up to the isolation cart. "I can take that in for you, old buddy," he said, opening the drawer to an isolation gown.

"That's mighty nice of you," said the aide. "Thanks. All these isolation patients are slowing our rounds down something awful."

"Not at all. Help a stranger, help yourself."

Roy pulled on the yellow paper gown, mask and gloves. Seeing the aide carry a pair of trays into another ICU room, he pulled the syringe from his lab coat pocket and squirted a small amount of arsenic-laced fluid into the coffee cup. Beside the cup, a lonely tea bag and a small pot of hot water waited to be added.

He knocked lightly on the door and carried in the breakfast tray. He saw Austin's husband and daughter seated beside the bed. The daughter looked a few years older than her picture on the mug in her mother's office. For a second Roy wondered how he could administer some arsenic to the girl, but decided bringing her a soda would look too out of place.

"That's kind of you to carry the tray in for the aide," said Austin.

"I was passing by, it was no problem," said Roy, placing the tray on the bedside tray. "Can I make you some tea?"

"Ugh, tea," said Austin. "Clear liquids. That's all right, my husband can help me, I'm still a little shaky."

As he turned to leave, Roy wished her a speedy recovery and left.

While Lawrence poured the hot water, Austin thought the resident—or was he a medical student—had a familiar voice. Probably she had heard him on rounds one day, with the mask she couldn't really see his face, but he did have rather vivid blue eyes.

Austin took a sip of tea, grimaced, set the cup down. 'This tea is *terrible*. I'm going to stick with coffee."

Her husband sipped the tea. Finding it too bitter, he added two sugars and some lemon juice. "Not too shabby," he said, sitting back and enjoying the tea. "Not too shabby at all."

22

Mimi and four other nurses stepped cautiously into a conference room at the union office in Center City. Alexandra Brayburn, the organizer in the Hospital Service Workers Union nursing division, was a tall redheaded woman with freckles splashed across a smiling face, a firm handshake and a no-nonsense way of talking. Brayburn welcomed them into the room. Mimi wished Lenny was with them, but he had assured her the nursing division would take good care of her, and he was always available by phone if she had a question the union rep couldn't answer.

"I am so very, very glad you're able to take the time to come down to the union office," said Alexandra. "I wanted you to see where we do business, and where you will be coming for meetings and such."

"It was kind of you to invite us, Alexandra," said Mimi.

"Call me Al, everyone else does."

"Lenny said you were a pro, and I know when he praises somebody, it's for real."

"Lenny Moss." Alexandra shook her head and smiled. "I wish we had a dozen more like him, we could organize every facility in the Delaware Valley."

Once everyone was seated, Alexandra sent around a sign-in sheet. As the nurses filled them out, she asked if they understood the process of signing nurses up. Most in the group were not clear.

"Well, in one way it's very simple, and in one way, it's very complicated. Under the labor relations laws, you have a right to organize a union. It's protected speech. But the bosses usually don't respect the law, so they take punitive action against the organizer."

"In other words, fire us," said Agnes.

"Yes, although the administration can target any nurse they suspect of participating in the union drive. That's where it becomes tricky. You want to begin with the nurses you know best and trust the most. Meet with them outside the facility, someplace where you won't be seen, and explain the campaign to them. In an ideal campaign, the bosses won't know what you're doing until you have enough signatures to call for a union vote."

Alexandra put a tall, free-standing pad on the conference table and uncorked a marker. "Now then, let's hear what your most pressing issues are. I'll list them, and then we can prioritize them and work on ways to frame them in a flyer."

"I hate the GPS units we have to wear," said Miss Kim. "I don't even want to go to the bathroom, I am afraid the dispatcher will hear me."

"You're not the first facility to be fighting the communications devices," said Alexandra "We have fought them in three hospitals and four nursing homes. So far, we have got them either eliminated, or we won the nurse's right to turn them off during breaks."

"We work short all the time, especially on the weekend," said Margot, a plump young nurse with a sweet, high-pitched voice that belied her tough attitude. "I've been ordered to stay over on a twelve hour shift an extra four hours more times than I can count. That means I worked for sixteen bloody hours! And the one time I called out sick for the next day's shift, I was written up for abusing the sick-out policy!"

Other nurses joined in with more complaints: patronizing, disrespectful supervisors, no paid days to go to a conference, no allowance for uniforms—it was a long list.

Mimi said, "The biggest, baddest issue for many of us is that pregnant nurses aren't allowed to switch assignments so they don't have to care for a Zika case. That is totally unfair. In fact, it's criminal. One nurse on my ward was potentially exposed, and she's in her third trimester. She is scared to death, literally, and that's not good for mom, *or* the baby."

Everyone chimed in with their agreement.

"We've brought that issue to labor relations in every facility we represent," said Alexandra. 'Even though the Labor Relations Board has not ruled on this particular issue, we feel we are on solid grounds arguing the health and safety aspect. Three of our facilities have granted waivers, the others are under discussion."

"That should be issue number one," agreed Agnes.

Alexandra wrote a number "1" and circled it on the note pad. After further discussion she set numerical values to the rest of the issues. The group spent the rest of their time talking about the best way to frame the issues so they resonated with the largest number of nurses.

"We don't want to be inflammatory at this point," Alexander cautioned them. "And we don't have to use insulting language. The issues by themselves speak volumes."

Once all were agreed on the issues they would employ to press the union campaign, the union organizer promised to type them up and email a flyer to everyone who attended. She reminded them to be careful how they gave them out, and not to be caught with copies in their locker or their purse.

"You mean the hospital might search our bags? Our pockets?" said Miss Kim, aghast at hearing that police tactics might be employed.

"Well, they won't go so far as to strip search you," said Alexandra. "But everything else is fair game as long as you are on hospital property. So be sure to stash any flyers or union cards in a safe place that can't be linked directly to you." She turned to Mimi. "Any last questions for me?"

Mimi looked at each of her co-workers. Agnes opened her mouth to speak, but then shut it. "Go ahead, Aggie, tell us what's on your mind."

"Well..." The nurse looked around at her colleagues. "I

don't want to be a spoilsport or insult the union, I know you've done a lot of good things for the service employees..."

"No need to guard your words, Agnes." Alexandra held her hands out in a welcoming gesture. "If you have questions about professional nurses joining our union, I can tell you that issue has come up in every campaign for RNs we have organized."

"How did you get the nurses to join?" Agnes said. "Some of us, maybe a lot of us, aren't sure we belong in your union."

The organizer told her that in some hospitals, the RNs did not sign enough union pledge cards to warrant an election. Instead, they decided to join an all-RN 'professional' union.

"The United Nurses of Pennsylvania," said Mimi.

"Yes, the UNP." Alexandra said. "In some facilities the nurses have gone their own way. They are weaker for dividing the hospital workforce, but they felt they had more unity. Unity counts for a lot when you are voting to strike."

Mimi was relieved the meeting with the union rep had gone so well, even if Agnes looked like she wasn't 100% on board with the plan. Alexandra seemed like a solid person who could help them bring the union message to the nurses, and Lenny would be a wise counsel for the campaign.

As the meeting broke up, everyone thanked Alexandra for the union support. Leaving the building, Mimi took out her phone and sent Lenny a brief text message asking if she could call him that evening, she wanted his take on what they were planning to do.

While no longer anxious about how the meeting would go, Mimi was concerned about Dr. Austin, the doctor had looked like gravely ill when Mimi sent her to the ER Friday afternoon.

Well, there was nothing she could do about it until she returned to work on Monday. All she could do was wait and hope for the best.

After dropping off Miss Kim at her home in Germantown,

Mimi drove to Lenny's house to talk about the meeting, she still had a lot of questions about the campaign, and Lenny was always so clear on what they had to do next.

***

Mrs. Filtcher peeked out of her front window overlooking the porch and could not believe her eyes. There they were, seven neighbors, all working on the old wooden trim and railing. They were scraping peeling paint and filling holes with paste: it was just wonderful.

"How many cans of blue we got?" asked Desmond, sanding a section of quick dry spackling.

"Two cans of the blue. Looks like we can salvage them with a lot of thinner," said Abe, stirring one of the cans. "This looks like it's US Army surplus, it is really *thick*."

"Yeah, which war?" asked Lenny, who was up one of the ladders laying a layer of primer on the trim along the roof.

"Okay," Desmond said. "We use the gray-blue for the rails and the siding along the front, and the white for the trim."

Abe said, "Hey, remember that big snowstorm couple of years back? Man, we made history that day for sure." They recalled how the city had announced they would not be plowing the small streets for at least three or four days, so the block club organized a snow shoveling party. Somebody brought out a boombox, Patience served hot coffee laced with bourbon, and everybody got out their shovels and cleared the whole street.

"Even your buddy from the hospital joined in," said Desmond. "'Member? He came sliding down the street on skis!"

"That Moose is a good friend," said Patience. "One in a million."

Once the prep work was done, they dipped brushes in the paint and began brushing on the paint. "I think we'll need two coats on the porch floor," said Patience, on her knees laying a thick coat at the far end of the porch. Desmond agreed, they would come back Sunday after the first coat was dry to add the second coat.

Finished with the trim along the roof, Lenny left them to repair the screens. Knocking on the old wooden door, he slipped inside with pieces of screening and metal shears. "Okay if I check the screens, Missus Filtcher?"

"You check whatever it is needs fixing," she said.

Climbing the creaking wooden stairs, Lenny began with the bathroom. Sure enough, there was a tear along the middle of the screen. He cut a section, held it over the tear and patiently threaded a thin wire along the edges while Mrs. Filtcher looked on.

"You boys are such a blessing for an old lady like me."

"We don't want you to catch that Zika virus, it's a nasty bug."

Mrs. Filtcher went downstairs to make lemonade for the crew while Lenny went on to the next room. By noon all the painting was finished and all the torn screen repaired. Desmond went around to the back door and called Mrs. Filtcher out to check the work. She followed him along the alley between her twin and the neighbor's. Standing on the sidewalk in front of her house, a stretch of broken concrete she wished she had the money to repair, the old woman clasped her hands together and nodded her head up and down.

"It's wonderful, boys, just wonderful. I can't thank you enough." When the crew packed up their equipment and prepared to leave, she insisted they stay for sandwiches and lemonade. "I made tuna salad, and liverwurst, too," she said. "Oh, and there's a couple of old bottles of beer in the fridge. Do you suppose you boys could do something with them?"

Lenny laid the ladder in the alley and followed the old woman to the back yard, where the cold drinks and sand-wiches were laid out. He made a note to bring his push mower and take a crack at the yard soon as he had the time.

23

Lenny was sitting on his front step talking with Desmond when he saw Mimi pull up in her little two-seat car, a ten-year-old Honda Insight.

"Hey, what does that car run on, rubber bands?" he asked.

"Hah, hah." Mimi followed Lenny into the house as his partner in the block club headed off. "I'm glad you said I could come over, we had our first meeting with the union organizer."

"Great, how'd it go?"

"Okay, I think. Alexandra seems like she really knows what she's doing, that was kind of reassuring. We put together a list of our grievances, she's going to write up a flyer and email it to me and Agnes, we'll start to give them out on Monday."

Lenny asked Mimi if she'd like a beer. "Got anything stronger?" she asked.

"Bourbon."

"That'll do, with a couple of rocks, thanks."

As Lenny went to pour the drinks, Patience came downstairs and greeted the nurse. "I heard you had a big meeting today, good for you," she said.

Mimi filled them in on the discussion and the plan to start giving out flyers and union pledge cards on Monday. Patience urged her to be careful and assess the nurse's loyalty to the administration before giving out something in writing. "You have to go real slow in the beginning. And you don't want to be caught with any union materials in your locker. We can help give them out, I travel all over the hospital when I'm shooting portable x-rays."

Mimi let the whiskey warm her throat and ease the tension she'd been feeling since going down to the union hall.

She told them she understood she couldn't keep any union materials in her locker, or even her purse. "That mean old Joe West is capable of anything," she agreed, referencing the infamous chief of hospital security.

"Most of our union members will be behind your campaign," Lenny said. "They're beginning to see we have the same issues. The same grievances." He told her of his meeting with Human Relations, and how the director had made a couple of concessions, but he couldn't give in to all of them. Like allowing pregnant workers to stay out of the Zika rooms.

"The thing that scares the bosses shitless," said Patience, "is for the whole ever-lovin' hospital to be organized in one big union. You better believe they'll do anything to stop it."

"Which means," said Lenny, "they will fight even harder to keep the nurses from joining. It's their worst nightmare."

Mimi described the discussion about the RNs at other hospitals joining an all-RN union. Patience cautioned that feelings of superiority and privilege were deep in the nursing staff. "It won't be easy convincing them, that's why you have to start with co-workers that you trust. And prepare yourself for the worst: some nurses will snitch to the Director of Nursing."

Lenny told her they had to deal with snitches in a few of their campaigns. Mimi admitted she wasn't surprised and promised to be careful. Drinking the last of her whiskey, she said, "Well, I better be getting on home, my old man isn't used to me going to a lot of meetings. All he knows how to cook is macaroni and cheese. From a box."

"He'll get used to it," said Patience. "Trust me, he wants you working in a safe environment, and the union is the only way to make that happen."

"Boy, is that ever the truth," said Mimi, stepping to the front door. "Even the doctors are getting sick. Yesterday I sent Doctor Austin to the ER, she looked like death warmed over. I'm really worried about her."

"Was she exposed to Zika?" asked Lenny.

"Maybe. I'll know more when I get to work on Monday."

Standing together on the front porch, Patience put her arm around her husband and watched Mimi pull away. "What a cute little car! What do they call it?"

"It's a Go-car, you pedal it with your feet. It has a rubber band for overdrive."

"Why don't we get something like that, but with four seats?" said Patience, ignoring her husband's wisecrack. "I bet it gets like a hundred miles to the gallon."

"It gets five miles every time you wind it up."

Patience poked him in the ribs. "You promised to sell your dad's car a whole year ago. It's time to let it go, Lenny. "

He sighed, knowing she was right, as usual. The women were always right. He would just have to trade in the big Buick and settle for something small and sensible.

And cheap.

***

Lawrence was telling his wife it was time for him to take their daughter home. "I need to feed this little girl some lunch or she'll stop growing on us. We can't have that, can we, Bethany?"

"How about we stop for pizza on the way home?" said the child.

As he stood up, Lawrence felt his stomach knot up. He broke out into a sweat as a wave of nausea swept over him.

"Dear, are you all right?"

"I feel a little queasy. Yikes, I hope what you've contracted isn't contagious."

"I hope so, too. Perhaps you should see the ER doctor before you leave."

"No, no, it's not that bad, just a little cramping is all. I'll be fine soon as we're home, I've got something I can take for it."

"Like good old Jack Daniels," said Austin.

"Jack Daniels with *ginger ale.* Don't you always say ginger ale is the best thing to settle your stomach?"

Austin didn't bother to correct her husband's remark, he had been enjoying his whiskey and ginger ale as long as she'd known him. And since he almost never had a second drink, even when they were at a party, she couldn't criticize him too much this time.

With a kiss on the cheek from Lawrence and a hug from her daughter, Austin lowered the head of her bed a few degrees, turned off the overhead light and closed her eyes. "I am dead tired," she mumbled to herself, then regretted using the word 'dead.' Not while she was lying in a hospital bed with an illness her physician couldn't identify.

***

In his small studio apartment Roy gently pulled the glass lid off the slow cooker and pulled out one of the petri dishes. Holding it up to the light, he smiled to see the beautiful cream colored colonies growing in the blood agar. It had been a stroke of genius, holding back blood tubes on the last four ambulance cases with fevers. He'd bet they had infections, and sure enough, the blood he'd cultured in soup broth, first boiled to make it sterile, was growing like blazes. Under the microscope, the slide he'd made confirmed the bacteria was a gram negative rod— just the kind of nasty pathogen he needed.

He checked the other dishes, all of which were growing robust colonies from the other blood samples. He had several species of gram positive bacteria thriving in the cultures. There was no sign of any fungal growth, but those were prickly little critters, difficult to grow in his primitive laboratory.

All in all, Roy was pleased with his progress. By Monday he would be able to bring poor old Dr. Austin a devastating attack to her immune system. One that produced such a massive infection, all the antibiotics in the world would be unable to fight them off.

24

Louis Feekin looked down at the tiny figure in the isolette, his heart swelling with love. He'd given his heart to his
daughter even before seeing the hazy images of the ultrasound when the baby was in her mother's womb. Even before
he or his wife could feel the baby kicking in the womb. The
instant the pregnancy test came back positive, he gave up his
heart to the baby, not even caring if it was a girl or a boy.

While Catherine's fears from the possible Zika exposure
had locked up her heart, Louis's had opened up more and
more. He was determined to do everything he could to see
that their daughter survived. Thrived, even, whatever disability she might suffer due to the premature birth. And there
was no damned way he would take any bullshit excuses or
lame explanations from anyone on staff: he wanted the best
care delivered twenty-four seven, and god help the caregiver
who slacked off an inch.

"How long will she be in the intensive care unit?" he asked
the nurse, a young Filipino nurse with a bright smile. The
doctors had finished their rounds, allowing visitors into the
big room filled with isolettes.

"We're waiting for the tests for virus to come back. That's
our protocol, but the doctors haven't seen any sign of Zika in
your baby."

"Okay, and then...?"

"Mainly it depends on how mature the baby's lungs are.
When a baby is born very early, the lungs haven't developed
enough to provide all the oxygen she needs. Your baby is
right on the edge: she's not *too* premature, but she's not close
enough to full term to survive without supplemental oxygen."

Louis put his hand on the plexiglass top of the isolette.

"Think we'll know today?"

"Mmm, probably not today. Tomorrow, maybe, but the signs are positive. Very positive." The nurse handed Louis a kit. "This is for collecting breast milk. The lactation nurse will assist your wife and help her express her milk, but it'll be good if you encouraged her, too."

"Sure," said Louis. "I'll do anything you need. They told me in the classes that breast milk is way better than formula." He looked down at the kit. "I'll work on it, we'll get it done."

"Thank you. And please give your wife my warmest wishes. She's welcome to visit her baby any time."

"I've asked her to go to the NICU. I've *begged* her to go, but she's so damn depressed..." He shuddered to recall the image of his wife, the sheet and blanket pulled up over her face, not wanting to get out of bed to see her baby. Not wanting even to talk about the little girl, so deep were her fears.

"I know, Miser Feekin, your wife is so afraid she's exposed her baby to the Zika virus. We don't believe she has, the baby has shown no clinical signs of exposure or infection, but until the viral cultures come back, I'm afraid she won't be convinced."

Louis thanked the nurse for her support and made his way back to the Postpartum ward, hoping Catherine was at least sitting up and showing her face.

***

Moose attacked the old peeling paint with broad powerful strokes, running the paint scraper up and down the porch. He and Lenny and Desmond were working on another porch, the last for the weekend.

"You sure you got enough primer and topcoat for this one?" asked Moose.

"Plenty," said Desmond. "We may have to thin some of the paint with turpentine, it was sitting in a basement for a hundred years, so it's dried up pretty good."

"Nothin' like the old oil based," Moose said. "It gives the best coating."

"I agree," said Patience, who was patiently applying primer to the wood railing at the front of the porch. The uprights were square at the base and top, round in the middle, making it a tedious job to cover every nook and cranny well. "But you have to be careful the paint isn't so old it's got lead in it."

She tucked a loose strand of hair up under the kerchief covering her head, dipped the brush and went on to another section.

The elderly couple's granddaughter came out with a pitcher of beer and glasses. "My gran said you can have all the beer you want, so long as you don't fall off o' no ladder."

Moose promised the young girl they would be very careful on the ladder. He stopped scraping to take a long taste of the beer. Seeing Lenny pour his beer over ice cubes, he asked, "You still drinkin' your beer on the *rocks?* Man, I don't get that at all."

Lenny explained that a really cold beer absorbed more heat in the stomach, plus, being diluted a bit, he took in less alcohol. "If I'm gonna work all day I have to keep my head clear," he said.

"Be the first time," Patience offered. "I was so proud of Malcolm, wanting to come out and help us. But he'd end up getting more paint on himself than on the porch, and it isn't even water-based paint."

"There's something wrong with that boy," said Lenny. "He volunteered to give up a morning of cartoons to work with us. That's unnatural."

Patience gave Lenny a look of scorn, so he focused on the painting and said no more.

As he rolled another band of primer, he filled Moose in on Mimi's Saturday meeting with the union organizer for the nursing division, wondering aloud how many nurses Mimi and Miss Kim had reached this weekend. Moose repeated his doubts that they would collect enough signed pledge cards to hold an election. "A lotta nurses don't want to associate with us service workers, they put themselves up on some kinda professional pedestal. It'll be a miracle if they came around."

"I have to agree with Moose." Patience adjusted her head scarf and paused in her work. "Sometimes when I ask an RN to help me position a patient in the bed for a portable, they do it, but some of them act like it's robbing them of their precious time."

"It's a problem, we can't discount it," said Lenny. "But their grievances are so deep, like those GPS units they have to wear, eventually it's going to wear down their resistance to joining our union."

Moose said, "My pop used to say, eventually is a long old time away. In the meantime, what's to stop another union from coming in and offering them pie in the sky?"

"You're talking about UNP," said Lenny. "They only have the RNs organized in two Philly hospitals, plus a couple in the suburbs. I haven't seen any signs of them trying to organize any more facilities in the city."

Moose said, "You just wait. Soon's they hear the nurses are signing pledge cards for our union, they'll come swooping down, try and steal our nurses away."

Lenny didn't like to think about another union poaching on their drive, but he'd seen it happen too many times to not know it was a real possibility. A possibility he had no way of stopping. On top of a potential threat from UNP, the current labor relations board was tilting so far to the right it was breaking the back of the labor movement. He turned his attention to the painting, estimating they would be ready to put on the topcoat about the time the pitcher of beer was empty. Once the painting was completed, he had a bottle of Evan Williams and a pot of beef stew waiting for him at home that would ease his cares and prime him for a nice long nap.

***

Mimi and Kim sipped their glasses of lemonade, listening to the two co-workers list their grievances with their supervisor. The union organizer had reminded them to spend more time listening than talking, so they were careful to wait and let the women vent.

"The GPS has got to go, that's my biggest beef," said Marilyn, a middle-aged mother of three with over ten years on the job. "I mean, isn't there a law against eavesdropping on somebody? How can they get away with this kind of crap?"

Her friend Louise, who worked on Six North with Marilyn, agreed. "I can't stand how little they respect us. I wouldn't treat my children like that, and I can be pretty darn hard on my kids."

Having vented a long list of complaints, Marilyn asked Mimi if it was true what Miss Burgess had been telling them that if they joined the union, they would have to work by the same rules as the service employees. "They say we would have to punch in at a time clock. That's not how a professional is treated, I wouldn't like that at all."

Louise asked weren't the RNs supervisors over the service employees, and therefore not eligible to even be in a union? "My head nurse tells us we make out assignments and supervise the aides and clerks and housekeepers, so we don't even qualify for being in a union."

Mimi told them those were all lies the administration told to intimidate and confuse the nurses. She pointed out that the head nurse did all of the hiring and firing, not to mention making out the evaluations and the time schedules. "Those are real supervisor responsibilities," she explained. "The head nurses and assistant directors wouldn't be in our union, only us RNs."

"And the non-professionals," Marilyn pointed out. "We'd be in the same union as those people."

"Yes, yes, the same union," Miss Kim said, "but not the

same division. We will be in the nursing division. We will have our own union leadership."

Pouring everyone more lemonade, Louise said, "If the service workers go out on strike, will we have to go out on strike, too?"

Mimi said it was true, they would be asked to join the other union members if they voted to strike. "That doesn't sound fair to me," offered Louise. "Why should we lose our pay for somebody else's benefit?"

"But with the whole hospital under one union, the administration would have to settle even before they went out on the picket line," said Mimi. "We might not even have to walk out if we're all together!"

Kim added that if the nurses stood with the service workers when they had a dispute, the service workers would stand with the nurses when we take a stand.

"Nurses can't go out on strike," Louise said. "It would mean abandoning our patients. We'll all lose our licenses to practice! We might even go to prison!"

Miss Kim explained that when nurses go out on strike, they give the hospital plenty of time to prepare: the hospital can discharge patients, transfer patients, or hire temporary staff to replace them. She assured them no nurse can be charged with abandonment for taking part in a labor walkout.

Marilyn and Louise still looked skeptical. When Mimi asked them to sign pledge cards, which they needed to qualify for a union election, the two women took the cards but did not sign them, promising to think long and hard about what was the right thing to do.

Mimi drove Kim back to her apartment, having completed three visits to nurses that day. Three nurses had signed cards, two openly refused, and others like Marilyn and Louise had made no commitment to join, though it looked like they were leaning away from signing.

"Lord almighty, I never thought this union business would

be so tough," said Mimi. "We've got a whole lot of work ahead of us."

Kim was quiet. Not unusual for her, the young nurse often held back expressing her thoughts or feelings. When they arrived at her apartment, Kim said, "The head nurse on Six-North has been talking bad about the union. I think she knows what we are doing."

"How could she know anything? We've been careful not to talk about it at work."

Kim pursed her lips, holding back her thought. Before closing the car door, she said, "Some nurses talk to the boss. We must be careful."

Mimi drove on to home, wondering what nurse might have snitched to Miss Burgess, and what, if anything, she could do to protect herself from the retaliation she was sure would be coming her way.

**

Standing in the hallway outside the sewing room, Joe West, James Madison Chief of Security, watched as an engineer stood on a ladder, his head above the tile ceiling. He was installing a router to carry the signal for the GPS units. Once installed, the dispatcher would be able to listen in on a nurse's conversation while inside the sewing room.

Having made sure no service worker was around, West was satisfied that no one knew of the installation. He planned to instruct the dispatcher to make no calls to the nurse while she was in the basement, that would alert her to the new system capability. As long as the GPS stayed silent, the nurse would never suspect she was being monitored.

As the engineer replaced the ceiling tile, concealing the device, West took out his wallet and gave the man a tip, instructing him to tell no one what he'd done, and that keeping his job depended on utter secrecy.

25

Five AM. Quiet in the ICU. Three of the nurses are bathing patients, the curtains drawn discreetly around the beds, leaving the open area empty of staff. A fourth nurse is busy printing labels for the morning lab work, which she and the other nurses would soon be drawing. With her attention focused on the lab orders so as not to mix up any of the requests, the nurse did not notice the young intern (or was he a medical student?) coming through the ICU. The lab-coated figure, looking like one of a hundred medical personnel roaming the hospital, silently passed the nursing station and made his way to Rachel Austin's isolation room at the end of the ICU.

Donning a mask, he slipped into the room with its glass partitions and drew the curtain around the bed, making it look like the other patients receiving their morning bath. He saw by her slow, regular respirations and her heart rate of sixty that Austin was sleeping soundly. Peacefully, even.

With a satisfied smile, Roy took the syringe from his lab coat pocket. He pulled off the cap and injected the contents into the intravenous port. As he watched the milky substance ooze down the transparent line, he heard the alarm go off on the IV pump. The poison was so thick that it was clogging up the catheter in the vein.

Quickly he stabbed the access port on the intravenous bag, withdrew 10 cc's of fluid, and flushed the line. That worked fine, most of the poison disappeared into the blood stream, but the pump was still beeping its alarm, and Roy didn't know how to reset the IV pump.

Looking over the digital message on the face of the machine, he saw a button to reset and pressed it, silencing the alarm. Out of the corner of his eye he saw Austin stir in the bed. With eyes half open, she looked over at Roy.

Austin mumbled was it time for breakfast? Roy told her to close her eyes and go back to sleep, it was not yet morning. He hurriedly opened the curtain, slipped out of the room and closed the door. Daring a quick look back, he saw that Austin had closed her eyes and was back asleep. He was confident she would not even remember his entering the room, let alone fiddling with her intravenous pump.

Roy hurried to the exit, pressed the plate on the wall to open the doors, and walked through without looking back. He did not notice the nurse at the station who saw him step out of Austin's room and remove his mask. He was a handsome young fellow, she wished he had stopped at the station to chat. Probably he had to hurry to collect his notes for morning rounds.

Wondering if the doctor had awakened Austin, she stepped down to her room and looked through the glass. The patient was sleeping soundly, all the numbers on the monitor were in the normal range. The nurse was relieved that Austin was doing so well, she was one of the nicest doctors in James Madison.

***

Lenny began his Monday morning like too many recent mornings, working alone, his partner Little Mary having been again pulled to another ward. He filled his stainless steel bucket with soapy water, dropped in a clean mop head and started on the hallway. It was always better to begin at seven, right at the start of his shift, before the ward filled up with medical teams rounding, orderlies picking up patients for tests and procedures, and nurses pushing their med carts up and down the hall.

He saw Mimi coming out of the nurses' locker room heading for the nursing station to take report from the night nurse. She wasn't wearing the hated GPS unit around her neck. "Hey, Mimi, aren't you missing something?" He pointed to where the unit would normally hang.

"I don't have to put it on until I take report. I have like a whole blessed thirty minutes of peace and quiet."

Asked how many porches his block club had painted, he told her six, with three more to do the following weekend. Mimi told him she had visited several nurses on Sunday. They had good talks. Very honest. Some still had their doubts about joining the union.

"At least they listened to you," said Lenny. "Most people aren't won over the first time they hear about the union drive, it takes a lot of discussions. And even then, often they don't come around until the bosses put one nail too many in their coffin."

He cautioned her once again to be careful who she talked to, and to not push the union while she was on duty. "In the current political environment, the few safeguards we had as union organizers are being stripped away. The NLRB is becoming the National Labor Restrictions Board."

Lenny asked how Catherine was doing. Mimi told him she'd delivered early Saturday morning, the baby was in the NICU, a preemie.

"Aw, that's sad news. Mom's doing okay?"

"Physically, yes, but her husband told me she's way depressed, she's worried the baby caught the virus. There's no clinical sign the baby has the infection, but she's worried half to death about it."

"Well maybe once she's certain the baby will be all right, she'll come around."

"I sure hope so, post-partum depression is a serious condition, it's not easy to treat." As Mimi took out her pen and paper to join the night nurse for report, she asked, "Nine-thirty in the sewing room?"

Lenny agreed.

The nurse sat at the station beside the night nurse and began to take report, while Lenny continued with the mopping. Though he wasn't well versed in Greek mythology, he vaguely recalled some poor bastard pushing a huge rock up a mountain.

***

When Moose came through the ward with the breakfast trays, he told Lenny there was no sign yet the administration was hiring extra hands in the kitchen. "They're talkin' overtime. Man, we need time *off,* hard as we've been working these last couple of weeks."

"It's the same in my department, I didn't see any temps punching in this morning."

"So what're we gonna do?"

"Let's meet for a break in the sewing room, kick it around." In a lower voice he added that Mimi would be joining them again.

"I know somebody I'd like to kick around, that's no lie," Moose said as he carried two trays into a room.

Feeling the same anger and frustration, Lenny channeled his feelings into the campaign to bring the registered nurses into the union. If they could pull it off it would be sweet revenge. Sweet, and empowering for the union.

He passed an isolation room, where Carlton was restocking the cart. "Yo, Lenny, I gotta tell you what I did this weekend!" Carlton added a stack of yellow gowns and latex gloves.

"Lemme guess. You were out catching mosquitoes for your experiment."

"Almost right. No, I talked with one of the ear, nose and throat nurses in the clinic. I told her my idea, and she said your breath actually starts way in the back of your throat. So if you want to change your breath, you got to change the bacteria that's growing there."

"Okay..." Lenny had a host of things to do, but he didn't want to be rude to his friend.

"So I made me a weak bleach solution. About the strength of the water in a swimming pool. I gargled and swallowed it so it would kill off anything growing down there, and then I sucked on a mouth full of antiseptic breath mints. The ones with menthol."

"And as a result your girlfriend dumped you for another guy?" said Lenny, an impish look on his face.

"Very funny, Ursula thinks this time my idea is a good one. So I sat out on my front steps at twilight and stayed for a couple of hours, and guess what: not one single fricking mosquito bit me!"

Lenny had to admit, the results were impressive. He told Carlton if he was serious about pursuing his theory, he needed to work with someone in public health or infectious disease, they could put together a real medical study. "I'll talk to Doctor Auginello for you, he's the expert on the Zika outbreak. If he thinks your breath mint idea is worth pursuing, I'll put you in touch with him."

Excited at the prospect of participating in an actual scientific study, Carlton left the ward pushing his stock cart and singing a happy tune.

Lenny wished he could enjoy a mood like that.

***

As he was preparing to hang a ten o'clock antibiotic, nurse Gary Tuttle heard the heart monitor chime at the nursing station. Tuttle was a soft-spoken young man whose quiet voice induced some listeners to lean in to hear him clearly. Looking at the display, he saw that Rachel Austin's heart rate was over 120 and her blood pressure was below 100 systolic. He hurriedly donned an isolation gown, mask and gloves and entered her room. The patient was breathing rapidly with pursed lips, a sign of oxygen deficit and acidosis. Silencing the alarm, Gary lowered the head of the bed and raised the legs, bringing an extra supply of blood to the heart on its return journey from the limbs. As he increased the infusion of the IV fluid, he asked Ausin how she felt.

"Like I've been run over by a truck, forward...*and* backward." Her voice was weak, she was clearly having trouble catching her breath.

"I'll set up nasal oxygen for you," he said, unpacking an oxygen set and dialing up the flow. He gently set the tubing around her head, the little prongs pointing into her nares to deliver the much-needed oxygen.

"You're...a good nurse...Gary," she said, laboring to breathe.

"Save your breath for Doctor Auginello, he'll be getting a computer alert by now, I'm sure he will be down to see you soon."

The nurse hurried to the on-call room behind the nursing station, where he told the ICU Fellow, who was about to start his long-delayed breakfast from a tray dietary left for the doctors in the ICU. "She sounds septic," the Fellow said to Gary. "Run a liter of saline in and draw a fresh chem panel, I'll page Doctor Fahim."

Taking a mouthful of cold scrambled eggs, the Fellow paged the ICU Attending. Then he called up the patient's drug regimen on the computer and considered what other part of their therapeutic armamentarium he could call on.

***

Fifteen minutes after the computer sent an alert to all of the therapeutic services involved in Austin's care, including pharmacy, Dr. Auginello entered the ICU and approached the nurse.

"Gary, what's going on with Doctor Austin, her numbers are alarming."

"Her heart rate is up to one-twenty, blood pressure is down and her temperature just spiked to one-o-three." The nurse called up the computer program with all the vital signs laid out.

"She had no fever or hypotension during the night, isn't that right?"

Gary confirmed the patient had been normothermic and normotensive since arriving in the ICU. Until now.

Auginello joined the ICU Attending and his team, who were making their own rounds. Dr. Fahim, the ICU Director, agreed the patient was looking septic. He ordered a second rapid infusion of intravenous fluids, blood pressure support with a continuous infusion of norepinephrine and a new set of blood cultures.

"I suggest you draw one set from a peripheral stick and one set from the IV line," said Auginello.

"You're thinking of line-sepsis?" asked Fahim. "That would be an awfully rapid onset of a catheter-induced infection, don't you think, the line was only placed Friday night."

"But it was placed in the ER," said Auginello, the inference being that IV line placements performed by the Emergency Room staff were not always as rigorous in their antiseptic technique as the procedures done in the ICU.

"I've never seen any good data on that theory," said Fahim. "Have you?"

"No, I haven't, but even if the technique was scrupulous, it's still a possible source of infection."

The nurse hurried to draw the two sets of blood cultures, one from the IV line, one from a vein. As soon as he was done he ran the IV fluid rapidly and hung the medication to support Austin's blood pressure. He, like the doctors was puzzled at the sudden onset of fever and hypotension. Maybe the tests for the Zika virus had been wrong, maybe she did have the infection. But if that was the case, why weren't the anti-viral drugs turning her around?

At the station, Auginello admitted to the ICU team that he was more puzzled than ever by the progression of their patient's disease. It had begun with GI complaints: nausea, vomiting, diarrhea and dizziness, and then unexpectedly turned to an inexplicable episode of profound hypoglycemia.

"You are sure the nurse did not make a medication error?" asked Fahim. "It is the simplest explanation for an extremely low blood sugar in a patient who is not diabetic."

"No, I don't think so, though you can never be entirely sure," said Auginello. "And even if there had been a medication error, that doesn't explain this new septic picture. Not with all of her admitting cultures coming back negative."

Fahim agreed, the case was puzzling. "Shall we test her for your old nemesis, disseminated TB?" The ICU Attending well remembered the difficult case he and Auginello had treated of a young man with tuberculosis that had infected all of his major organs. The hospital's computerized diagnostic program had placed TB at the bottom of its list of possible diagnoses, and Auginello had taken a lot of heat from the Chief Medical Officer over his decision to treat TB. Happily for all, the diagnosis had proven correct and the patient was saved.

Auginello declined to treat for TB yet, he wanted to wait for more culture reports. But he agreed she needed a central IV catheter placed, given the need for adrenalin-based IV medication and the large volumes of IV fluids.

"There is nothing more that you can do for her, my friend," said Fahim. "It is time for the waiting game. And the praying, if that suits you."

Hiding his anxiety, Auginello knocked gently on the doorframe and stepped into the ICU isolation room. He found Dr. Austin bundled beneath several cotton blankets, shivering as if she were laying on a block of ice. Auginello confirmed she had moments ago received a dose of ibuprofen for the rigors, the medicine should relieve her shaking in time.

"Good morning, Rachel, I see you had a rough night."

"What in the name of all the gods in the night sky is happening to me, Michael?" Austin said between chattering teeth. "I feel like death warmed over. Is this a viral infection, bacterial, fungal or what?"

"The cultures have been negative so far. Gary drew new cultures this morning, we'll have to wait and see what they grow in the Micro lab."

"You're changing my antibiotic regimen, aren't you? I'll be dead. . . by sundown if you don't do something."

Auginello confirmed he was bringing in the big guns, with broad coverage for bacteria, virus and fungal infections. He admitted he was even entertaining the idea of treating her for disseminated TB, although that diagnosis was so unlikely, he probably could not justify adding TB meds to her already heavy drug regimen.

"It's not . . .TB," agreed Austin. "You can order a PPD, but...it will come back...negative."

Auginello agreed to do the simple TB test, he was so desperate to find the answer. "I'll run by the Micro lab and see if any of the blood culture broths are turning cloudy. I'll check on your vital signs and lab results throughout the day. If your condition worsens, I'll have to get a central line and start you on pressors."

Austin told him to do whatever he had to do, the chills were draining her of energy. She had no doubt if Auginello didn't get control of her infection she would soon be making a date with Dr. Fingers, the chief pathologist.

26

On the Maternity Ward, Louis sat holding Catherine's hand, relieved that at least she was sitting up and taking a little tea with sugar. He heard a knock on the doorframe and saw the lactation nurse come in. Irma was a slender young woman with a bright, beaming smile and a can-do attitude.

"Good morning Missus Feekin. Hi, Mister Feekin. How are you feeling this morning? I see you're taking your tea, that's good, the fluids will help you."

Catherine was slow to speak, finally saying she did not have any energy, she just wanted to sleep all day long.

"She's worried about the baby," Louis added. "The doctors keep assuring us our baby is fine, there's no sign of any infection, but Catherine still worries. It's making her sick."

Irma offered to help her patient express her breast milk so the baby could enjoy the health benefits of a mother's milk. Catherine agreed to try once more, although she had no enthusiasm for the task.

With her husband's support and Irma's encouragement, Catherine managed to produce a small amount of milk using the pump. The nurse held up the little bottle as if it were gold. "You see, you did it! You're giving your baby the best part of you!"

Seeing his wife found no comfort in her modest milk production, Louis followed Irma out of the room as the nurse carried the expressed milk down to the neonatal ICU. "Irma," he said, "isn't there something more you can do to lift Catherine out of her funk? I'm worried sick about her. More than I'm worried about the baby, even."

Irma stopped and considered his question. "Well, the doctor did put in for a psychiatric consultation. And she did see a therapist. That's pretty much all of the resources we have."

Louis's eyes were pleading and close to tears. With a shaking voice he said, "You've got to do *something*. ANYTHING. She's not bonding with our daughter, she's drifting away!"

Irma's durable smile faded as she struggled with the issue. Finally, she told him there was a new program that James Madison had recently introduced in cases of premature births. She wasn't sure the OB service would approve using it with Catherine, the new program wasn't approved for general use. When Louis asked what this new program was all about, Irma said she would explain it all to him after speaking with the OB doctors. She promised to let him know if Catherine and her baby were approved later in the day.

Louis returned to his wife, wondering what this 'new program' was all about, and praying it would bring Catherine out of her emotional shell.

***

Lenny settled into one of Birdie's battered folding chairs and sipped his coffee, a toasted bagel in his lap. Moose tilted his head at the sight. "No donut today?" Lenny told him he was trying to cut down the sugar. Moose pointed out the bagel turned to sugar as soon as it was digested, to which Lenny just shrugged. "Leave me one good vice, please." Birdie suggested that his vices were too numerous to count.

The conversation turned to the health and safety grievance the union had filed on Friday. Birdie asked how soon the hospital would respond. Lenny told her they had five business days to reply, but if they went over, the union had little they could do about it. "If they don't address the issues in a serious way the union will hold a press conference in front of the hospital and give the press a copy of the grievance. That will give them some bad publicity."

"That's all they care about," said Birdie. "The president has no shame. He only cares about making money. Look at those new 'executive suites' he put in for rich Main Line patients: gold plated fixtures, private duty nurses around the clock. It's disgusting."

"But it brings in big bucks," said Moose.

"Money they don't spend on staffing," Lenny added. They discussed holding an informational picket line along with the press conference. All agreed it was the right thing to do, although they had to give the hospital the five business days to respond to the complaint.

A knock on the door interrupted the discussion. Mimi stuck her head in the door: "Okay if I join you?"

"Always, Mimi." Birdie opened a folding chair and made room for her beside the sewing table. The nurse told them she was getting more and more discouraged. Few of the nurses she visited over the weekend had signed pledge cards. Some took the card and promised to consider joining the union, others were skeptical, even frosty, and declined the offer.

"I tried to tell them we were stronger together, but it didn't really sink in," said Mimi.

"You can't turn around an attitude in one visit," said Moose, "old grudges die hard."

Birdie reminded Mimi that a union campaign was a long, tough fight, not something you won overnight. "You've got to get to know the nurses. It's all about building trust."

Lenny added there will be tough days ahead. Threats from the bosses, even terminations. But the friendships she made in those fights will last her whole life. He ended saying, "You have to steel yourself. Someone will betray you, that's part of the struggle. It'll break your heart, but it will make you stronger in the end."

Mimi left her friends not feeling very encouraged. She told herself it was good to be prepared for the worst, she just wished it wasn't Mother Burgess they would have to deal with, the woman had a heart of stone.

On second thought, Mimi decided the Director of Nursing had no heart at all.

In the communications room, a wary dispatcher had seen that one of the nurses had gone to the basement. At the start of the shift Joe West had ordered him in no uncertain terms to watch for any nurse venturing anywhere near the sewing room. With the new transmitter hidden in the hallway ceiling, the dispatcher was now able to hear any conversation the nurse engaged in.

Having turned his microphone to mute so the GPS would not produce any sounds and switched on the recording mode, he now had an audio file of the entire nurse's conversation in the room.

Per instructions, he paged Joe West STAT, at the same time emailing the security chief the audio file, now labeled Rogers, Mimi. He felt a twinge of guilt for spying on the nurse, she sounded like a nice person. The dispatcher was grateful he didn't know her. Didn't even know what she looked like, he only knew her voice, which was rather pleasant. Almost musical. He wondered if she sang in a church choir. Well, there was one nurse he was never going to meet for a drink.

Then he recalled the crushing credit card debt he had incurred and the late payment warnings. The bonus West had promised would take a nice chunk out of it. That made his conscience just a little bit easier.

He restored the microphone function so he could send requests for assistance just as a patient on Seven South pressed her call for assistance button.

***

Dr. Auginello walked slowly down the Seven South corridor, his mind searching for answers to Austin's mysterious clinical picture. He knew he was missing something, but was damned if he could find a single disease process that fit Austin's clinical picture.

"Watch the wet floor!" a voice called to Auginello. The distracted physician stopped in his tracks just before planting a foot on a section of gleaming wet tiles, a yellow caution sign clearly announcing the warning to step to the other side of the hall.

"I'm sorry Lenny, I was lost in thought."

"Yeah, I could see that. You gotta be careful, if you slip and fall and break your neck, the paperwork I gotta fill out is a royal pain in the arse."

"I'll be more careful, I wouldn't want you to have to strain yourself filling out an incident report." The worried physician stood still for a moment, his mind turning back to the issue at hand.

"Looks like you've got something on your mind," said Lenny, sinking his mop in the bucket of soapy water.

"I do indeed. It's Rachel Austin."

"The Family Medicine doctor. Yeah, Mimi told me about her. She's not getting better?"

"No, her condition is deteriorating, and I haven't any idea what the diagnosis is." Because Auginello had worked closely with Lenny on several challenging investigations in the hospital, the physician had learned to trust the wily shop steward's opinion, as well as to share confidential information with him.

"It's not the Zika virus?" asked Lenny.

"No, the symptoms don't fit, and the viral test was negative." Auginello explained to his friend that Austin had presented at first with GI symptoms: nausea, vomiting, diarrhea, loss of appetite. Then she had a seizure, a condition she had never exhibited in the past, and accompanied by a profound drop in her blood sugar.

"Some infections can alter your glucose metabolism, but I still don't have a single positive culture." He added that today the signs of infection were alarming, even life threatening, so he was throwing every drug he had at the offending pathogen, but still couldn't say what it was.

Lenny pulled his mop out of the bucket and ran it in broad strokes over another section of the floor. "Well, you know I have kind of a jaundiced view of life, even in the hospital. Actually, especially in the hospital."

"Because you've encountered some bad people doing bad things."

"That's right," said Lenny. "We don't have to debate theology or legal bullshit, but I think you'll agree there are some cruel, selfish people in the world who don't mind hurting others to get what they want. Some of them even enjoy it."

"In other words..."

"In other words, when you draw up your list of possible diseases that could be making Doctor Austin as sick as she is, you have to add to it the hidden hand of some person or persons with an evil intent."

"Somebody out to hurt her."

"Yeah, hurt her, or worse. Someone out to get her admitted to the morgue."

Auginello poked his tongue in his cheek, processing the ugly suggestion. He didn't like the idea that someone could be deliberately harming Austin. But he'd seen enough evil in the world to have to entertain the idea.

"Tell you what," said Auginello. "I'm still looking for a natural explanation for her clinical picture. But if you'd be willing to keep your eyes open, just be on the lookout for anything or anyone unusual connected to Austin, somebody who doesn't belong around her care, you'll let me know, all right?"

"Of course. I'll spread the word among my co-workers, one of us is always around serving meals, transporting a patient, mopping the floor. We'll keep an eye on her, and I can maybe poke around a bit, see if I can learn something useful."

As Auginello started to walk away, Lenny asked if he could

run something by him. "It might be kinda crazy, but I promised a friend I'd ask you." He explained Carlton's theory that mosquitoes were attracted to humans by the smell of their breath, and if people could disguise their breath, the bugs would not bite them.

"That's a very interesting theory, Lenny, I don't know it there's been any research on it, but I'll ask the med student on my service this month to do a literature search. Maybe it's been studied."

Auginello headed for the Microbiology department, hoping Lenny was wrong about an evil hand producing the illness in Austin, and realizing that more often than not, his friend was right on target.

27

Lactation nurse Irma Cedeno approached the NICU Attending physician with caution. The doctors were making rounds, always a tense time, and Dr. Blackthorn could be prickly, even on her best days.

As the team stepped away from an isolette, Irma asked if she could have a moment. Blackthorn did not tell her 'no,' though she didn't invite the nurse to speak, so Irma asked if Baby Feekin could be enrolled in the new papoose program.

"She's right on the edge of needing the NICU," said Irma. "The baby started on oral feeds, and she tolerated it fine. I think—"

"The papoose program has not been approved by the New Procedure Committee," said Blackthorn. "We have only approved it for three babies on a case-by-case basis."

"Yes, I know," said Irma. "But you see, the baby's mother has a serious case of postpartum depression. She's been worried her baby acquired the Zika virus—"

"Baby Feekin does *not* have a viral infection!"

"I understand that, but mother is still scared. I think enrolling her in the papoose program would help her depression in a big way. And the baby is exactly the right number of weeks to qualify for the program."

Blackthorn consulted a resident, who reviewed Baby Feekin's weight, gestation age and urine production. Satisfied the baby met the criteria, the OB Attending told the resident to write an order to 'papoose the baby,' then she went on to the next baby and listened to the report.

Suppressing a smile—smiling on rounds sometimes irritated Blackthorn—Irma hurried away to tell mother and father the good news.

***

Louise looked up and down the corridor at the entrance to the Executive Suite to be sure no one who knew her was nearby. Having told her co-worker Marilyn she was going for a quick cup of coffee, she slipped into the Director of Nursing office, where the secretary told her to go on through to see Miss Burgess.

With a shaky hand Louise opened the door and stepped inside. Burgess and the Six-North head nurse were seated there, as grim-faced as a judge and executioner about to sentence a prisoner to death.

"Sit yourself down, Louise," the head nurse said. She was a humorless woman who dressed ten years younger than her age. "I believe you have news for us about the disloyal girls who have been spreading stories about a union. Isn't that right?"

"Yes, ma'am," Louise said. The frightened nurse sat with her hands in her lap, looking at the floor.

"You are still interested in the assistant head nurse position, aren't you?" asked Burgess, impatient to get the information out of the frightened nurse.

"Yes, I would like that very much, ma'am. It would mean weekends off, and no more twelve-hour shifts. I just worry—"

"Your only worry should be the safe and professional conduct of the nursing staff in this hospital," said Burgess. "A nursing union would destroy the trust between the leadership and our girls. Your coming forward is the best thing a nurse could do for our James Madison family."

Biting her lip, Louise realized she was good and truly trapped. If she refused to tell about her meeting with Mimi and Kim, she would not only not be given the promotion but, in all probability she'd be written up over and over until the director had grounds for firing her. And that would make it difficult to find another job.

She wrapped her fingers around the hated GPS unit, fearful the dispatcher would be listening in.

"Don't worry about dispatcher," said the head nurse, "they work for us."

"Well, you see, I was at home in my apartment with Marilyn and..." Louise slowly went over her meeting with the union advocates. She had no knowledge of how many other nurses had been contacted, or any idea how many nurses were supporting the union drive. The head nurse told her to stay close to the two disloyal nurses and report back to her whenever she had new information, then she told the nurse to get back to her station.

A shaken Louise hurried back to the ward. Sick to her stomach, she didn't know how she would be able to look Marilyn in the eye, let alone work with her day after day. They were friends, they often double dated. How could she face her co-worker?

As she stepped back on the ward, Marilyn asked her how was her coffee. Louise shrugged, not trusting her voice, and not looking her co-worker in the eye.

***

After dismissing Louise, Burgess called Joe West. "Mister West, we have two malcontent nurses thinking they can organize a union in my hospital. The leader seems to be a Missus Mimi—"

"Rogers. She's an RN on Seven South, I know all about her," said West.

"You do?" Burgess was startled, she thought for once she had beat the security chief in uncovering some malefactor. "How...?"

"The nurse visited the sewing room in the basement," said West. "That's where they hold their meetings. I have an audio recording of her meeting with her union cronies. I will have the audio transcribed and bring you a copy within an hour."

Burgess looked at her colleague sitting across the desk, dumbfounded. The Director didn't know how West managed to collect such information, she only knew he was the most dangerous man in James Madison.

***

As Lenny was climbing the stairs from the basement to the seventh floor, avoiding the elevator at Moose's insistence, he cursed his friend for urging him to exercise more. Stopping at the last landing to catch his breath, he recalled the nurse who had been poisoned by a psychopathic doctor and nearly died. The bastard had given her arsenic, which the doctors didn't identify until it was almost too late to save her. Always suspecting the worst in life, Lenny decided to ask Auginello to test Austin for poison, it was an obvious potential cause of her nausea and vomiting.

But the other symptoms were baffling: seizures, low blood sugar, fever and shock...Lenny was not a medically trained individual, he didn't have any idea what could cause all of these widely varying symptoms. But he had a good idea who could figure them out.

28

After collecting the materials for the new premature baby papoose program, Irma hurried to Catherine's room in the Postpartum ward, where she found mother and Louis. Setting the bundle on the bedside table, she explained how Dr. Blackthorn had learned about a treatment for premature babies in Venezuela. The country's hospitals and clinics lacked the resources to provide isolettes and the intensive support found in American hospitals. They had to find a low-cost method of supporting preemies that provided the right environment, especially warmth and nutrition.

Their innovation was to copy Mother Nature: specifically, the pouch of the kangaroo, where the baby kangaroo that was always born too immature to survive in the world were kept warm and supported in the mother's pouch.

The fragile babies could suck at the mother's teat, providing them with nutrition, while the warmth and physical pouch held them safe.

The OB physicians wrapped the mother's chest and abdomen with a soft cotton blanket. The premature infant was nestled in the papoose, where it was warm. Held in an upright position, the baby could nurse, sleep and listen to her mother's heart beat, just as the baby did while in the womb.

Irma concluded with: "A study found that preemies raised in the papoose had a better survival rate than babies placed in isolettes in a neonatal ICU. The researchers were not sure why, but they thought that the sound of the mother's heart and the warmth of her body were the perfect environment for baby. Isn't that wonderful?"

The lactation nurse unwrapped the bundle. She showed Catherine and Louis the soft cotton wrap that would hold her baby, explaining that a nurse or Louis could change the baby's diaper without taking her out of the papoose, and that baby could nurse whenever she was hungry.

Louis looked at his wife, hoping the proposal would lift her spirits. Catherine picked up the papoose and ran her fingers over the fabric. "It is wonderfully soft, isn't it? But Irma, are you sure my baby is ready to leave the Neonatal ICU? She won't have the oxygen or the intravenous fluids...she won't be on a heart monitor. Are you sure she's mature enough to survive on just...me?"

"We tested her oxygen saturation on room air, it was in the acceptable range. And your baby is taking her formula, so we don't *really* need the IV access. What she needs more than anything is contact with you, her mother." The lactation nurse did not add that Catherine needed the contact with Baby Lilly just as much as the baby needed her. She looked into Catherine's eyes. Waited. Hoped mom would consent to the plan.

Catherine looked at her husband, who kept quiet, not wanting to trigger any argument. With a long sigh, Catherine agreed to try the papoose, at least for a day and a night. If the baby showed any signs of distress Catherine would walk her back to the NICU herself.

Louis could hardly contain his relief. He was sure this would lift his wife's spirit and help her bond with their daughter.

***

Miss Burgess looked over the transcript of Mimi's meeting with the detested union troublemakers as Joe West stood ramrod straight in front of her desk. The creases of his navy blue trousers were as sharp as a knife, in contrast to the wrinkled, ill-fitting business suit that Burgess wore.

"I should have thought a nurse we gave a job to, with all

the benefits and opportunities, would know better than to get involved with this union garbage," she said. "It makes me sick, one of my girls turning on me."

West said nothing. He had delivered the record, there was no need to comment. All that he required was instructions on how to deal with the traitorous nurse.

After giving out a long sigh of disgust, Burgess told West to continue watching any nurse who descended to the basement and met in the sewing room, she would deal with Mrs. Rogers personally. She ordered her secretary to bring her the nurse's record of attendance, including how many days were in her sick time bank. Then she called the director of the pharmacy and told him she needed him to scrutinize the narcotic records for Seven South. Asked what she was looking for, Burgess said, "I'll know it when I find it, just get me the file."

Looking up from her desk, she saw that West had silently left. Annoying, but she had to admit there was something to be said for not wasting time on small talk. She was too busy for that kind of crap anyway, she had an employee to break, and a workforce to bring to heel.

***

Just before noon Lenny was cleaning a discharge bed, raising the mattress and being sure to remove any blood or other fluids from the underside when he heard a knock-knock-knock on the open door.

"Lenny, you need to see me about something?" Regis stepped into the room. "What's goin' on?"

"How're you doing, Re'ege, thanks for coming by. Everything okay in pathology?"

"Yeah, it's all cool. I told Doc Fingers I'm ready to take a crack at the pathology tech program, the full scholarship is too good to pass up."

"Serena must be pleased."

"She's the one kept pushing me to go for it. She wants me to get into a job that has a future. I'm doing it as much for her as for me."

"Married life," said Lenny, dropping his rag in the bucket of soapy water. He congratulated Regis, telling him he was one-hundred per cent certain the tests would be something his friend could handle.

Lenny's face switched in a flash from happy to serious. Making sure no one was outside the door to overhear, he told his friend he had a favor to ask.

"Anything for you, Lenny."

Lenny asked if Regis could talk to the chief pathologist about Austin's case. He explained that Doctor Auginello couldn't make sense of all the weird symptoms she keeps developing. He mentioned her nausea and vomiting and her dangerously low blood sugar, followed by a massive infection. "Doctor Auginello has no idea what's causing all this disease, none of it fits anything he's seen before. I'm afraid there's a criminal explanation for it, which is something the doctors don't like to think about. I thought maybe your boss could suss it all out."

"You're on another case, huh?" Regis showed a wolfish grin. "I'm on it. I'll get back to you soon's I hear from the doc. Anything else I can do?"

"Just keep your eyes wide open when you make your rounds. If somebody's trying to kill Doctor Austin, we can't let that happen. She doesn't belong on a damned autopsy table."

29

At lunch time Mimi wanted to look in on Dr. Austin in the ICU, but she only had 45 minutes and she was starving. She hurried to the ground floor and made her way out of the hospital through the Emergency Room exit, since it led directly onto Germantown Ave and the fast food restaurants just down the block.

As the nurse approached the exit she stepped aside to allow a pair of EMTs to wheel a patient in on a stretcher. There was something familiar about one of the paramedics: he was the same young man she'd seen on her ward taking notes during surgical rounds. What, she wondered, was he doing working as an EMT? He probably started out as a paramedic and kept working part time while going to school. That must be a wicked schedule. Her respect for the young man was even greater.

Leaving the hospital, she hurried to a Chinese restaurant, where she ordered a crispy tofu stir fry with vegetables and brown rice, her favorite. Sitting at one of the little round tables to wait for her food, she reviewed her weekend meetings with the nurses. It hadn't gone nearly as well as she had hoped: few of the nurses signed pledge cards. They were angry at the administration for the abuse they suffered, that part was okay. But several nurses were reluctant to join the same union as the service workers. Unity. Solidarity. All for one and one for all: they made perfect sense to Mimi, but to several of her co-workers they were only empty slogans.

Mimi thought the Chinese take-out place could be a good place to meet nurses, the dreaded GPS unit didn't transmit from here: the dispatcher wouldn't be able to hear their conversation. Not that they had much time for lunch, staffing was always short. But at least she could call her sisters on other wards and ask them to lunch, there was nothing suspicious about that.

She asked herself: what would it take to win them to the union? How could she break through their stubborn ideas about being 'professionals'? Lenny had often said, every worker is a professional, every job is a skilled job. Why couldn't the nurses see that?

Picking up her food, she savored the spicy aroma as she hurried back to the ward. In the elevator, she peeked inside to confirm the girl at the counter had given her hot sauce *and* soy sauce. What was spicy tofu without them?

***

Having given all the participants time to fill their plates from the luncheon buffet, Dr. Auginello reviewed the month's Infection Control statistics, including admissions for Zika virus and hospital acquired infections. Although admissions for the virus had been steadily increasing throughout the month, he pointed out on the graph that the rate had leveled off in the last five days, hopefully a sign that the public health mosquito eradication efforts were starting to pay off.

Auginello brought up the issue of the temporary supplies that he and Katchi had introduced. Dr. Slocum repeated his objection to the inexpensive commercial fans used for creating a negative pressure room, as well as use of masks not specifically tested for N95 respiratory isolation.

"We cannot have James Madison cited by the Department of Health or the CDC charging us with putting our patients at risk!" Miss Burgess, seated beside him, supported the Chief Medical Officer.

Auginello told Slocum that he had tested the fans and the masks and found they met the required safety margins, *given the public health emergency*. Katchi, who had agreed to play the 'bad cop' at this meeting, reminded Slocum that if the hospital had approved the funding to convert more rooms to full grade negative pressure when Engineering asked for it last winter, they wouldn't have had to resort to desperate measures. And as for the masks, the entire Delaware Valley was short on approved masks, they had no choice but to improvise.

Auginello told them he had informed the DOH by phone of all their emergency measures, and the Director was more than comfortable with them. She even told him they were going to pass on the strategies to the other facilities in the region, including nursing homes, which are always short of funds anyway.

Hearing no further objection from the other representatives at the monthly meeting, Auginello went to the last two items: the use of bleach for disinfecting horizontal surfaces in isolation rooms, and the proposed restriction for pregnant women caring for confirmed or suspected Zika patients.

Katchi admitted that too strong a solution would degrade the environment, especially wooden furniture. Burgess reminded them that in the past patients had complained that the odor had irritated them. One patient with a history of asthma had an attack and needed emergent treatment.

The Risk Management director suggested that they weigh the unlikely risk of another patient suffering an asthma exacerbation against the more likely risk of an employee acquiring a Zika infection. Given that formula, clearly the risk of infection was far greater.

Katchi asked why couldn't the policy include a restriction against using bleach in the room of any patient with chronic pulmonary problems: asthma, COPD, emphysema, and so on. Dr. Blackthorn in OB pointed out that bleach would be inappropriate for premature children or children with any disorder that weakened their pulmonary system.

After more discussion, Auginello framed a policy that included all of the exemptions that had been brought up. Put to a vote, the majority supported it.

Going on to the last agenda item, Mr. Freely from Human Resources argued strenuously that pregnant staff not be required to care for confirmed Zika patients. He pointed out that it was not only immoral, it could put the hospital at risk of a major lawsuit. Risk Management supported him, as did the Recruitment and Retention Director.

Only Miss Burgess argued against the policy proposal. She said if her girls could get out of caring for one kind of isolation case, what would stop them from demanding they never go into any room with a communicable case in it? Freely pointed out that the issue did not only concern the nurses, all the hospital staff involved in patient care were involved. "And Miss Burgess, surely the images of the babies with such severe neurologic deformities must give you pause about sending 'your girls' in to care for the Zika patients."

Dr. Auginello pointed out that the two measures he had proposed would ameliorate the conditions cited in the union's recent health and safety grievance. When Slocum asked how the ID physician knew about a union matter that was confidential, Auginello told him that all the union members were discussing the grievance, it was public knowledge. The nurses were relieved to hear about it as well. The wily physician did not need to tell Slocum or Burgess that the grievance could only draw the RNs closer to the service workers union.

After discussing the staffing difficulties that might occur by exempting pregnant employees from entering the specified rooms, an issue that Burgess raised with great passion, Auginello called for a vote. Burgess looked at Dr. Slocum, who usually sided with her, but the CMO demurred. "Whatever the committee decides," he said. The vote was unanimous but for the Nursing Director's No vote.

As soon as the meeting broke up, Auginello asked his secretary, who had been recording the minutes, to email the two policy changes to the Executive Board. Usually a vote by the board only happened during their monthly meeting, but Auginello wasn't going to wait that long. He requested an immediate vote by email, something he didn't recall ever happening before.

The ID physician figured it was about time the old farts moved into the 21st century and vote by email, the staff couldn't wait.

As the meeting broke up, Auginello took the medical student assigned to his department aside and asked him to conduct a literature review of mosquitoes and breath. "Gordon, see if anyone has studied altering the scent of human exhalation as a way to prevent the host from attracting the mosquito. Somebody on staff came up with the idea that if we masked our breath, we would not be bitten."

"That's a cool idea," said Gordon, who promised to get to the medical library and start the search right away.

***

Roy, in his doctor outfit, looked with deep satisfaction at Dr. Austin's lab values on a computer in the medical library. The lactic acid and pH levels indicated septic shock from a massive infection. It was unfortunate that he couldn't visit the woman and watch her sinking into a shock state. Couldn't enjoy seeing the ICU doctor put her on a respirator and blindly try to reverse the slow journey to the morgue.

And there was the post-mortem! If only he would be allowed to take part in that pleasure. To cut open her chest and rip out her lungs, heart, liver. To see her laying on the autopsy table, her body open and leaking blood down the side gutter into the drain.

He thought about the superior physician he would have become if not for Austin's meddling. He may never earn his medical degree, but he was damn sure she would never care for a patient again.

30

On Tuesday morning as Mimi stepped onto the ward, she stopped to count the number of yellow isolation carts. There were three. That was down from five the day before, was the Zika epidemic finally getting under control as Dr. Auginello suggested? Probably not. Probably there were ten more isolation patients in the ER waiting to come upstairs, she would find out soon enough.

Twelve more hours of running to stay in place. *Lord of mercy, we do so need that union.* She settled in at the station and took out a blank sheet of paper for report. The night nurse told her she had been down to see Catherine on the Postpartum unit and was thrilled the new mom and baby were doing so well. "And that papoose she wears, have you ever seen anything like it?"

"It's wonderful, isn't it?" said Mimi. "Louis has been coming by and keeping me up to date."

"Personally I don't see how Catherine sleeps with the baby strapped to her belly, but I guess the doctors know what they're doing."

"Uh-hmm, I know they do. The papoose has been used for years in Venezuela. The moms there know what they're doing."

Taking notes and prioritizing her morning tasks, Mimi couldn't wait to get a break time so she could visit her friend. It was such a godsend, the papoose, god bless the lactation nurse for advocating for it. And for Doctor Blackthorn for giving permission.

***

Before starting on his morning rounds, Dr. Auginello went to the Microbiology lab, anxious to see if there were any results from Dr. Austin's latest blood cultures. Greeting the techs on the early shift, he went to the warming cabinet and found the bottles of growth medium, the modern version of 'chicken soup.' Auginello was surprised to see that all the bottles were cloudy.

"This looks like an awfully rapid growth," he said to Frieda, who was under one of the hoods smearing liquid from another bottle onto an agar plate. "There must have been an awfully large inoculum in the culture specimen."

"You want me to plate them for you?" she asked.

He told her to go ahead and plate all of the bottles on agar. Knowing it would take time for the bacteria to grow sufficiently to produce colonies they could view under the microscope, he asked her to run antigen-antibody tests as well.

Although the antigen tests would not give him antibiotic resistance or drug sensitivity, they would identify the species, and that would help him target his antibiotic regimen.

As he was about to leave, Frieda asked if the Zika outbreak was finally ending. "Calvin in virology tells me they're getting less and less viral cultures, is that right?"

Auginello told her the DOH was reporting that visits to the ER had leveled off. "It looks like the city's mosquito abatement efforts are starting to pay off."

"Hallelujah," said Frieda. "All this overtime is great for my bank account, my credit card is nearly paid off, but a body can only take so much time staring into a scope. I've forgot what my little boy looks like!"

Auginello assured her the epidemic couldn't last forever. Thanking the tech for making his request a priority, he hurried to the ICU to check on Austin. Although her lab work showed that the septic picture was improving, he knew that a patient's status could turn in an instant. He needed definitive culture results if he was ever going to make a correct diagnosis.

Unless Lenny was right, and Austin's roller coaster illness was not the result of an infection, and if *that* was the case, the doctor knew the treatment was way beyond his authority. It would be up to Lenny and the police to figure out who was behind such a monstrous act.

***

Mimi told the other RN on her ward she was going to peek in on Catherine on her morning break. Hurrying to the Postpartum ward, she found her friend walking back and forth in front of the window, her gown bulging out even more than it would if she were still pregnant.

"Hi, Catherine, how are you feeling?" As she gave her friend a hug, Catherine warned her not to squeeze too tight. "I have my baby with me. Come, see." She untied her hospital gown and lowered it, revealing the papoose wrapped around her chest and abdomen.

"Oh my goodness, Louis told me about the papoose, but even so, it's amazing!"

"It's a new protocol for preemies that Dr. Blackthorn started. It's still experimental, I'm not *really* supposed to be enrolled in the program, but Irma the lactation nurse begged for permission to get me and Lilly into it and the doctor gave the okay."

Catherine explained how the physicians in Venezuela lacked modern neonatal facilities, so they copied the practice of the kangaroo. Their babies were born too frail to survive on their own in the wild, so they lived their first month of life in mama's papoose. More than the baby's care, Mimi was thrilled by the improvement in Catherine's spirits.

"I can't believe James Madison would try a low tech practice like this, they always go with the newest gadgets and computer programs."

"I know. But I bet the insurance companies will love it, it

will save them oodles of money."

"Isn't it always the ever-loving bottom line?" said Mimi. She confessed she could only stay for a moment, but as long as she was there... The GPS unit prevented her from asking her friend if she would sign the pledge card for the union, so she showed a card to her. Catherine signed it and gave a thumbs up.

"I'm going to be discharged tomorrow if baby keeps doing so well, isn't that wonderful?"

"Wow, so soon, and you with a preemie. Those insurance people don't play, do they?"

"The lactation nurse is going to make regular visits, and I have to come to the clinic three times a week, so the OB doctors will be keeping a close eye on baby Lilly."

Mimi pried open the top of the papoose just enough to see Lilly's face. "She looks so happy in there. What baby wouldn't, having her meals available twenty-four seven."

"They think the baby hearing my heart beat like she did in the womb is part of why the babies thrive."

"Those isolettes are kind of a sterile environment," said Mimi. "The babies in the NICU don't get much tenderness, that's for sure. All those lights and alarms and people talking, it isn't very restful."

Congratulating her friend, Mimi asked Catherine to send her hugs, gentle ones of course, to Louis. "He must be thrilled to see you up and about, you look so much brighter." Catherine agreed, her husband was happy. Not that her postpartum depression was miraculously gone, she still felt the weight of it. The depression was like a quicksand that kept sucking her down, paralyzing her. But with Lilly squirming and nursing and making little baby sounds, squeezing her with those little fingers, she was definitely seeing the world in a brighter light.

"And you know the funniest thing, Mimi? My baby never cries. She's totally happy!"

31

Security Chief Joe West stepped silently into the dispatcher room. The Chief had a well-earned reputation for sneaking up on staff. A worker would turn around and there the man would suddenly be, standing right behind in his crisply ironed navy blue suit, a pair of silvery handcuffs dangling from his belt. West would give an order and then disappear as silently as he came. Workers joked that he was a ghost. That he had secret passages like in an old haunted house movie through which he would shortcut his way from ward to ward.

The dispatcher looked up, saw West and felt his throat tighten. "Yes, sir?" the young man said.

"Are you closely monitoring those three nurses I told you about? I want to know where they are every minute of the day."

"Yes, yes sir I am." The dispatcher opened a note pad and showed West the three names: Mimi Rogers, Myung Kim and Agnes Smiley. "They are all at their nursing stations. All GPS units are functioning."

"If any one of them goes to the basement, you will page me STAT. Is that understood?"

"Yes, sir, understood. One of the nurses has gone to the Postpartum unit to visit a co-worker, but there was nothing suspicious in their conversation."

"Be sure you record all of those conversations, I want to hear every word."

"Yes, sir." The dispatcher felt an urge to snap a military salute, but he was afraid the chief would think he was joking with him, and you didn't joke around with Joe West, the man was never seen to smile. Sneer at times, but never smile, and he was never known to laugh.

Joking aside, there was no pleasing the man anyway, whatever you did he found something to criticize. The young dispatcher wished he could work in another department at James Madison, the spying on the nurses left him feeling dirty at the end of his shift. But what else could he do, he needed the job, and if he didn't carry out West's orders, there was always somebody else ready and willing to take his job.

Life sucked. Work sucked. And he wasn't even in the damn union.

***

In the afternoon Dr. Auginello was rounding on the ID consults with his team when he got a call from the Microbiology lab. Frieda was on the phone, and she was agitated. "Doctor Auginello, I have the results of the Antigen-Antibody tests, and they are totally weird. I don't even know how to enter them in the computer!"

She told him the cultures of Austin's blood had come back positive for four different bacterial species, two gram negative, two gram positive. "I've never seen anything like this. How do you get four different species in the blood stream? And even more weird, the culture drawn from the line had heavier growth than the one from a venous stick. What the heck is going on?"

Immediately recognizing how Austin's cultures could produce four different pathogens, Auginello told her he would explain it all later. He thanked Frieda for her enormous help, then shared the new results with the ID Fellow, who said, "The stronger growth in the intravenous line culture, it is a line infection, isn't it?"

"Yes, that's right, the source of the infection is definitely the intravenous line, but it's not a simple contaminated line or a sloppy insertion, it's intentional." He explained the possibility that an unknown person was visiting harm upon Dr.

Austin. Asking the Fellow to finish rounds, Auginello hurried to the ICU, where he needed to revise the antibiotic regimen. He had no doubt about the source of the infection. His alarm was not only the four bacteria species that he had to battle, he knew that Austin was at risk of acquiring even more infections if they didn't act immediately to protect her from the monster who was stalking her. God only knew what other medical catastrophe would come down on his friend, Rachel Austin.

***

In the ICU, Dr. Fahim and his team were standing outside Austin's room reviewing the lab results when Dr. Auginello approached them. "Well, there is some good news, Michael," said the ICU Attending. "We can discontinue the isolation, the viral studies are all negative, and we have now four pathogens to explain her sepsis."

"If you can call that news good," said Auginello, more worried than he had been when the provisional diagnoses had been Zika virus or disseminated TB. The ID physician pulled the blue Respiratory Isolation sign from the door and slid it into the cart. Nurse Gary Tuttle wheeled the cart to the dirty utility room where the Central Stores clerk would remove, clean and restock it for the next case.

"We need to broaden the antibiotic coverage, she is still septic as hell," said Auginello. Fahim agreed. His resident entered the new medication orders in the computer and Gary went to the drug locker to see if they had the new drugs on hand. He was relieved to find the Vancomycin, while one of the nurse's aides volunteered to go down to the pharmacy for the other antibiotic they didn't stock, so the patient didn't have to wait for the messenger service.

As Fahim went on to the next patient for his rounds, Auginello stopped him, saying "Samir, there is something else." He led Gary and the ICU medical team to a quiet corner where no one could overhear and explained that in his opinion, some evil individual had brought on all of Austin's medical problems.

"What, *all* of them?" asked Fahim, his usually cheery face drawn with anger and disgust. "This is an abomination! This will not stand!" He asked Auginello what could they do.

"I'm going to speak to someone more knowledgeable about criminal matters. He will bring in the police, so you can expect a visit from them some time today."

"Ah, you will speak with Lenny Moss," said Fahim. "That is good, Lenny knows the criminal mind, he has had to deal with the president of this beleaguered facility for some time."

The ICU Attending instructed his on-call resident to keep a close eye on Dr. Austin and to be suspicious of any visitor that he did not personally call in for consultation. Gary agreed to alert the night nurses when he handed his patients over, they would also be vigilant and not allow anyone in the room they could not vouch for.

Auginello left the ICU encouraged that at least they had a plan for protecting Austin from further injury. He hoped the added antibiotics he had selected would prove to be the right ones, without the sensitivity reports back he couldn't know if any of the bacteria were resistant to the drugs. But he'd called in the big guns: if they didn't work, he didn't have much left to use. And he didn't believe in the efficacy of prayer.

Now he had to find Lenny and get him to call in the police.

***

After mopping the entire length of the Seven South hallway, Lenny began on the patient rooms. He chose the empty rooms first where patients had left the ward for a procedure. That would lessen the chance one of them complained about the bleach solution he was using.

Little Mary stood in the doorway watching him. "Don't

you just love the smell of that bleach?" she said, a satisfied smile on her face.

"It's still the best." He had found a special satisfaction in using the weak solution on the floors and on the bedside tables of the isolation patients on his ward. As much as he was tempted to increase the strength of the solution, he knew that a stronger odor would just bring on more complaints, so he kept it to a one-to-ten ratio, still confident he was killing any viral particles lingering on the horizontal surfaces.

"I'll pull a round of trash liners from the rooms, the night crew didn't get around to them. Again." She plucked two liners up. "Least ways you're not working alone today."

"Yeah, not yet."

"You just can't ever be the optimist, can you, Lenny?"

As Lenny wheeled his bucket out of the room and placed the CAUTION WET FLOOR in the doorway, Mary reminded him of the time he was called down to the kitchen to deal with the exploding toilet. "That was one unholy mess for sure," she said. "I heard you had to be hosed down in the morgue b'fore you got rid of the smell."

"It wasn't quite *that* bad, but it was pretty smelly. The waste pipe had backed up and blew refuse out of the toilet and all over the room. I had to mop the fricking *ceiling*. It was nasty."

Just then Dr. Auginello approached and asked if he could talk to Lenny in private. Mary went on with her trash rounds so Lenny could talk to the doctor. They found an empty room, both patients were downstairs at physical therapy. Auginello told Lenny about the positive blood cultures. "The fact that the cultures drawn from the IV line had a heavier growth tells me that's where the bacteria entered the blood stream. But a new IV line doesn't produce a massive infection with four different specie when it's only been in place for twenty-four hours, even if the insertion was not done with the proper antiseptic technique."

"In other words, somebody spiked the line."

"Exactly. It's the most horrific thing I've ever seen: injecting four different bacteria species into a patient's blood stream. It's barbaric."

"Well, it tells us a lot about the perpetrator. He has to be someone with a medical background. Someone who knows how to grow the fricking bugs in the first place." He thought about what it would require. "Or, someone who works in a lab."

"Oh, no, not someone in our Micro lab, I can vouch for everybody there. They've all been pulling massive overtime handling all the extra specimens. My people are one-hundred per cent dedicated to the patients, I'm sure of it."

"Okay, it's not someone from *our* lab, but there are plenty of other labs in Philly. I see people coming through with boxes lined to keep them cool or warm or whatever, they all work for private companies."

"That's true, we do send some specimens out that our lab can't adequately culture or analyze. And there's the Medical Examiner, they have their own lab as well."

"So we're looking for somebody who works for a laboratory or who has the training to set it up on their own."

"It doesn't exactly give us a name and an address," said Auginello.

"No, but we know more than we did before. I'm going to talk to Doctor Austin's secretary as soon as I go off shift, maybe our perpetrator visited her office." Asked about contacting the police, he told Dr. Auginello he would send a text message to a Philadelphia detective he had worked with in the past. That news reassured the physician, who felt he was way out of his depth. "Be sure to give him my contact information, I'll help in any way I can," said Auginello.

Due at the outpatient clinic to supervise the ID Fellow and resident, he hurried off, leaving Lenny to contact the police.

32

After hanging up his mop and punching out at the time clock, Lenny made his way to the ICU, where he found that Gary was well aware of the danger to Dr. Austin. The self-taught sleuth was relieved that everyone in the ICU would be on guard for any unwanted visitor. Thinking through possible scenarios, he told Gary, "We need a plan, Tuttle. If the bastard comes by to harm Austin again, and I believe he will, what will you do? I mean, you can't make a fricking citizen's arrest."

Gary thought he would call hospital security to interrogate any suspicious visitor to the ICU, but Lenny wasn't happy with that. "If we involve security we have to deal with Joe West, and he's a bastard, I don't like the idea of working with him."

The nurse asked what alternative did they have, but Lenny couldn't come up with anything "Lemme think about it, I'll call you if I get a brainstorm."

He took up a broom and made the appearance of sweeping the floor as he made his way to Austin's room. He knocked gently on the door and slipped into the room, closing the door behind him.

"Mind if I come in, Doctor Austin?" he asked, pushing the broom ahead of him.

Austin waved him in, too short of breath and too fatigued to talk. She used the bedside control to raise the head of the bed a few degrees, thankful that oxygen and the liter of IV fluids Gary had infused into her bloodstream had her feeling a little better.

"I didn't know...you were working in the unit today."

"I'm not, I'm working with Doctor Auginello. About your,

uh, particular condition." Seeing she was puzzled by his vague expression, he said, "You mean, Doctor Auginello didn't tell you about how you got so sick?"

Now Austin was more alert. She realized important information had been withheld, and she didn't like being left in the dark. "What's going on, Lenny?"

He explained that he and the ID physician believed her mysterious run of symptoms had not been caused by a natural disease, they developed at the hand of some malevolent agent. Somebody was trying to harm her. Or worse.

"Oh my god, are you *serious*? This is insane, who would want to do me any harm, I'm a Family Practice physician? I *heal* people, I don't make enemies."

"That's no doubt true, Doctor Austin, but somebody has a big time grudge against you. Somebody has been hurting you. Can you think of anybody who would want to get revenge for something?"

Austin closed her eyes and pondered the question. It was unthinkable. Impossible. But the bewildering series of illnesses had puzzled her and all the physicians caring for her, so the explanation that Lenny was offering, however bizarre, seemed to explain what had happened to her.

"Honestly, Lenny, I can't think of anybody who would hate me so much they would want me this sick. Or dead, even. I'm sorry."

"That's okay, it was a long shot. But let's approach it from another angle. Have you noticed anybody who doesn't belong hanging around you? Spying on you, that sort of thing?"

Austin puzzled over his last question. She began to say "No," but then held back. "I haven't actually *seen* anybody out of place around me or my team, but my secretary *did* report that a resident dropped off a set of articles for me. It was kind of odd, because I hadn't asked anyone on my service to collect those articles, and this resident wasn't even on my team. At the time I didn't give it much thought, but now that you mention it..."

"Okay, that's something, I'll talk to Siobhan, see what's up. Meantime, if you think of anything else, let Doctor Auginello know about it, he knows how to reach me."

Promising to keep her informed of any new information, Lenny left the ICU and hurried to the Family Practice office, hoping the secretary had not left for the day.

***

Although he didn't know the secretary in Austin's office well, Lenny had advocated for her once when she had used more sick days than she had saved in her bank. The office manager had been willing to let her borrow from future accrued sick days, but the hard-ass in the time keeping office refused and docked her pay. It took a grievance and citing past hospital practices to get Siobhan her money.

Knocking on the office door, he stepped in and greeted the young woman. "Hey, Siobhan, I'm glad you're still on duty."

"I work 'til six, Lenny, not like you housekeeping folks. No crack of dawn for me, thank you."

"You okay with your sick days this year?"

"Yeah, it's all good, thanks, I haven't called out in, like six months. Doctor Austin has me on a new medication that's doing wonders for my chronic anemia. I actually started dancing again."

"Really? That's great, what kind of dancing? Ballet? Polka?"

"Ha, ha. No, it's traditional Irish dance. It's very vigorous, you need a lot of stamina to do it well. I'm just a beginner."

Lenny looked around the office to be sure there was no one nearby. "Listen, I've been asked to look into Doctor Austin's condition. About how she got to be so damn sick. You okay with my asking you about her?"

"Of course, Lenny, *anything* to help Doctor Austin." In a

whisper Siobhan added, "Are you thinking she's the victim of foul play, you being the famous detective of James Madison Hospital?"

"Famous? I don't think so, I just stick my nose in places it doesn't belong, and don't make a crack about my nose, I've heard it since I was a kid."

"I would *never* say something disparaging about your nose, Lenny. Never!"

He asked if he could look in her office. The secretary accompanied him down to the room and stood watching as Lenny looked around.

"What exactly are you looking for?"

"I'm not sure. Have you seen anyone suspicious or out of place coming around in the past few days?"

"No, nobody suspicious. Why?"

"It's probably a wild goose chase, but the doctor was complaining of nausea and stomach pains, and that can be caused by somebody putting something bad in her food."

"Oh my god, you mean, she was *poisoned?*"

"Not necessarily, it's just something I have to consider." Seeing the coffee mug with the little girl's picture on it, he asked where Austin brewed her coffee. Siobhan told him they had a coffee pot in their break room, and that everyone drank from it.

"Nobody else complained of nausea and throwing up?"

"No, no one."

He saw the mug on the desk with the child's face on it. Bending down, he sniffed it. It smelled of coffee.

"Doctor Austin told me a resident or student who wasn't on her team came by and left her some articles, but she doesn't remember asking for them. That ring a bell?"

"Yes, that was a Doctor Baumann. A very nice young man. He left them on her desk."

"Did you see him in the office? Were you with him when he was in this room?"

"Uh, no, I stayed at my desk. Why, do you think—"

She suddenly raised her hand and pressed the open palm to her mouth. "Lenny, if I thought I allowed some monster to come into the doctor's office and...and..."

Lenny tried to reassure her, saying it didn't mean the man was guilty, he just had to track him down and make sure he was legitimate.

Picking up the coffee mug, he asked if it would be okay if he borrowed it for a while. Assured that the doctor would not mind, he wrapped it in a clear trash liner, promising to keep Siobhan informed and asking that she call him right away if she spotted the man.

Leaving the Family Practice suite, Lenny sent Dr. Auginello a text asking if they could meet right away in the ICU. Lenny needed to talk with this Dr. Baumann, and he was sure Auginello would want to be there when he did.

33

Lenny found Gary Tuttle at the ICU nursing station. The nurse was reading lab results with the on-call resident. Asked if anything had changed with Dr. Austin, Gary told him she was stable and there had been no suspicious visitors to the unit.

A moment later Dr. Auginello entered the ICU and joined them. Lenny reported what he had learned from Siobhan about a Dr. Baumann leaving medical articles that Austin did not recall requesting, or even knowing the resident. Adding that the doctor had gone down to Austin's office alone, Lenny showed them the empty coffee cup he had taken from the office.

"Can you have this tested for poison?"

Grim-faced, Auginello accepted the item and promised to have it tested. He hoped it was a wild goose chase, students and residents copied articles for their Attendings all the time, but he agreed they had to check the man out. STAT.

Auginello asked the operator to page Dr. Baumann, STAT.

Time seemed to stand still as they all stared at the phone. When it finally rang, Auginello picked it up. "Infectious disease, Doctor Auginello."

"Uh, hello Doctor Auginello, this is PGY-2 Nathan Baumann. You paged me, sir?"

"Yes, I did. Are you in the house?"

"Yes, I am in the neurology clinic, we're just finishing up."

"Good. I need you to come to the ICU right away, can you do that?"

"Yes, sir, of course. Uh, may I ask what is so urgent, I'm not doing an ID rotation this month."

"I'll explain when you get here, just collect your things and meet me here STAT."

Auginello hung up. Turning to Gary and Lenny, he said, "One thing I'm not clear about."

"What's that?" said Lenny.

"If we think this Baumann is the perpetrator, what do we do?"

"Gary is my secret weapon, we'll handle it until the police show up."

The ID physician looked at Gary. He saw a slightly over-weight man in his mid-thirties, not especially tall and not intimidating in his demeanor. The nurse always struck him as a gentle soul who never raised his voice in anger. Was he really some sort of lethal weapon, or was Lenny making one of his usual wisecracks? Auginello reminded himself that people often held secret talents nobody would ever suspect.

For just a moment, he wished that he had one.

***

Dr. Nathan Baumann pressed the metal plate on the wall outside the ICU, waited as the double doors swung open and stepped into the ICU. He was wary of Dr. Auginello, whom he had heard expected nothing but a first-rate performance from the students and house staff who rotated through his ID Division.

Stepping up to the station, he held his hand out to shake Dr. Auginello's hand, then recalled that the Infectious Disease department had recommended all hospital staff refrain from shaking hands during the Zika outbreak, since touching palm to palm was an efficient way of transmitting the virus person-to-person.

With a slight bow, the young resident identified himself. Auginello led him and the others back to the on-call room behind the nursing station. There he asked if Baumann had left copies of several medical articles in Dr. Austin's office. Baumann said he had not.

"I haven't done a rotation to Family Practice yet, that's on my schedule for the winter. Why, what's this about?"

While Auginello continued to question the resident, Lenny snapped a photo of the young resident's face. He phoned the Family Practice department, relieved when Siobhan answered the phone. He told the secretary he needed her cell phone number, he was going to send her a photo and she should stay on the line.

Entering the number into his cell phone, Lenny sent her the picture of Baumann. She told him she didn't recognize the man in the picture. "That's not the Doctor Baumann who came to the department," she said. "He had more hair, and he was more handsome, I don't know who this doctor is."

Lenny thanked her and hung up.

"It's not Baumann," he said. "She says the man who left the articles had a full head of hair and was more handsome." To Baumann he said, "Sorry about the more handsome bit."

"That's all right, I'm used to it, why do you think I went into medicine?" Relieved that he was not in any trouble with an Attending, Baumann asked, "Does this have anything to do with my hospital ID being stolen?" He explained how he had been in the ER on a neurology consultation when he discovered someone had taken his ID badge from the lab coat he had left hanging on the pole of an isolation cart outside the room.

Satisfied that Baumann was not a suspect, Auginello sent him off with his thanks, ordering the young man to speak to no one about the incident.

Turning to Lenny, Auginello suggested it was time to notify the police of their suspicions. Lenny agreed. He sent a text to Detective Joe Williams, whom he had worked with on several investigations. In the beginning their relationship had been antagonistic, but over time the detective had grown to trust Lenny, while Lenny had seen the benefits of sharing information.

Lenny promised to report back to Auginello on the conversation with the police. In the meantime, the ICU doctors and nurses would be extra vigilant watching for anyone suspicious, especially on the long night shift.

Saying good-bye to Gary and Auginello, Lenny didn't bother to mention a phrase that had popped into his head, a common expression hospital staff used to describe the long hours from midnight to morning: *the graveyard shift.*

***

Since Regis Devoe had told Dr. Fingers that Lenny suspected foul play in Dr. Austin's mysterious illness, the pathologist had ordered toxicology tests on the patient's blood and urine. When the young man brought the lab results to him, Fingers was not surprised when the urine came back positive for poison, Lenny never engaged in wild speculation. When the wily shop steward had a suspicion, there was always a sound basis for it.

With a heavy sadness tinged with anger, Fingers called the ICU to inform Dr. Fahim in the ICU: arsenic. A classic choice, easily mistaken for a gastrointestinal disorder. Classic, and deadly. Then he paged Auginello, taking some heart in knowing at least he was not reporting a post-mortem result.

While the two physicians talked, Regis sent a one-word text to Lenny: ARSENIC.

34

Having stayed late at the hospital working with Dr. Auginello, Lenny reached home to find Patience had already served Malcolm and Takia their dinner. The children were upstairs doing homework, or at least they were supposed to be. His wife had left out the bottle of Evan Williams and Lenny's favorite glass. He poured himself a double, added two ice cubes and sank into the stuffed chair in the living room.

"You want some dinner? I left the meatloaf in the oven on low for you."

"Thanks, yeah, that would be super. Did you cook any potatoes?"

'Yes, sweet potatoes, I'll heat some up, you enjoy your drink."

"Thanks, dear. Did I tell you you're the best wife in all of Philadelphia?"

"I thought I was the best in the whole Delaware Valley."

"You are! I'll even throw in the Jersey shore."

"You better not be comparing me to the housewives of New Jersey!" she called from the kitchen.

Lenny picked up his drink and spoke to it. "Jeez, a guy can't even compliment his wife anymore."

Patience was just carrying his dinner in from the kitchen when the doorbell rang. Lenny got up, went over and opened the door to find the tall, imposing figure of Philadelphia Detective Joe Williams standing there.

Williams saw that Lenny was holding a drink in his hand. "I hope you haven't killed the bottle, Moss."

"I'm fine, thanks, and how are you, Detective Williams?" Lenny made room for Williams to come in. "Aren't you on duty?"

"I'm always on duty. A man's gotta have a few vices."

The detective took a seat on the couch while Lenny poured him a drink. "You want anything in it?"

"Yeah, whiskey, two fingers."

"I never understood what the hell that means. Is that an index finger and middle? A thumb and Freely?" Lenny handed Williams his drink, then settled back in his chair. He picked up his fork, stopped. "Have you eaten?"

"No, but I've got reservations for eight, thanks." Williams took a sip of the bourbon. "You still drinking that bottom barrel crap?"

"Evan Williams is not the bottom of the barrel! Heaven *Hill* is the bottom."

Taking a forkful of meatloaf, Lenny took a moment to collect his thoughts. With Patience joining them, he filled the detective in on what he had learned and what he suspected, including the fake Dr. Baumann, the suspect coffee mug and the arsenic report.

Williams scribbled in his pocket notebook, nodding at times but otherwise keeping a deadpan face. When Lenny was finished, the detective asked if Austin had any idea who might want to harm her. Lenny reported she had no idea.

"Don't forget some folks hold unreasonable grudges," said Patience.

"How do you mean?" Williams asked.

"I mean, sometimes a woman will break a man's heart and not even know what she's done. Sometimes a man keeps his desires to himself and she doesn't even know what he feels about her."

"Someone paranoid, maybe," said Lenny.

"Or somebody with a big ego who resents rejection," Patience said.

Lenny agreed lost love could be a motive for murder, but there are other things you can lose as well. "Money. Position. Maybe a doctor lost a position in Family Practice to her. Or an award, even."

Williams agreed all those motivations were possible, but for now they had nothing specific to go on. "I know you'll both be keeping your ears to the ground," he said. "You can find evidence I can't. I want you both to keep me informed of whatever comes your way. Agreed?"

"Of course," said Patience.

"As long as you keep us in the loop on your end, too," Lenny added.

Williams finished his drink, rose, shook hands with Lenny and Patience and bid them good night. He promised to interview Austin in the morning, figuring she was too sick to be all that helpful tonight.

"It's a shame you can't spend the night in the ICU," said Patience. "Doctor Austin would be a damn sight safer."

Williams promised to speak to the security officer in charge at night and be sure they made extra rounds in the ICU.

***

In the hospital parking lot, Mimi started the engine as Miss Kim buckled up her seatbelt. As she pulled out onto Germantown Avenue, Mimi asked her friend what was the emergency she had sent in a phone text. Miss Kim had trouble finding her voice, she was so upset by the news she had to share.

"It is bad news, Mimi. Very bad. A nurse from the United Nurses of Pennsylvania is giving out pledge cards. She showed me the card! I could not believe my own eyes!"

"*Say what?!*" Mimi couldn't believe what she was hearing. "Who? How? Where?"

Kim told her two of the nurses in the OR and three in the PACU had already pledged to the other union. "My friend Mae Lin was taking report from the Recovery nurse and she asked about joining our union, but Hazel told her she would never join an unprofessional organization that has janitors and ward clerks and dietary aides. She was very angry."

"Saints preserve us! Don't they realize we're stronger together?" Mimi felt a terrible weight on her shoulders. The weight dragged her down like an anchor on her heart.

"What are we going to do?" asked Kim. "Do we give up?"

"Not me, Kim, I'm not ready to throw in the towel. We have a bunch of pledge cards signed. We need to hustle up more pledges before that *other* union gets a foothold. We aren't beaten yet!"

Reaching Kim's home, Mimi bade her friend good night. She drove out onto Germantown Ave, so thankful her hubby was home waiting for her. She wondered what he had warming in the oven for her. It was just as her mother had told her when she and Louis had gone over to her mom's apartment for dinner. After dinner Louis had without a word bused the plates and started in washing them.

Mimi's mom whispered to her then, "Marry this one, dear, a man who's at home in the kitchen will never stray from the nest."

Mimi smiled to recall the moment. At the time she thought Louis had been a little cheeky asking what seasoning mom had used in the meatloaf and what herbs were in the salad. But she soon learned that Donald loved to cook and was always asking experienced cooks what they put in their dishes to bring out the flavor.

***

Roy walked through the hospital corridors with complete confidence, his white lab coat, dress shirt and tie and resident's ID giving him access to any department, any door, any room. A stray thought brought a smile to his lips: Why did he have to stop with Austin? This could be the start of a whole new career. He could steal ID badges in hospitals all over Philadelphia. Find people he thought deserved punishment: a corrupt politician (and aren't they *all* corrupt), a wife beater, child molester. A gentrifying scumbag real estate agent...the list of possible victims was endless.

What an exemplary hobby to take up, a real-life comic book hero without a cape. An avenging angel. A doctor without a degree. His future was bright. *What can be imagined can be executed.*

Finding an unused portable computer on the orthopedic ward, Roy entered the password he'd stolen on rounds from a surgery resident. He called up Austin's lab work, expecting her septic picture to have worsened. With any luck, she might even be transferred to the morgue for a post-mortem.

The news was sorely disappointing to him. Her lab works were not getting worse. Her blood gas was still acidotic, but the values were not critical. Her kidney function was still poor, the BUN and creatinine were still high, but the trend was inching downward.

Those bastards in Infectious Disease must be doing cartwheels, he thought. So smug and full of themselves. The deadly inoculum of pathogens had failed. It was time to develop a new methodology: one that was foolproof. One that put both her feet in the grave and still kept the foolhardy physicians in the dark.

This was going to take some serious thought. Some research, even. Electrocution came to mind, but he couldn't imagine how to implement that in the hospital. Unless...

If he could find some excuse for applying the defibrillator.... Or perhaps he could suffocate her with a pillow, the classic method. But as long as she was on a heart monitor the ensuing rapid heart rate would trigger the alarm. Besides, he couldn't afford to be there at the moment of death, that would be suicidal.

Suicide.

Why hadn't he thought of that before? He would set up a

death to look like a suicide, complete with a note, written on a computer, of course.

So many possibilities. Roy left the orthopedic ward and made his way to the main entrance, feeling pleased with himself and optimistic that with careful planning the plan would eventually come to fruition.

35

As soon as Mimi arrived on Seven-South she looked for Lenny, finding him at the janitor's closet filling his bucket with soapy water. The pungent smell of bleach filled the room.

"Lenny, I'm glad I caught you early, I heard the most terrible news last night about our union campaign."

"Oh? What's goin' on?" He screwed a fresh mop head onto a handle.

"Miss Kim told me the United Nurses of Pennsylvania has been talking to our nurses. They even gave out their own pledge cards! How can they *do* that, Lenny? That's not right!"

"Poaching is an old problem in the labor movement, it happens all too often. I haven't heard of the UNP doing it, but you never know, a couple of James Madison nurses who don't like the service workers union probably called when they heard about our union drive and asked them to come in."

"What sort of union are they?" asked Mimi.

"They're not a bad organization, they've won some good contracts for their members, but they do appeal to the elitist attitudes of some of the nurses."

"That's so stupid. It feeds into the administration's tactic to divide and conquer."

"I know," said Lenny. "It's the oldest trick in the book. Unfortunately, it still works for them."

"What do we do, Lenny? How can we stop them? Can we file a lawsuit or something?"

"No, they have the same right that we do to try and organize the nurses. All you can do is make your case and try to get the number of pledge cards you need to call for an election before they do."

"Lord have mercy. Like it wasn't hard enough getting them to sign already. I've been so busy talking to my co-workers, I haven't had time to visit Doctor Austin. Have you heard how she's doing?"

Lenny admitted the doctor had been awfully short of breath when he spoke to her, but he wasn't a medical person so he couldn't say what her condition was. "At least we know someone stole a resident's ID badge, that's how he got into the hospital and moved around without raising suspicion."

"I'm so glad she's safe, now, that's the main thing. God in heaven, what is this world coming to?"

Mimi went out and hurried to the nursing station, where she picked up the hated GPS unit, turned it on and opened her notebook to take morning report. As she wrote the date at the top of the page she cursed quietly under her breath, almost wishing the dispatcher could hear just how pissed off she was.

***

In the ICU Dr. Auginello asked the on-call resident if there had been any problems with Austin, medical or otherwise. The young resident assured him there had been no unwelcome visitors, and the patient's sepsis was slowly improving.

"How about her renal function?"

"Her creatinine is coming down, her urine output is over thirty cc's per hour, although it's still not prodigious."

Auginello smiled at the resident's choice of words, he was an avid reader who loved Dickens and always appreciated a well-turned phrase.

Auginello reviewed the lab values with the resident. The trends were positive. As much as he hoped they'd dodged a bullet with the broad spectrum antibiotic coverages, he knew all too well that bacterial infections could rear up and strike back with a vengeance. Then he discussed the arsenic poisoning with the resident, the ICU Fellow and the nurse.

"Arsenic is almost always administered by mouth, so you have to keep a close eye on her diet. There must be no opportunity for someone to interfere with Doctor Austin's food or drink. Understood?"

Gary promised to speak to the dietitian. He would suggest the dietary aide be sure the cart was kept in sight from the moment it was loaded until the food was served in the ICU.

Auginello didn't know how he was going to break the news to his patient. But he had held back too long from informing his patient of the danger she was in.

A gentle knock on the door and he entered the room. "Morning, Rachel, how are you feeling?"

"Michael! God, it's good to see you. I think I've taken a step back from the grave. I still feel like crap, but not like I'm dying, so I suppose that's a positive sign."

"Very positive." He looked down at the urine bag hanging on the bed frame. It was dark amber, he wanted pale yellow.

"Can't you tell the nurse to discontinue this damn Foley? I never knew how uncomfortable they are. Every time I move in bed the thing pulls on me, you can't imagine what it feels like."

Auginello smiled a satisfied grin: a patient complaining about a urinary catheter was usually on the mend. "One day when you're a hundred percent better and *not* in the hospital I'll tell you about my own near-death experience as a medical student. I learned what an unpleasant experience it is to have a Foley inserted...by an intern. Nurses are much gentler."

He proceeded with a physical exam. The edema in Austin's ankles had improved, though he could still leave an imprint from pressing on the soft tissue. Her heart tones were good, lungs clear, skin warm and dry. All the signs were good.

"How are my labs? My renal function is improving, isn't it?"

"All the trends are positive. Just one or two surprises."

"Like somebody trying to kill me, you mean?" She tilted her head to the side and cast a serious look at him.

"How did you know?"

"Lenny told me. He had several questions for me, too."

Auginello apologized for not informing her earlier of his suspicions. "There was arsenic in your blood and urine. It wasn't a surprise."

"Shit! What a son of a bitch! Michael, you have *got* to catch this bastard. I mean, today!"

Auginello assured her that the police were involved and that Lenny and his friends were watching out for her, the perpetrator was bound to be caught before long. He explained how someone had stolen a Dr. Baumann's ID, no doubt giving the perpetrator access to the hospital. But they had no line on who that suspect could be.

"Doesn't the hospital have video cameras all over the damn facility? They must have *something* on tape."

"The police have somebody reviewing the hospital video logs with security, but apparently that's a tedious job, it will take some time to review them. Just keep in mind, you're in a safe place and you're getting better. That's what matters most."

"Yeah, well I don't *feel* so safe."

He put a hand gently on hers. "I'll talk to Fahim, I'm sure he'll be willing to keep you here at least a couple of more days, as much as to keep you safe as to monitor your vital signs. We'll keep the current antibiotic regimen, unless the cultures indicate resistance. That doesn't seem likely, given your improvement to date, but we'll make that determination when we need to."

About to leave, he asked, "Can I get you anything? Is there anything you need?"

"I'd kill for a good cup of coffee."

"Alas, all I can offer is the cafeteria's mud. Sorry."

"Then it's tea for me. With lots of honey."

Auginello left the room to consult with the ICU team. Then he planned to go by Seven-South and see if Lenny had found anything new.

***

As soon as he'd made sure the autopsy suite was clean and ready for any unexpected case, Regis left the Pathology department and made his way to Seven South, where he found Lenny cleaning the discharge room of a patient who had died during the night. The night nurse had to take the body down to the morgue herself, Messenger service said they couldn't spare anyone, so the cadaver had remained on the ward for several hours. Lenny was wiping down the overbed table when he heard a knock on the door frame and looked up.

"Hey, Re'ege, got any news?"

Regis confirmed what he'd reported in a text message, that Austin's blood and urine had tested positive for arsenic. "The coffee mug, I guess it's from the doc's office? That had arsenic residue, too," said Regis. "Doc Fingers said the arsenic explains the patient's nausea and vomiting. He figures she had at least two doses. If she got any more..."

"Yeah, I get it," said Lenny. "The bastard switched to injecting her with a bunch of nasty bacteria. That's what put her in the ICU." He told his friend about the resident who had his ID stolen, which explained how the perpetrator was able to move around the hospital freely.

"This is one smart son of a bitch," said Regis. "We got to stop him before he comes back and tries something else. It'd be a sorrowful shame if the doctor ended up in my department, her caring for so many —"

Regis stopped in mid-sentence as Dr. Auginello approached them. "I better get back to my department," he said and headed off the ward.

"Lenny, I just came from the ICU, Rachel Austin is doing better, there were no incidents during the night. No intruders."

"Good news. Did you hear Doctor Fingers found traces of arsenic in the coffee mug?"

"No, I haven't talked to pathology yet, thanks. Good thing you picked it up."

Lenny pointed out that they had a witness who saw the criminal: Austin's secretary, Siobhan. The challenge now was to find a face to show her and finally identify the bastard before he administered some new form of poison.

"Hmm." Auginello's face grew long. "Do you suppose she's in danger as well?"

"Now you're starting to think like me. Yeah, I think she is, I'll go down on my break and give her a heads up."

Auginello thanked him and hurried off for rounds, while Lenny got back. The crafty shop steward realized he had to learn a whole lot more about the good Dr. Austin's history, because somewhere along the way she may have pissed somebody off big time.

And judging by her statement to him, she didn't even realize what she'd done.

36

Detective Joe Williams showed his badge to Dr. Fahim
in the ICU. With permission from the Attending Physician
to visit the patient, Williams looked through the clear glass
window and studied the patient. He saw a full-figured woman
with auburn hair sitting up in bed reading a journal. Medical,
he assumed. The heart monitor above her head traced a
repeating hieroglyphic on the screen, steady as a metronome.

A knock on the door, she looked up, saw a tall man in a suit
holding a badge up to the window. With a wave of the hand,
she beckoned him in.

"Doctor Austin, I'm Detective Joseph Williams. I've been
reviewing your case, can you spare a few moments?"

"Pull up the chair, detective, I've got all the time in the
world. I had no idea being an inpatient was so totally *boring*.
When I'm discharged I'm going to ask Patient Relations to
give out decks of cards, crossword puzzles, anything to stop
the boredom."

Williams got down to business, asking if she knew of
anyone who might wish her harm. She didn't. He asked
about colleagues in her department, jealousies, disgruntled
employees, followed by patients who had died with families
putting the blame solely on her.

"I've had more than a few patients on my service die, as
you'd expect, most people die in a facility these days, not like
the old days. But no, I haven't had any lawsuits, knock on
wood, or angry letters accusing me of killing grandma or letting grandpa wither away. Nothing like that, ever."

Williams made notes in his pad, saying, "Uh-huh" and
"Okay" from time to time. When Austin asked if he knew
about the stolen ID badge, he confirmed he knew the story

from Lenny and he had already spoken with her secretary. "But without a photo array of suspects, her description of the man doesn't help us all that much, it fits half the doctors in the facility: young, white handsome male."

He asked if her marriage was happy. Austin laughed, saying her husband would be lost without her, there was no way he would ever do her harm.

The detective suggested that she search her memory for anyone who might hold a first class grudge against her. It could be years old, some people could hold a grudge their whole life long. Austin promised to give it serious thought.

When he thanked Austin and closed his notebook, she asked him how long he thought it would take for the police to apprehend the person. Williams confessed he had no idea, it could be a day, a week, there was no telling. He told her his officers were reviewing videotapes from several locations in the hospital. Hopefully they would find someone who didn't belong, and that would put them a step closer to identifying the suspect.

"Well I hope you put in the overtime on this one, I'm not looking forward to any more poisons or inoculations with virulent bacteria, thank you very much. I just want to get back to my patients and not have to worry every time I step into the hospital."

***

With Baby Lilly snug in her papoose, Catherine bent to pick up her Freely suitcase, but her husband Louis leapt at it and took hold, a plastic bag filled with maternity items in his other hand. Irma took Catherine's hand and walked with her out of the room.

"Now you know I will be coming to visit you tomorrow. And if you have any issues or questions or *anything,* you call me right away, you hear?"

Catherine promised to be in touch. With a kiss on the cheek from the lactation nurse, she and Louis entered the elevator and made their way down to the main entrance. As she walked carefully down the broad marble steps, Catherine heard Louis tell her that the news that morning was the Zika epidemic seemed to be tapering off. There were still mosquitoes carrying the disease, still new cases coming into the hospitals and doctor offices, but the numbers were definitely declining.

The new mother put her hands gently on the papoose. She realized that the cotton swaddling not only kept Lilly warm and safe, it also protected the baby from any mosquitoes that might be around. She let Louis open the passenger door of the car for her, something he never did before. She was beginning to realize this motherhood thing had its advantages. Best of all, she was off work for three months.

37

Mimi was relieved, the last bed bath was completed. She and the nurses' aide Malvina lifted the patient out of bed and settled her into a reclining chair. While Mimi placed a security vest on the patient and tied it securely at the back of the chair, the aide stripped the bed. Together they placed new sheets on the bed, adding a waterproof pad to keep the sheets dry, the patient was incontinent of urine...and stool.

The nurse checked her watch. "My goodness, is it lunch time already? This morning just flew by!"

She told the other RN she was going out for Chinese take-away, offering to pick something up for her or the aide. Getting no takers, she hurried down the stairs and walked to the ER, that was better for her, the main entrance had too many head nurses and suits coming and going. Given her union activities, Mimi tried to avoid contact with the bosses as much as possible.

As she passed through the ER, she thought there weren't as many patients crowding the hallways on stretchers. Maybe the Zika outbreak really was coming to an end, what a blessing *that* would be!

There were three ambulances in the slots outside the ER entrance. She hurried down the ramp they used to wheel the stretchers up to the door and past the triage tent standing in the parking lot. Out of the corner of her eye Mimi caught sight of a familiar face coming out of the tent with a patient: it was that diligent medical student she had seen on rounds the week before, only now he was working as a paramedic. He was wearing dark sunglasses and a baseball cap, but even without the white lab coat she would have recognized him anywhere.

Well, she thought, he really is a hard-working sort: doing a tour as a paramedic *and* going to medical school. His experience in the field was bound to give him an advantage over the students with money who only had college behind them. As Mimi hurried down the sidewalk toward the restaurant, she didn't notice that Roy had seen her at the same time she had looked at him. Seen and stared at her through his dark glasses. He could tell right away she had recognized him, their paths had crossed twice while he was making his 'rounds.'

The nurse couldn't suspect anything sinister about him, she had smiled when she saw him, as if she admired him. How could that be? He thought, the stupid woman must think he was moonlighting as an EMT while going to medical school. People were so incredibly stupid.

Now he had a potential second victim to send to the morgue. A nurse, who could be easier to kill? If she was single, or if she was married but unhappy with her partner, it would be easy to get her alone in a bar. Or a hotel room. Yes, a hotel room, he liked that scenario, it had the ring of a classic dark movie.

I'm the star of my own movie.

"Hey, Roy, you joining me or what?" His partner was pushing the patient on a stretcher to the ramp for the ER.

"Sorry, got lost in thought," he said, quickly taking his position at the head of the stretcher.

"Got a girl on your mind?"

"As a matter of fact, I do. A lovely nurse who can't wait to meet me for drinks."

"Lucky girl."

As he dropped the ambulance form at the desk for the ER clerk, Roy knew exactly how he would have to deal with the nosey nurse. She may not know today who he was and what he had done, but he couldn't take the risk that she didn't eventually put two and two together, and in his case, that came out to twenty years to life in a state prison.

And prison was no place for a free spirit.

***

Lenny Moss was pissed. Not an unusual state of mind for him, but today the anger was deep and wide. The housekeeping supervisor had finally relented and given the staff permission to use a weak bleach solution for disinfecting the horizontal surfaces, and the word was, the Zika outbreak was starting to turn. But they were still criminally understaffed, burned out and fed up. The hospital hadn't hired more staff, hadn't brought in temps from an agency, and were balking at approving much overtime.

He looked down the hallway and counted four isolation carts. Okay, that was down from seven the week before, but the workload was still too fricking much, especially when half the time they pulled Little Mary to cover another ward or a clinic.

As he helped Moose collect the lunch trays, he remembered with a smile his former housekeeping partner, Betty, and how she always saved leftover food from the trays to take home. "It's for my dogs," she had told Gary Tuttle when the nurse had worked on Seven South. But Lenny knew the food was for her grandchildren whom she was helping raise while her daughter got her life together. Apparently, the young woman was clean, had graduated from Philadelphia Community College and was in a job training program with one of the big pharmacy chains. Good for her, he knew it was a great relief to Betty, who was now retired.

"I heard 'bout the nurses signing with that Pennsylvania nurses union," said Moose. "Guess you're kinda disappointed."

"Yeah, I was hoping we could get them into the nursing division of our union. Would've given us a hell of a punch. Imagine marching on the president's office with nurses joining us."

"Too much like right," said Moose. "Too much." He went on to collect the last of the trays, leaving the isolation rooms for the aides to discard the paper trays in the trash.

Lenny was thinking about his own lunch when he spied Dr. Auginello's lanky figure coming down the hall. The doctor didn't stop to look in on a patient.

"Lenny, you have a minute?"

"Sure. Step into my office."

He led the physician to the janitor's closet, where he upended two empty buckets. "It ain't plush, but it is private," said Lenny, leaving the door cracked. The smell of bleach tickled their noses. "Thanks for getting approval for the bleach, it's just what we needed."

"You're sure your people are keeping the dilution to one-to-ten?"

"They know, make it too strong, they lose the use of it."

"Good. Good." Auginello stretched out his long legs, which was not easy, given the small dimensions of the room. "Anything new with the investigation?"

"I wish I had something for you. I passed around the description of the guy who left the articles in Doctor Austin's office, but it's pretty vague. Besides, we can't be sure he's the one we're looking for."

"When you hear the sound of hoofbeats, don't always think of coconuts," said Auginello.

"Monty Python," said Lenny.

"Exactly."

"The police are looking over videos of the hallway at the ICU entrance. But with so many medical staff coming and going, it's going to be hard to identify the perp," said Lenny.

"The number of students and house staff *is* daunting. And we have pharmacy interns, physician's assistants, respiratory therapists...it's a heck of a long list."

"Well we have to break this nut open, we can't have some deranged bastard roaming the hospital, he could kill one of the patients, a staff member, anyone he wants."

Lenny thought for a moment. "You know, somebody this determined...someone who's willing to take the kind of risks he's taken, he's got to have some monster chip on his shoulder."

"A grudge."

"Big time. How about you look into Doctor Austin's history? She must have been involved in some kind of dispute. Maybe an unexpected death, angry family member blames her. Somewhere she pissed this guy off, we need to find out who it was."

Auginello agreed, he would look over Austin's medical school, her internship, residency and graduate studies for Family Practice, see if there's anything that stands out.

They parted, both men worried the threat looming over Austin was still there.

38

When she returned to the hospital with her take-away lunch, a burly security guard stopped her inside the ER. "Ma'am, you need to come with me," he told her. The flat affect in his voice left Mimi no doubt she had to comply.

As she walked beside the guard, Mimi felt fear taking over. Scenarios flowed through her mind: of losing her job. Losing her license to practice. Losing their home. It was all so horrible. So devastating. She said a silent prayer, asking Jesus for the strength not to fall apart and break down crying. Not until she got home and felt the arms of her sweet husband Louis holding her. He always told her things would work out. She didn't always believe him, but she loved to hear him say it.

Sure enough, the guard led her to the office of Miss Burgess, Director of Nursing. Joe West was standing behind the desk beside the director. When Mimi reached the monster desk in front of Mother Burgess, West said in his clipped, flat voice, "Take a seat, Miss Rogers."

"Missus Rogers, thank you." Mimi settled into a straight-back chair, whispering "Jesus, take my hand" under her breath. It seemed like the kind of chair the police would have in a room where they interviewed murder suspects. "I have to get back to my ward, my co-worker will be asking where I am."

Burgess said, "Another nurse has taken over care of your patients, you don't have to think about them any more."

"Taken over? What in god's name are you talking about? Are you saying I'm not going back to my ward? What is going on?!"

She turned around, saw that the burly guard was standing in the doorway and meant business. A sickening feeling took hold of her. She felt weak and nauseous. She wanted to find a bathroom and put her head in the toilet to throw up.

Joe West leaned over the desk and pressed the button on an open laptop computer. The sound of Mimi's voice suddenly filled the room. She was talking to Lenny in the sewing room, talking about how they were going to ask more nurses to sign pledge cards. How they would be visiting nurses on their day off and meeting with the union organizer.

"What's going on?" said Mimi. "How did you... I mean, that's not legal. It can't be!" Anger welled up in the nurse, driving the fear from the pit of her stomach. "You have no right to record my conversation! That is outrageous!"

Joe West let the hint of a smile, more like a smirk, bend his perennial scowl. "We have every right to record our employees while they are on duty. The law is very clear on this. Monitoring staff is an accepted practice."

Burgess pointed a meaty finger at Mimi. "Conspiring to form a union while on duty is a clear and present violation of employee conduct. You have been warned on more than one occasion. In writing."

She pulled out a sheet of paper and slid it across her broad desk. It was the last page in the Standards of Professional Practice that she had signed when she was first hired. Burgess had highlighted in bright orange a sentence that warned against engaging in any labor or political organizing within the facility while on duty.

West informed Mimi that she was suspended for three days, pending final termination. A board of James Madison administrators would review the charges against her and make its recommendation, she would receive the final notice of termination by certified mail.

"The security officer will accompany you to your locker on Seven South. He will observe you emptying your locker. He will confiscate any property belonging to the hospital. He will then take you to your car and observe you leaving hospital property. You will not return to James Madison again unless it is for medical treatment."

Although Mimi wasn't sure her legs would support her weight, she resolved not to show Burgess or Joe West any sign of weakness. She held her head high as she stood up, pulled the hated GPS unit from around her neck and dropped it on Burgess's desk. As she turned and walked to the door, the burly guard opened the door and walked behind her like a looming shadow as she made her way to the elevator. They rode together in silence to the seventh floor.

Walking down the corridor and entering her ward, Mimi told the guard she needed to use the toilet. "Are you going to follow me in there?"

The guard shrugged, obviously not the chatty type. She pushed open the staff bathroom door, stepped inside, saw the room was empty. In case the guard had the nerve to poke his stupid head inside, she went into the stall, closed and locked the door and took out her cell phone.

Who to call first? Louis? No, Lenny. First she had to talk to Lenny Moss.

Once Mimi was out of the Director's office, Burgess called the suspended nurse's head nurse and ordered her to bring the log for their narcotics usage to her right away. When the Head Nurse asked if there was a problem with their count, had any narcotics gone missing or unaccounted for, Burgess told her to leave all that to her, she was sure there would be a few discrepancies, there always were. And all she needed was two or three ambiguous entries for her to put nurse Mimi Rogers out of work. And without a license to practice nursing.

***

When Lenny got the phone call from Mimi, the nurse was so shaken up, she could barely speak. He tried his best to comfort her, but she didn't hear much of what he said, he was sure, the shock of being suspended or fired always knocked a worker out like a blow to the head. It was a fearful blow, and few withstood it without falling apart.

The call over, he phoned Alexandra at her union office and spoke to the organizer in the nursing division. She promised to reach out to one of the union lawyers and to visit Mimi at her home as soon as possible. Lenny proposed that he meet them there after work, and Alexandra readily agreed.

Now angrier than he had been since the beginning of the Zika outbreak, Lenny attacked long black streaks in the old marble floor with a vengeance, alternating between a bristle brush and mop. His long strokes with the mop often calmed his nerves, but today there was no therapy in them, it was all cursing and fury. It was all heartbreak and a vow to fight back. Hard.

Once the floor was as clean as it was ever going to be, Lenny had a new thought that intrigued him. It was outside the box, but those were often the best ideas. He wondered if there was a chance the UNP union might join his own HSWU in filing a complaint of unfair labor practice. He hadn't seen other cases of competing unions joining together in such a complaint, but going on the principle that a united front was more powerful in a campaign than a divided one, he thought it couldn't hurt.

If Alexandra gave him the go-ahead.

If the UNP rep would even talk to him.

If the charges against Mimi were labor related, because if Mother Burgess found something in the nurse's practice that was outside the labor issue, that would be beyond his union's reach.

Watching the beefy security guard escort Mimi off the ward, Lenny tried to give her an encouraging look, but the nurse was so distraught, he was unable to make eye contact.

For causing her that much pain, Lenny vowed to get even, one way or the other.

39

Dave Rambling, one of the union lawyers, pulled up to Lenny's house on his motorcycle with Alexandra riding behind him. The loud rumble of the motorcycle brought Malcolm out onto the porch. "Can I ride the bike?" the boy asked as the lanky young man dismounted and approached the house.

"Sorry, lad, I don't have a helmet that'll fit your head. You've got to grow a bit before you can ride with me."

Alexandra pulled off her helmet and showed it to Malcolm, who tried to claim his head was almost as big as hers, but she just laughed and tucked the helmet beneath her arm. The boy tried appealing to Lenny, but Lenny wasn't buying it, although Rambling was kind enough to let the boy sit on the bike, as long as it wasn't moving.

Mimi arrived a moment later. Inside, Lenny poured drinks for everyone, having stopped at the State Store on his way home from work.

Rambling explained to Mimi what was involved in filing a complaint of unfair labor practice with the NLRB. He warned her it was a slow process, the Board was not likely to rule very quickly, which meant Mimi could be out of a job for a prolonged period. "There's no guarantee they will rule in your favor," he added, "the Board has been staffed with Republican hacks since Trump was elected."

They discussed additional legal strategies, as well as reaching out to the *Daily News*. Patience suggested contacting the *Philly Tribune*, which catered to the African American population. Although they had no evidence the attack on Mimi was racially motivated, they thought it was worth trying for an article in the Trib.

"What about social media?" Mimi asked. "I mean, just how much can I say on my personal online page? Will it hurt my chance in the courts?"

Alexandra told her that social media stories were a mixed blessing. They were great for informing coworkers, friends and members of faith-based organizations. But if the language was especially critical or engaged in name-calling it could backfire big time. "You're better off leaving the messaging to the union for the moment," she said. "Just report you are suspended with the possibility of termination and that the union is taking your case. People can reach the union by email or messaging if they want to know more."

Mimi was ready to call for a job action, but Lenny knew the registered nurses were nowhere ready to risk their own jobs when they hadn't even voted in the union. Even more worrisome, he believed the suspension would scare a lot of nurses out of signing pledge cards.

Patience said, "Why don't we ask the UNP people to support our petition to the NLRB?"

"But I wasn't organizing for *them*, I was organizing for your union," said Mimi.

"True, but we do have a common interest here. If James Madison can get away with firing you for organizing, they can do the same for the nurses who signed UNP pledge cards."

Alexandra thought the proposal would be dead on arrival, but Rambling pointed out there was nothing to lose by asking, the worst the UNP organizers could do would be to say no. So Lenny agreed to call the union and make the pitch.

Pouring another drink for Mimi, Patience said, "The men don't understand how women think: we don't huff and puff and get all territorial, we just get the job done." She and Mimi clicked their glasses and smiled.

"Girl power," said Mimi.

"Amen to that!"

***

"You sure you're okay sleeping in my recliner?" Louis set a cup of tea on the little table beside the beat-up leather chair that he loved to sit back in and watch a game on the TV. The chair was well worn but still comfortable. Catherine had threatened to throw it out for years, complaining the worn leather looked shabby, but Louis wouldn't hear of it.

"I'm fine, dear, the chair is just the right thing for me and Lilly."

Louis kissed his wife on the cheek and shuffled off to bed with a yawn, muttering to himself. Catherine took a last sip of the tea with cream and honey that Louis had prepared for her, then she pushed back on the chair. Her legs were raised up, a great relief for her tired feet, while Baby Lilly slept in the papoose, nestled between her breasts.

Catherine closed her eyes and was immediately asleep. In her sleep she dreamed her baby was nursing at her breast. Opening her eyes, she looked down into the papoose to see that the baby was indeed taking her fill of mother's milk. As mother looked down, the baby looked up into Catherine's eyes, and Catherine felt a tender, aching love that suffused her entire body. It was like a soft tide of warm water that flowed through her body. She had never known anything like it. Never dreamed she could feel so connected to another human being.

She stared down into her daughter's face, tears of joy streaming down her cheeks. Catherine didn't even bother to wipe her face, it was such a relief to feel the depression beginning to lift, and such a release to be loved so completely.

***

Detective Williams looked down at the drawing he'd set on his kitchen table. The kitchen was where he liked to sit and think about a case while a pot of New Orleans style gumbo on the stove cooked away, filling the room with a fragrant aroma. It seemed when his stomach juices were really flowing his imagination was triggered as well.

The drawing was the police sketch artist's work. Siobhan O'Shea had worked with the artist to make the drawing. The face was as she had described him, rather generic. The man looked like any number of young residents or medical students: white, dark hair, handsome face. The only distinctive characteristic she had come up with was his eyes, which she had described as "blue. Very blue...vivid blue."

So that was what the hospital security guards were watching for: some white male appearing to be a student or resident with vivid blue eyes. Not the best lead he'd had to work with, but not entirely worthless either.

Williams went over Austin's medical and school records, looking for signs of conflict: a letter, comment, report of anything outside the norm, but there was nothing. Austin hadn't testified in any employee termination. She hadn't been part of any lawsuit or charges against a hospital. There was no coroner's report linking her to an unexpected death.

He looked for a hospital staffer who would gain by her death with a promotion, but there was no one, she was a faculty member, but not a chair. She didn't even head a committee. Austin was a hard-working physician who put in long hours caring for her patients. She even made house calls now and then to her long-term patients.

Whatever reason the perpetrator had to try and kill the woman was not evident in her written record. Which meant he had to throw out the documents and burrow into her brain: somewhere in her memory there was an incident: a breakup with a boyfriend or spurning of a man's overtures that had tipped him into a revenge fantasy.

Frustrated, he put the records away and served himself a bowl of New Orleans style gumbo over rice. The first spoonful, like the first sip of a fine whiskey, made him smile. If only his case could come together so well.

40

On his morning break, Lenny made his way to the ICU, where he found Gary Tuttle carrying a cup of coffee out of the break room. "Yo, Tuttle, how's Doctor Austin?" he asked.

"Slow improvement." The nurse beckoned for Lenny to follow him down to the patient's room, where Austin was sitting up in a recliner chair, her husband on a white plastic and metal seat beside her.

"You do know they use that for toileting, don't you, dear?" Austin was telling her husband, who looked down to see the slots where a bedpan could be inserted beneath the seat. He shrugged his shoulders and sipped a cup of coffee.

Gary placed the cup he'd just brewed on the overbed table. "Two sugars, spot of milk," he said.

Austin leaned forward and inhaled the aroma, smiling. "Ah, at last, a real cup of coffee, thank you, Gary."

When Lenny reported there was nothing new on the investigation, Austin's smile faded. Her husband pointed out that at least she was safe and getting better, but that didn't mollify his wife.

"I can't spend my life looking over my shoulder, wondering if the sandwich I'm biting into or the coffee I'm stirring is going to kill me. You have to catch this maniac."

Lenny asked once more if she could recall any incident she was involved in that upset someone in a serious way. Austin looked up at the ceiling, searching her memory, but came up blank.

"I've gone back in my mind all the way to high school, for god's sake. I'm not the kind of person who gets into fights. I don't trade insults, I trade information."

Lawrence was looking at his cup of coffee. He was trying

to imagine what kind of a person would engage in such cruel and diabolical acts. "Rachel, do you remember you telling me a story about a medical student who was drummed out of the program? It was, I don't know, four, five years ago. He—"

"Oh, yes, I *do* remember. He was examining a post-partum woman who was in a coma, she'd suffered an embolic stroke, poor thing. When I came into the room he was performing a vaginal exam, which wasn't in and of itself suspicious, although he should have had a supervising physician with him. It was the fact that he wasn't wearing exam gloves that made me suspicious. He wasn't wearing gloves at all."

"You went ballistic. I remember you cursed when you got home that day, which was not your usual mode of speech, you were really livid. There was a hearing..."

"Right, a hearing. Several other physicians and even a few students testified that the student was inappropriate in his examination of women patients. In the end, they dropped him from the program."

"What was his name?" asked Lenny.

Austin poked around in her memory. "I don't remember, it was years ago. Raymond, maybe? Roger, I'm not sure."

"Can you track him down, Lenny?" asked Lawrence.

"I can't myself, but I know someone who can. We'll find him. Trust me, we will find this bastard."

Lenny hurried out to the station, where he asked Gary to page Dr. Auginello. "Ask him to meet me on my ward, I have information that I think is going to crack this case wide open."

As the nurse reached for the phone, Lenny noted the GPS unit suspended around the nurse's neck. Something about that device troubled him, though he couldn't quite make out what it was. But it nagged at him as he stepped to the exit and punched the metal plate on the wall. The automatic doors opened and then closed behind him. Lenny realized it was all too easy for the perpetrator to enter the ICU, even with the nurses and doctors on alert. They had to nail the bastard before he came back.

***

Dr. Auginello was examining a man with a post-operative wound infection that so far had resisted the antibiotic regimen. The problem was that the resistant bacteria had colonized the patient's colon, and antibiotics were unable to eradicate them in that dense environment.

The ID Fellow asked if a stool transplant would help. Auginello put his hands in the pockets of his lab coat and considered the question. "You're thinking, if instilling non-pathogenic bacteria colonies into the gut is an effective treatment for C-diff colitis, why not use it for driving out virulent microorganisms. I admit, it's logical. But you know many a logical idea proved to be ineffective in clinical practice. Or worse."

He instructed the medical student to conduct a literature search for articles that explored seeding the microbiome of the gut as a strategy for treating chronic skin or bone infections. The student who took notes asked the ID Attending if it was okay if he also pursued the question, did changing the odor from a person's breath block mosquitoes from finding their host.

"So far I haven't found much research into this question, Doctor Auginello. I think it could be a terrific research paper. It might even bring in grant money."

Auginello told the student he was free to pursue the question, but he should focus on the question at hand first.

Three loud chirps from his cell phone told Auginello he was being paged, the old pager having finally been replaced by an app on his phone. The message read: "See Lenny 7 S STAT."

Telling the Fellow he would rejoin him on rounds as soon

227

as he could, Auginello hurried to Seven South, hoping it was good news, there was precious little of it around these days.

***

Mimi carefully placed the job application on the desk, stepped back, took a deep breath and waited. The woman behind the desk, a young woman dressed in maternity clothes, picked up the form and looked through it.

"Union organizing, huh?" she said.

'Yes. It's like I told you, I've been asking the RNs to sign pledge cards for the HSWU. The head of security, this mean, cruel man named Joe West must have had the sewing room in the basement bugged or something, because he had a recording of me on my break talking about the union."

The young woman shook her head in disgust.

"So, do you think you'll have work for me? For real?"

"As long as you hold your license, sure, I can use you. I only wish I could send you down to James Madison, wouldn't that be a kick, you walking in there on an assignment with my agency. But they'd have you arrested and then drop my contract, so we better not go down that road."

"That's fine with me, Miss Bondi, I don't want to make trouble for you, or for me!"

The owner of the nursing temp agency suggested they wait until the hospital notified Mimi if she was permanently discharged or returned to duty. Once they had that decision the agency could begin giving her assignments. "You'll have to start working nights in the nursing homes. It's not glamorous, but it pays well."

"I'll take whatever I can get, thank you. Thank you so very much."

Relieved that she would have income, unless Mother Burgess had her license suspended, Mimi left the agency, hopeful but still afraid.

41

"You paged, me, Lenny, what's the latest?" Dr. Auginello had left his Fellow to continue rounds and headed straight to the Seven-South housekeeping closet, where he found Lenny rinsing his mop in the sink. The pungent smell of bleach tickled his nose as he entered the room.

"I'm glad you could come right over, thanks." Lenny turned over two plastic buckets so they could sit. "I talked to Doctor Austin again this morning, and she remembered an incident with a medical student. A male student."

"Okay..."

"The student was doing a gynecological exam on a woman in a coma. Austin came in and found him, and aside from the student doing the exam without supervision, he wasn't wearing gloves."

Auginello shook his head in sadness. "It's one of our profession's dirty little secrets. Not that it happens often, thank the gods, but there's the rare deviant who finds sexual pleasure in his exam of female patients. Especially unconscious ones."

Lenny explained that there had been a hearing where doctors and medical students testified that the guy was inappropriate over and over again. In the end they kicked him out of the school.

"Did Doctor Austin remember the student's name? I might have come across him in the ID Division."

"No, she didn't remember. She thought it could have been Raymond or Roger, something like that, but she couldn't be sure."

"The insulin shock gave her brain a heavy hit, that probably impaired her memory."

Lenny asked the doctor if he would try and find out more from the medical school. Auginello was friends with the Dean and immediately promised to speak to him that morning. "There's no time to waste, Lenny, every hour this creep is roaming the hospital puts Austin in danger."

He hurried off to the medical school, feeling for the first time they were making progress in this horrendous case, and grateful to have Lenny and his co-workers watching out for his friend.

***

Catherine opened the brightly wrapped package as Mimi looked on with glee. The box contained three books for babies, with thick pages Baby Lilly could explore with her mouth as well as with her eyes.

"I love the Pat the Bunny the best," said Mimi. "My girl loved to feel the soft fleece in the page."

Catherine pulled out a box with a colorful toy. Opening the box, she found a series of plastic circles all intertwined. It looked like a prop from a cheesy science fiction show.

"How lovely, this is just the right size for her little fingers," said Catherine. She peeled open the papoose and shook the toy above Baby Lilly, who looked up for a few seconds and then closed her eyes.

"She naps quite a lot," explained Catherine. "It's so funny, Mimi. It's a little like when she was in my womb. I feel her poking around, squeezing my boob or kicking her feet."

"I think the best part is how the baby can hear your heart beat."

"Yes, that's what they believe." Catherine poured Mimi a second cup of tea. "I'm so glad Louis is at work, he tries to hide how worried he's been, but I can tell. This morning he put on socks that didn't match: that's a sure sign he's got a lot on his mind."

Mimi asked Catherine if her mood was better, she seemed a lot brighter. The new mom admitted the depression was still with her. It was like a threatening storm on the horizon. A cold wind that still sent a chill through her. But being home, with Louis and with Lilly, and knowing there had been no Zika exposure helped her fight off the blues.

"But what about you, Mimi? That evil Mother Burgess, she makes me so mad I could just spit."

Mimi confessed it had been a bad blow, taking away her hospital ID and escorting her out of the hospital, and there was nothing she could do about it. At least in that moment. "The union is filing a complaint, but that takes a long time. I signed up with an agency, I'm supposed to start working tonight."

"Wow, that's wonderful news! Where will they send you?"

"Rototua Nursing Home, out in Bedminster. They said I'll be the charge nurse for the whole damn place, isn't that crazy?"

"It sounds like a lot of work."

"They have LPNs to give out the oral meds and aides to handle the bedside care. I'm to hang the IV meds and mix the enteral feeds. That, and supervise the staff."

"Boy, it sounds like a precarious place, I hope there are no emergencies."

"You and me both, girl. You and me both."

Mimi took up her cup of tea and sat back, relieved for her friend, scared she would never again take morning report from her good friend.

***

Lenny was climbing the stairs on his way back from lunch, cursing his friend Moose for pushing him to avoid the elevator, though it was a curse tinged with affection. His cell phone chirped twice, meaning he'd received a text message.

Surprised he had good reception in the stairwell, Lenny reached into his pocket for the phone. As he called up the message, the thought that had nagged at him when he left Gary Tuttle in the ICU suddenly became clear in his mind.

The GPS units had never received signals in the basement since the day the new owners took over and made James Madison a private institution. That was how the nurses could meet there and speak freely. So how did Joe West get the recording? He must have installed a transponder in or near the room, the bastard.

He decided to visit his friend Ali Patel in the IT department. If there were any new GPS signals coming in from the basement, Ali would be able to track down the transponder.

Grim and tired from the walk up the stairs, Lenny emerged onto Seven-South out of breath but with the first sign of optimism in Mimi's case.

42

The Dean of the Medical School was unhappy. He adjusted his bow tie, moved his glasses up higher on his nose and clasped his hands together on his broad mahogany desk.

"Michael, I am to be sure entirely sympathetic to Doctor Austin's plight, the thought that somebody would try to harm her, in our institution is monstrous, simply monstrous. But there are issues of confidentiality. Liability. The records of our medical students can't be handed over to you on nothing more than a vague suspicion that the young man *might* be implicated in these charges."

Auginello poked his tongue in his cheek, thinking, did he want to be diplomatic or did he want to be blunt? He decided there was no time for beating around the bush.

"Arthur, the police are investigating the assaults on Rachel Austin. They have a sketch of a suspect. If you simply let me look at the students' ID photos, we can clear this whole thing up in a matter of seconds."

"The police are involved?"

"Yes. A detective will be seeing you today with the sketch. But I need to know right now so that security can watch to be sure the man doesn't come anywhere near Austin."

After chewing his lip and tapping his desk with fingertips, the Dean buzzed his secretary and instructed her to bring him the files of all students who were suspended from the program over the over the last ten years.

While they waited, the Dean asked the ID Division chief if reports in the news were true that the Zika outbreak was finally waning. Auginello told him the admission rates were down, as were the number of positive viral tests. When the Dean brought up the emergent use of consumer-grade fans and painters' masks for personal protective equipment, Auginello thought he saw a twinkle in the old man's eyes.

"Desperate times," Auginello said.

"Indeed. I always preferred an outcome-based solution to problems. Provided we follow ethical guidelines, of course."

"Of course."

The secretary came in with a stack of file folders. Leaving Auginello to sort through them, the Dean excused himself for a meeting. It didn't take Auginello long to find the student that Austin had testified against, there were a dozen supporting statements. The review committee had voted unanimously to expel the student.

His name: Roy Reading.

His ID photo, if not an exact likeness to the police sketch, was close enough to make Auginello confident he was the one they were looking for. The ID physician took out his cell phone and snapped a photo from the hospital ID clipped to the folder.

They were getting close, he was certain.

Leaving the Dean's office, he sent a copy of the photo to Lenny, asking him to forward it to the detective. That would put the whole affair in the hands of the police where it belonged.

***

Lenny had no sooner forwarded the photo of the disgraced medical student to Siobhan in Dr. Austin's office when his phone rang. Stepping into his 'office,' he listened to Siobhan's excited voice saying "It's him! It's him! It's Doctor Baumann, or whatever you call him. God, I hope he never comes back to *this* office, I'd be scared to death."

"I think that's unlikely, this guy has always done things on the sly, he hasn't openly attacked somebody."

"Open of closed, I'm still scared, Lenny."

"Well, it is better to be safe, Siobhan. Don't stay in the office alone, be sure there's someone else there with you. And just be aware of your surroundings when you come and go to work."

"From now on I'm getting my boyfriend to drop me off and pick me up. And I'm locking the damn door to the office, they can buzz me to come in!"

Hanging up, Lenny sent the photo of the medical student to Detective Williams and followed it up with a phone call. He told the detective how Siobhan confirmed it was the same person who came to the doctor's office to "drop off some journal articles." Williams promised to follow up on the lead right away.

"You'll call me when you have the bastard in cuffs, right?" said Lenny.

"Give me some time to check him out, for Christ's sake. We don't know he's the perpetrator. At this point the best we'll be able to do is question him."

"Are you kidding me? The photo's a dead ringer for the sketch!"

"I hear you, Lenny, but we have to have actual physical evidence that he committed a crime before we can arrest him."

"I don't fricking believe it. This is a load of crap!"

"It's procedure, don't blame me, I don't make the rules. And don't go off and do something on your own, all right? We'll find him and bring him in for questioning. Just be aware, this is a long, slow process. Be patient."

Lenny made no such promise before hanging up on the detective. He wasn't about to wait for the slow wheels of justice to grind their rusted way forward, it left Austin in danger, not to mention Siobhan, who was a potential witness.

No, the times called for quick action, and fuck the slow-motion police investigation.

***

235

Seated at a computer terminal in the medical school library, Roy scowled at the latest lab results for Austin. The infection was responding to treatment, her septic picture had improved. Roy was surprised, he had been convinced his intravenous cocktail would do the trick. But he wasn't discouraged, it was merely a temporary setback. Nobody knew of his role in her string of illnesses, so he had all the time in the world to administer a new lethal dose.

And there were so many choices. So many drugs that could kill her. An opiate overdose would work well, though Roy wasn't confident he could easily purchase a pure specimen. This would require some serious contemplation.

Roy considered the nurse who had seen him on her ward as a medical student and in the ER as an EMT. She had definitely taken notice of him in the ER, but did that really make her a threat? She had no way of knowing how he was exacting his revenge on Austin, so at the moment all the dumb woman could conclude was that he held two jobs.

But once Austin was dead, what if the autopsy even hinted at 'foul play'? Unlikely, his method was well thought out and perfectly executed. But even so, the best laid plans, blah, blah, blah. Roy realized it was better to be safe than sorry: better to eliminate a possible threat than to let it fester and grow.

The first order of business: her name. Noting the date when the nurse saw him in his EMT uniform, Roy opened a computer file of the patients on her ward. Next, he looked for the signature of the nurse on the day shift in the medication administration record: "Mercedes Espinoza." Did the nurse look like an "Espinoza?" He didn't think so.

Going on to another patient chart, he found a different signature: "Mimi Rogers."

"Mimi." That sounded right. She was black. It wasn't a classic black name, it didn't have an African sound to it, but she was the only other RN on duty that day, so it had to be her.

Going to a popular social media site, Roy typed in the name and James Madison Hospital. In seconds the nurse's face showed up on a profile. It was her all right.

He read her profile information. There was no home address, but he learned she had a husband and a daughter. Photos showed her in a row house: North Philly? Could be West.

This was going to take a little research. But Roy was undaunted. He would find out more about the nurse, follow her home from work, maybe. When the timing was right he would administer a fatal blow without the nurse knowing it was coming, and *then* he would administer the coup de grace to Austin. That way, if any suspicion ever did arise over her death, unlikely and improbable as it was, the witness who saw his double identity could not point him out to the police.

Logging off of the computer, he decided to take a walk past the morgue just for the pleasure of it. After all, that would be Austin's final destination. He wanted to have a clear image of the place since he wouldn't be able to attend the autopsy in person.

43

Lenny walked downstairs to the first floor and made his way to the Information Services department, where he greeted a woman he had helped with a disability claim. "Hey, Ziralda, how's the job?" She told him she was doing great, no more hassles from the boss about her battery-powered wheelchair. "Is Ali here?"

"Where else would he be?" She pointed to a cubbyhole in the back of the room. Lenny found his friend working with three different computer screens, the young man's eyes darting back and forth as he typed furiously on his keyboard.

"Yo, Ali, got a minute?"

Reed thin, with jet black hair combed straight back, a high forehead and piercing black eyes, Ali spun around in his chair and placed his palms together in a greeting. "For you, my friend, I have all the time in the world."

Lenny quickly explained his dilemma: he understood that the transponders which connected the GPS units the nurses wore around their necks with the dispatcher were not installed in areas where nurses didn't provide direct care: there were none in the laundry, central stores, the sewing room or pharmacy, and so on.

"But one of our nurses who was suspended said Joe West played a recording of her speaking about the union drive while she was in the sewing room, and the sewing room..."

"Is in the basement." Ali spun around and opened a new program on the big screen in the middle of his desk. "You are correct, we service all of the networks. I'm not aware of any new installations, not that it's my department per se, but..."

He typed in a command, scrolled down a page, frowned and leaned back in his chair. "There *is* a new signal from the basement. Curious. I can't say from here *exactly* where it's located. Sorry."

"That's okay. Do you think we could find it?"

"We?" Ali gave his friend a skeptical look. When Lenny put on a pleading face, Ali flashed a wide grin. "Sure, why not, it's in our department's wheelhouse. Let's take a look, it's not far."

They walked down to the basement and along a narrow hallway that had pipes and electrical conduits running along the wall. The floor was streaked with black strips where dirty wheels had rolled over. It hadn't been cleaned in a long time.

They entered a wider corridor and followed it to the door for the sewing room. Ali looked up and down the corridor checking the ceiling. "No antenna here." Lenny suggested they look in the room.

With a knock they stepped in. The room was empty, Birdie was out on her lunch break. Ali and Lenny looked up at the ceiling. Again, no antenna was visible.

"Curiouser and curiouser," said Ali, rubbing his chin. He studied the ceiling more closely. "That ceiling tile in the corner. See it? It's not perfectly flush with the others."

Lenny grabbed a chair and set it beneath the tile. He stood on the chair, with Ali holding it steady. Pushing up, he lifted the tile and slid it to the side. "Fuck me."

"Yup, there she blows." Ali confirmed, it was a transponder equipped to relay a GPS signal.

Lenny had the smile of a wolf sniffing out its prey. When Ali asked him why he didn't look pissed off, Lenny said he believed West had finally hung himself by going one step too far. He took out his cell phone and took several photos, then he replaced the tile, stepped down and took more pictures of the ceiling, the room, and even a shot of the door taken from the corridor.

Walking out to the elevator where Lenny would ride it to his floor, Ali said, "You know, my friend, you always told me what a scumbag that Joe West is, but I never thought he'd stoop this low."

"There's no bottom to his treachery," said Lenny. As he rode the elevator up, Lenny worked out a plan for Mimi's defense. It felt right. He would call Rambling at the union office to run it by him just to be sure, but Lenny felt good about his tactic, it was the one chance they had to save Mimi's job.

***

When his shift was over, Lenny punched out, then made his way to the ICU, he wanted to talk to Gary Tuttle about Austin's safety. Coming into the unit, he spotted the tall figure of Dr. Auginello at the nursing station talking to Gary. Lenny asked the physician what was the latest on Austin's condition. Auginello confirmed she was getting stronger each day, the infection seemed to be under control. "Her kidney function still hasn't returned to normal, and there may be long term damage to the brain from the hypoglycemic shock, but all in all, not a bad prognosis."

"I like your optimism," said Lenny, having noted several times in the past that the good doctor was a born pessimist. Lenny explained that the police were trying to track down the suspect medical student, but even if they found him, there was no actual evidence that would justify an arrest. Yet. Auginello was furious.

"He's a slick son of a bitch, that's for certain. If you hadn't put a bug in my ear to look for a malevolent hand, I might have never suspected foul play."

"You would've figured it out eventually," Lenny said, tactfully not mentioning that the correct diagnosis might have only come from the autopsy.

Gary showed Lenny the photo of the suspected medical student, Auginello had made copies. "We're all keeping our eyes out for this guy, he won't be getting near Doctor Austin, you can count on that."

"That's great," said Lenny. "But how long can we keep her here?"

Auginello told him the ICU Attending was okay holding Austin in the ICU for a few days longer. Lenny walked down to the isolation room at the end of the unit and looked in. "She seems safe enough. But what's going to happen when she transfers to the ward? Or goes home. Or back to work."

Gary followed Lenny's gaze into the isolation room. "You believe he's going to keep on trying until he kills her, don't you?"

Lenny nodded his head.

"Well then," the nurse continued. "Why don't we let him try?"

Auginello opened his mouth to object, then realized where Gary was going. "A trap. That idea sounds good in a TV police show, but I don't want to put her in danger. Not even in an environment like this."

Gary suggested we put the proposal to the patient, adding, "She won't really be in danger, doctor: she won't even be in the room."

Entering the isolation room, Auginello told Austin that they believed they have identified the perpetrator, but at that point the police had no evidence that would justify an arrest. "I'm worried the bastard is going to keep on trying to harm you, Rachel, in the hospital, your office, your home: anywhere you might be vulnerable. So Gary thought the best scenario would be to wait for him to try to harm you in a controlled environment, where the police could apprehend him in the act."

"That's an awfully dramatic proposal," said Austin. "You want *me* to be the bait? I don't think so."

Gary said, "No, Doctor Austin, you wouldn't be in the room, you would be safely settled in another bed." He explained, they would put one of the mannikins used for CPR classes in the bed. They would hook the EKG training machine up to the monitor so it looked like she was being monitored, and they would put a wig on the mannikin that looked like her hair.

"We keep the lights low and wait. Some time during the midnight shift he's likely to come in, and when he does, we'll have security waiting."

"I can get IT to set up a monitor screen in the on-call room," Lenny added. "That's where security will be waiting."

"And you will be transferred to a single room under a different name, safe and sound," Auginello added.

"The police will be involved in this, won't they?" asked Austin. Lenny assured her he would make sure Detective Williams was there every step of the way.

"I like it. Let's do it."

Auginello had a last doubt. "What if someone sees Doctor Austin being transferred out of the unit? If he got word somehow..."

"No worries," Lenny said, "I can guarantee nobody will see her leaving the ICU or in the hallway."

Ignoring the puzzled look on Auginello's face, Lenny winked at Austin and left the isolation room to go to the nursing station. He called Regis Devoe in the Pathology Department. "Re'ege, Lenny. Can you bring the morgue cart up to the ICU? What? No, nobody's died, it's for a little project of mine, I'll explain when you get here."

Hanging up, he went to inform Austin she would be riding to her new room in the covered morgue stretcher, no one would see her face. Auginello smiled at the news and went to talk to the Admitting clerk to arrange for the transfer under a pseudonym, but Austin's face betrayed a look of doubt. "It won't smell, will it? The cart, I mean."

"No worries," said Lenny. "They scrub it down with a bleach solution after every body is transported."

44

At home, Lenny told Patience about the latest developments in the Austin case and that Detective Williams was on his way over. Then he told her how he and Ali had found the transponder hidden in the ceiling of the sewing room.

"What a dirty bastard," Patience said, crossing her arms. "You going to use it against him?"

"Damn right. I'm going to represent her at the hearing." She reminded him it was always a good plan to bring a crowd to a hearing and offered to spread the word among the nurses she knew when she made her rounds shooting portable x-rays. "I'll ask Carlton to help spread the word, too, he goes everywhere delivering supplies."

"Good idea," said Lenny. "You need help with dinner?" She declined the offer but reminded him he had to do the dishes. All of them. "I don't like dirty dishes sitting in the sink all night, they smell up the kitchen." He promised to leave the kitchen squeaky clean.

The doorbell rang. It was Detective Williams. When Lenny told him of the plan to entrap the suspect, "Are you shitting me?" were the first words out of the detective's mouth. "How many times have I warned you, Moss, *don't play detective*. You have no authority to set up any kind of scheme."

Lenny pointed out the police wouldn't even know there was a criminal stalking Austin if he hadn't alerted Auginello. And he had found out about the doctor impersonator who visited the Family Practice offices.

"That doesn't mean jack, I found the same damn thing when I interviewed the secretary."

"Well, have you got a better idea? Have you even found what happened to the guy after he was kicked out of med school?"

Williams confessed they had not had any luck tracking down the suspect. It looked like he had changed his name. They were using facial recognition software to see if they could identify him on a current driver's license, but that was a slow process that would take some time.

"How long?" asked Lenny.

"No way to tell. A day, a week..."

"Screw the software. You can't leave Doctor Austin in danger for god knows how long. My plan is the best chance of stopping the bastard before he finishes what he started. You know it, I know it, Austin knows it."

Lenny went for a bottle of Evan Williams and glasses. He poured them both a healthy amount, added a few ice cubes and handed a drink to the Detective. Clinking their glasses, Lenny tried to get a read on the man's face. He could see Williams was troubled by the uncertainty of identifying the suspect. The entrapment plan was a good one. More to the point, it was the only one they had.

"All right," Williams said, putting down his glass, "I'll go this far, and *no farther*. I'll agree to moving Doctor Austin to another room under a fake name for her safety, that much is cut and dried. But posting an officer all night in the hospital, I'm not sure my Captain will go for it." Lenny opened his mouth to object, but Williams cut him off: "I'll make the case, trust me on that, we'll just have to see if he goes for it."

"Fair enough," said Lenny. He didn't tell the detective that even without a police officer keeping vigil, he had his own support team who would keep watch during the long night: the graveyard shift. But this time it was the creep who was going to get buried.

***

When Roy had looked over the Seven-South patient notes on the computer in the Medical School library, he noted that

Mimi Rogers was not working today. That meant she was off duty, he would have to wait for another day to follow her from work. Except...

He recalled that James Madison had a monthly newsletter. It was all bullshit news about new programs, people retiring blah, blah, blah, but it might have a searchable database. He found the newsletter on line and entered Mimi's name in the search option. She didn't show up until his fifth issue, but there she was, taking an advanced course on bereavement or some other dumb program.

The article didn't say much about her personally, but it did offer one piece that was promising: she was active in her church, including singing in the choir. With the name of the church, Roy realized he could watch for her attending the Sunday service, then follow her home. The more he could learn about her, the easier it would be to surprise her in some quiet out-of-the-way place.

He reached his hand into his lab coat pocket and felt the reassuring touch of the syringe. It had been so easy to put on the mask, surgical cap and surgical gowns, step into one of the operating rooms and help himself to vials of anesthetic. The syringe in his left pocket contained propofol, which would render the recipient unconscious in ten seconds. The other was a paralytic, which would block the nerve impulses that triggered breathing.

Ordinarily the anesthesiologist put the patient asleep before paralyzing him, since being unable to breathe was a terrifying experience. But for the annoying little nurse, Roy decided to paralyze her first and watch the fear overcome her as her lungs ceased to supply oxygen to the blood.

It was Thursday evening. If the woman was off today she was bound to be back on Friday, or the weekend at the latest. If he planned it perfectly, he could even kill two birds with one stone.

***

After giving report to the night nurse, including an explanation of the fake patient in the isolation room, Gary wheeled the old morgue cart into Austin's room. As he lifted off the canvas top which concealed the body that would take its last ride on the stainless steel stretcher, Austin tied her nightgown around her. Gary lowered the head of the bed and pushed the stretcher alongside.

"Gary, this is the craziest thing I've ever done." She reached her hand over to grab the edge of the stretcher. "God, this thing feels cold." Shifting her body across, she laid back on the platform. "What, no pillow?"

"Nobody's ever asked for one before," the nurse said with a wry smile. He placed a pillow beneath her head. "You don't have to cross your arms across your chest if you don't want to."

"That's not funny, Gary."

He lowered the canvas top and snapped it into place. "If it starts to feel stuffy, tap on the stretcher three times. You don't want to scare anyone with your voice."

He pushed the stretcher out of the room and wheeled it to the exit. With a whoosh the double doors sprang open and he was out in the corridor.

"Where are you taking me?" Austin asked from beneath the canvas.

"Seven-South, but you really should keep quiet."

"Thank god, it's Lenny's ward." Austin settled back in her dark hideaway, feeling confident for the first time that she would be safe and this long nightmare would soon be over.

45

"Gin."

"Again? I don't effing believe it." Moose laid down his cards, admitting defeat. Sandy added up his points and entered them in the score he'd been keeping. The old guard chuckled as he gathered together the cards and began to shuffle them.

"You got a marked deck?" Moose asked.

"In your dreams."

Sandy was dealing another hand when his cell phone went off. It was Lenny, checking on their status. Sandy told him yes, they had a good video feed of the isolation room. The mannikin looked real enough, given the low lighting and the EKG monitor displaying above the bed.

"You have plenty of coffee and food?" Sandy assured him they were set for the night. "No police, yet?"

The police had not sent anyone to help keep guard. Lenny cursed. He had faith that Moose and Sandy could call more security guards in STAT, apprehend the suspect and hold him until the police arrived. But there was always the chance the lunatic would be carrying a weapon: a scalpel, that would be a good guess, or a syringe with another kind of poison. Lenny wanted the police in the hospital ready to take charge.

"Maybe I should join you guys," he said, but Patience was nearby and overheard him. She told him he couldn't go to every person who was in trouble, he had to let others carry their weight sometimes. Much as he knew she was right, Lenny still grumbled. But he had to work in the morning, Moose and Sandy were off, so they could catch up on their sleep.

With a long sigh he agreed to stay home and wait. "My cell phone will be by the bed, wake me up if the bastard shows his face."

Sandy promised to call and returned to his game, while the nurse "assigned" to the fake Austin's care went into the room and hung an intravenous solution. Gary had suggested they do everything to make it look like a real person was in the bed.

***

Restless and unhappy he wasn't at the hospital with his friends, Lenny decided to call Mimi to let her know about his discovery of the clandestine transponder in the sewing room ceiling. When she told him she was working the 7pm-7am shift at the nursing home, he was relieved that she had found work so quickly.

"Yeah, it was a big relief. When I told the agency woman about how I was suspended, she was all for the union."

Lenny told her he was happy Mimi had found work so soon. Although he thought she had a good chance of being reinstated, the union's complaint to the National Labor Relations Board could take months to resolve.

"Months, Lenny? Really that long?"

"Actually, I have a plan to get you back way sooner." He told her how he and Ali had found the new transponder hidden in the sewing room ceiling. "The dispatcher was listening to you the whole time, the bastard."

"Lord have mercy, how can they *do* that? How can they be so totally evil?"

"It's all Joe West's work. I talked to Dave Rambling, the union labor lawyer, and Rambling agreed to threaten a lawsuit over the hospital's spying on you. He's also threatening to hold a big press release about the scurrilous tactics. Our hope is the hospital won't want the bad publicity and will take you back."

"That's great news, Lenny! You're the answer to my prayers!"

"I don't know about that, we're just doing what unions do: fight back."

After asking Lenny to thank the union lawyer for her, Mimi asked if he had any news on Doctor Austin. He told her she was making a good recovery and that they had moved her to a room on their ward under a fake name.

"That's a great idea, Lenny, changing her name. But how come the police haven't found the person who was impersonating a doctor?"

He told her they had the name of a medical student who had been expelled years ago due to a complaint Austin had filed, but the person seemed to have fallen off the face of the earth, there was no record of him shortly after he left school.

"He's obviously somewhere in the Philly area," Lenny added. "We just don't know who or where he is. My theory is he works in a hospital or a lab, because he has access to microbiology cultures."

"God, what a devil. I wish I was on Seven-South, I'd sure keep my eyes out for somebody like that." Lenny told her about the mannikin made up to look like Dr. Austin and how they were hoping to catch the perpetrator going into the ICU.

Admitting he was bone tired, Lenny promised to keep Mimi informed of any new developments and said good-bye. He joined Patience in bed, who had headphones on, listening to an audio book.

"Good book?" he asked, slipping under the covers.

She pulled one of the headphone speakers away from her ear. "What did you say?"

"I said I love you to death and I'm going to sleep."

"I love you, too." She settled the headphones back on and sat back in bed as Lenny turned away from her and closed his eyes. He was snoring within seconds. Even over the audio book, he could hear him and thought, *I have GOT to make an appointment with ENT and have him tested for sleep apnea.* She turned up the volume and resumed the book.

***

Having tired of playing cards, Moose had his sketch book out and was drawing caricatures, his favorite subject, while Sandy paged through a magazine, periodically lifting his eyes to the monitor that showed the isolation room where the fake Austin was receiving care. The nurse assigned to the room had gone on dinner break and the other nurses were all busy with their patients.

Sandy suddenly sat forward and squinted at the screen. A white male in a lab coat was pushing one of the portable carts toward the isolation room. The cart had a computer screen and medications. Sandy could only see the back of the man's head.

"Moose, check this out. That's not the on-call resident, is it?"

Moose studied the figure on the screen. "Hell, no, the on-call guy is bigger. Heavier, too, and he's got a shaved head, this guy's got hair."

Moose asked if they should call security for backup. "Let's go check him out first," said Sandy.

Slipping quietly out of the on-call room, they silently approached the nursing station and watched to see if the individual went to the isolation room. The figure stopped between the room and the bed in the open bay beside it. He read something on the screen, then wrote something in a notebook.

The figure stepped to the isolation room and looked through the glass door. He stood a moment peering in. Before he could open the door, Sandy and Moose grabbed him by the arms and turned him around.

Checking the suspect's pockets for syringes or other potential weapons, Sandy demanded, "What's your business with Doctor Austin?"

"What? Excuse me, what's going on?" His voice shook as

he looked at the two men holding him.

Sandy pulled the ID badge from the suspect's lab coat. "It's not Baumann. It says, "Bradshaw." He ran his finger over the badge trying to determine if the photo had been replaced. "Looks genuine."

"Of course it's genuine, who do you think I am, anyway?"

"That's what we're trying to find out," said Sandy. "What are you doing going into that room at two o'clock in the morning?"

"You let go of me and I'll tell you." His arms released, Doctor Bradshaw explained that he was on the Neurology service and was following up on Dr. Austin's case. "She exhibited signs of damage to her frontal lobe from the period of profound hypoglycemia. I was reviewing the progress notes in her chart."

"In the middle of the night?"

"Yes, in the middle of the night. I'm on call tonight, so I'm making use of the time. All right?"

"Okay," said Sandy, "but don't go into her room."

Promising to not enter the room, the resident went to the nursing station, where he made a few more entries in his notebook, then closed the chart and left without a word.

Sandy and Moose realized they were hungry, so Moose went for food from the vending machines while Sandy remained, this time sitting at the nursing station where he could see everyone coming in face to face.

46

Lenny got to work early so he could stop at the ICU before starting his shift. He greeted Gary Tuttle and learned about the one incident that turned out to be a legitimate resident. Assured the fake Austin would remain in the ICU, he took the elevator to Seven-South, too bone-weary to climb the stairs, and checked in on the real Dr. Austin.

"Lenny, any news?" were her first words to him. He admitted the ruse had not yet drawn out the perpetrator, but so far Admissions was going along with leaving the ICU bed with a mannikin instead of a real patient.

"Why can't the police find this guy? He's obviously in Philly *somewhere.*"

"They're still comparing his student ID with Pennsylvania license photos, but that's a slow process, apparently."

"It's crazy! I'm in danger and they're looking at pictures."

"Well, at least we have his photo, security is watching for him, so's the staff in the ICU and here. If he tries to get near you, we'll stop him."

"I sure hope so, Lenny, I want to live to see my daughter grow up and have kids of her own." Austin said she was surprised the hospital would allow them to keep the mannikin in the ICU isolation room. "The Zika epidemic must finally be waning, All summer we've been fighting to get infected patients admitted to the ICU."

"Guess so," said Lenny. "The hospital won't keep the room empty forever, but you'll be discharged anyway."

He went to the housekeeping closet and began setting up for work, enjoying the pungent smell of bleach added to the soapy water in his bucket. Little Mary was already at work picking up trash liners the night custodian didn't get to.

***

The Nursing Director stared at the file on her desk. It was so loathsome to her, she didn't want to touch it. Looking up at Joe West, she snarled, "This is *your* fault, West. If you hadn't hidden that transponder inside the ceiling, we'd be on firmer ground."

"The hospital is entitled to place the devices anywhere in the hospital we choose. There's no violation of any law. Besides, the nurses aren't covered by a union contract, they've got no basis for the complaint."

Mr. Freely from Human Resources cleared his throat. Getting a word in when Burgess and West were arguing was always difficult. "Let me remind you, the nurses *are* engaged in a union campaign. That gives them protections under current labor law. They can make a strong prima facie case that hiding a transponder, and I stress the word *hiding*, in an area where nurses do not provide care is unjustified from a human resources standpoint."

"Don't take their side, Freely," snarled West.

"I'm not taking a side, I'm simply explaining the law. The employees have a right to know when they are in a public space and when they are in a private one. Wearing the GPS unit puts the nurse in a public space, but she has a right to know when her voice can be overheard and when it cannot. They have a strong case, and in the court of public opinion, we will look very, very badly." He advised Burgess to reinstate Mimi Rogers.

West pointed out to Burgess that if she did take the nurse back, the Head Nurse would be able to find lapses in her work performance, everyone made mistakes. "She won't last a month," he said.

Closing the file folder without touching the written complaint, Burgess nodded her agreement. "But she comes back on probation. And I won't pay her for the time lost!"

"Very well," said Freely. He rose and left to notify Mimi she could return on Saturday, the following day, but she would not be receiving retroactive pay for the time lost.

***

At home after her first midnight shift in the nursing home, Mimi gave Louis a peck on the cheek before he left for his new job delivering furniture. Too tired to make breakfast, she poured milk into a bowl and was adding cereal when her cell phone rang. She didn't recognize the caller.

"Hello?" she said.

"Missus Rogers, this is Desmond Freely from Human Resources. I hope I find you well."

"Uh, thank you, Mister Freely. What's going on?"

"The hospital has decided to reinstate you. You may return to work tomorrow, Saturday, for your usual shift. But I have to inform you, you will not be receiving retroactive pay for the time lost. You may use your accrued vacation time if you wish."

"I'm back? I'm really back to work?"

"Yes, you are back, but Miss Burgess will have you on probation for the first sixty days."

Mimi didn't care about the probation, she was so relieved to be going back to work. After thanking Freely for the call, she notified the agency she would not be working with them for now, thanking the director for having faith in her. Then she sent Louis and Lenny a text message with the news.

Happy but exhausted, she stripped off her uniform and climbed into bed. As she sank into a deep, welcome sleep, a thought on the periphery of her mind tickled her brain, but it was so far away, and she was so very tired, she couldn't make out what that thought was.

Sleep overcame her, and all her cares dissolved into dreamland.

47

Dr. Auginello signed off on the ID consult. He was happy it was a diabetic ulcer and not another Zika case. "Anything in the ER I need to know about?" he asked the ID Fellow. The Fellow reported no new cases of Zika over the last 48 hours.

"So the epidemic is finally waning," he said. "Thank the gods for that. The city's mosquito eradication program has turned the tide."

"Uh, sir," said the resident who was on his ID rotation. "I reviewed the literature about mosquitoes and how they are attracted by the smell of the breath on their host. There has not been a lot of research about masking it, at least in the US. I think we could apply for federal grant money."

Auginello poked his tongue in his cheek and considered the idea. After a moment he said, "Have you ever written a grant proposal?"

"No, sir, I haven't."

"Well, our office manager has experience with that. You can talk to her and write up a proposal, I'll review it before she submits it to the CDC."

"That's great, thank you, Doctor!" said the Resident. "Uh, and when the paper is written summarizing our results, will my name be on that as well?"

"Yes, Gerald, your name will be on the paper. But...I want the name of the fellow who first came up with the idea on it, too."

"Of course. That would be a doctor..."

"His name is Carlton. I'll get his full name and affiliation for you when the time comes."

Auginello led his team on to the next patient, to Seven-South, where he smiled to imagine the look on Lenny's face when he asked for Carlton's full name and job title to go on a medical research paper.

***

When Lenny saw the text from Mimi he could barely contain his happiness. The threat had worked, Burgess had folded. He sent a message to Dave Rambling, asking him to forward it to the nursing organizer for the union. Mimi's firing had sent a chill over the union drive and Lenny was hoping the victory would help lessen the fear that had spread among the nurses.

He rolled out the buffing machine and attacked the old marble floor. The rhythm of the machine always relaxed him and helped him think.

Detective Williams still hadn't traced the missing medical student. Lenny suggested the police concentrate on people in medical jobs, but that hadn't borne fruit, either. For once he was stumped for a strategy to move the investigation forward.

Seeing Auginello and his team coming down the hall, Lenny switched off the buffer and greeted his friend. Auginello explained that his department was going to apply for a research grant on the idea Lenny had told him about, and he wanted Carlton's full name and job title.

"You're kidding. You want Carlton in on the research?"

"Not on the research per se. But it was his idea, it's only fair his name go on any paper that comes from the research."

"Holy crap, one of his crazy ideas is actually going somewhere. He's gonna flip out." Lenny gave the doctor the information about his co-worker. When the resident learned that Carlton worked in the Central Stores and had no medical or even college training, he was dumbfounded, but Auginello reminded the young man that many an important medical breakthrough came from amateur scientists. "Remember the Royal Society of London? They were amateurs for the most part." The resident was not in a position to argue, so he kept his mouth shut.

The ID Attending told Lenny he didn't think he could keep up the fake patient in the ICU isolation room much longer. While the Zika epidemic was winding down, there were plenty of other infectious cases who needed the room. Lenny suggested they transfer the fake patient to a room on a ward, but Auginello pointed out it would be a lot more difficult to monitor visitors, the isolation room in the ICU was ideally suited to laying a trap.

"One more day," said Lenny. "Can you get me one more day?"

Auginello promised to try, then he led his team in to Austin's room, closed the door for privacy, and listened to the Fellow's report.

***

After delivering a new admission to James Madison through the ER, Roy told his partner he needed time for a coffee. Finding one of the rolling computer stations unoccupied, he pushed it into a bay, pulled the curtain and logged in with the stolen password. He called up the Seven-South census and quickly scanned the medication administration report. Mimi's initials and signature were not there. He checked three more patients scattered across the ward, but still no sign of her.

That meant with the extra days off due to the twelve-hour shifts, the nurse had to be working tomorrow, Saturday. That was good news, the weekends had less staff on duty, it would be easier for him to visit the ward without being noticed.

Joining his partner in the parking lot, she asked how was the coffee. "Hot and sweet, just how I like it," Roy said. He climbed up to the driver's seat. "Buckle up, partner, I have a feeling we're going to be running the siren today."

"Always the optimist, Roy. You have any plans for the weekend?"

"I haven't decided. Beach, lake or mountains."

"Geez, it must be great to have so many options."

"Life is all about choices, my dear, and never regretting a one of them."

48

Looking forward to a day of great adventure, Roy took his time dressing. His navy blue pants were fresh from the dry cleaners, his pale blue shirt and striped tie a perfect match. The lab coat, freshly laundered, was as white as a cloud on a perfect Spring morning. Even his hair was combed back straight with a touch of gel to keep it in place.

He attached the name tag to the lab coat, took one more look in the mirror, and opened the felt-lined box that held his prize weapons. Two 50 cc syringes, one with the paralytic agent, the other with the anesthetic. Either one would render his victim helpless, but it was the paralyzing agent he favored. By using that, he could watch the terror fill his victim's eyes as she struggled without success to breathe. The hypoxia would build up quickly in the blood and tissues, sending the brain frantic messages. A slow death was always the best, it was just a pity cannibalism was so out of fashion.

First, he would eliminate the nurse. The suffocation would likely trigger a heart attack, so that would be the coroner's report. Then, when Austin was in a regular room and vulnerable, he would administer a powerful anti-coagulant through her intravenous line. She would bleed out from every orifice, there would be no stopping the hemorrhaging.

Yes, a slow death from hemorrhagic shock: that was a fitting end for the wretched Rachel Austin. And what could be more fitting for a pre-menopausal woman? It was perfect. It was poetry.

It was revenge of the bloodiest kind.

***

Mimi looked over her notes from morning report with deep satisfaction. *What a miracle, to be back on the old ward,* she thought. True, the threat to her job wasn't over. Mimi had no illusions, she realized that Mother Burgess would be scrutinizing her every moment at work. Give out a medication five minutes past the "limit" and she would be called into the Head Nurse's office. Leave the ward without a proper justification, written up. It was going to make organizing the union more difficult, but she would just have to use her days off more efficiently, make more visits, have more coffee and cake with co-workers.

And what a blessing that she was assigned to "Elizabeth Bennett," the name Austin had requested for her illicit transfer. Mimi could keep an eye out for any suspicious character hanging around the ward.

With a sigh she rose and went to ask "Miss Bennett" if she wanted to wash up before they served breakfast. As she walked down the hallway to Austin's room, she had that nagging thought again on the periphery of her mind: what was her poor tired brain trying to tell her?

***

Roy sat at a computer station in the Medical School library and called up the patient census on Seven-South. Scanning the medication administration log, he was pleased to see that 'MR' had signed for an insulin injection and an antibiotic. Excellent, the woman was back on duty.

He looked at his watch: 8:30 am. No doubt the nurses would be taking their morning break by 10, 10:30. That would be an excellent time to visit the ward. If Miss Rogers was gone on break, he could watch for her return by the elevator. And if she was alone on the ward, all the better to follow her until she was in a quiet little corner: the medication room, for example, or the supply closet. There were so many private spaces in the hospital, any one of them would serve his purpose perfectly.

Patience was the prince of triumph. He had all day, there was no need to rush. He went to the Operating Room for a surgical cap, mask and gown, the better to see her without being recognized.

***

Austin was picking at her scrambled eggs, taking small forkfuls and hesitating before swallowing them.

"Dietary is monitoring your meals, Rachel, they really should be safe." Auginello tried to reassure his friend that nobody could be tampering with her food. "You're under an assumed name and your doppelganger is in the ICU waiting to be bludgeoned to death..."

"That's not funny, Michael."

"No, I suppose it isn't. I was just trying to lighten your mood."

"You can lighten my mood by finding the bastard who put me in the hospital in the first place! I can't believe how inept the police are. This is my *life* we're talking about."

Auginello promised to call the Detective and receive an update on the investigation. He admitted the ruse in the ICU would probably be ended, Surgery was calling for the ICU bed for a patient with a post-operative wound infection that was life-threatening.

"I knew that wouldn't last forever. When does Surgery take over the room?"

"The patient is in the OR for debridement. He'll go to recovery for a few hours, but then they'll need the bed."

"Jesus Christ. This is a nightmare I'm never going to wake up from."

"Be patient, Rachel, we have good people working on this."

Just then Mimi knocked and entered the room. "How's the

breakfast? Tolerating it okay, Miss Bennett?"

"She's still wary of the food," said Auginello.

"I can't say I blame her, given all the poison she's swallowed. I don't want to have to take her down to the ER again in a wheelchair. I—"

Mimi stopped in mid-sentence. Her mention of the ER had suddenly loosened the vague thought that had been flitting around in her mind.

The ER.

She had seen that smart young resident on the ward, and then saw him in the ER working as an EMT. At the time she figured he was a hard-working med student who was working his way through school, but now...

"Doctor Auginello, do you have a picture of the medical student who was kicked out of the program for Doctor Austin's complaint about him?"

He showed her a copy on his cell phone.

"Holy mother of god, I saw that guy in the ER last week, he was working on one of the ambulances, he's a paramedic!"

"Damn," said Auginello. "Do you remember what service it was?"

"No, he was inside the ER, I didn't see what vehicle he was riding."

While Auginello called Detective Williams to notify him of the new information, Mimi called Lenny and told him how she identified the photo of the dismissed medical student as the same person she saw in an EMT uniform *and* a medical student outfit on the ward.

Lenny was heartened by the news. "This is great, Mimi, it won't take long for the police to check on all the EMT's in the city. They'll have him arrested today, I'm sure of it."

"I sure hope so, Lenny, for Doctor Austin's sake, I hope to god they catch him."

***

Lenny was setting out his painting tools, ready to spend another afternoon with the block club painting porches. He felt the bristles of an old brush, thought it would just do, when he thought about what a lucky break to hear from Mimi about how she spied the EMT who was also an apparent medical student. He *could* be a legitimate student who was working his way through school, but Mimi had identified the picture of the disgraced student as the EMT she saw in the ER. A paramedic job would be just the right place for a disgraced medical student, working under a new name, of course.

He stuffed his tools in an old canvas bag and was about to head for the designated house when a frightening thought struck him: Mimi had seen the suspicious EMT. Okay. Good. But what if the EMT had seen *her*? If he caught her staring at him, and if he'd seen her on the wards when he was in his medical school outfit, that could mean only one thing: Mimi was in as much danger as Austin, since she was the only one who could lead the police to him.

Throwing the bag of supplies on the porch, he called out to Patience he was driving to the hospital. "What's going on, Lenny?" she called back, hurrying to the front door.

"I think Mimi could be in danger. Call Detective Williams and have him meet me on Seven-South!"

Without waiting for an answer, he threw open the car door, fired up the big V-8 and pulled out into traffic. Green lights or red, he was not letting anything stop him.

49

Seeing Mimi enter the staff lounge, Roy silently opened the door and looked in. The room was empty, the door to the toilet, closed. Quietly entering, he stepped to the bathroom door, put his ear to it and listened. He heard a rustling and the sound of the toilet flushing. That was his cue.

He pulled the syringe with the paralytic from his lab coat pocket, pulled the cap off the needle, and held it above his head, ready to strike.

The sound of water running told him Mimi was washing her hands. Such a good nurse. So conscientious. It was appropriate she would die with such clean hands.

***

Lenny stepped out of the elevator and hurried toward his ward. Reaching the nursing station, he looked back into the medication room. Empty. The cart was in the room, so she wasn't likely to be in a room passing out meds.

A second cart was half way down the hall. Hurrying to it, he saw Mimi's partner Josephine hanging an intravenous medication. "Josie, where's Mimi?"

"Hi, Lenny. Isn't she at the nursing station?"

"No, I was just there."

"She didn't say anything about leaving the ward. Try the staff lounge, she's probably in the loo."

"Okay, thanks."

As he started down the long hall, Josephine called out to him, "Is everything all right?" He didn't answer, he needed to find Mimi before that bastard did.

***

As Mimi opened the bathroom door and took a step out, she gasped in surprise: Roy was standing in front of her. Her eyes locked on his for a second, then she spied the syringe in his hand. Putting up both hands in a defensive posture, she begged him, "Please, don't...please."

She felt the syringe plunge into her neck. The shock stunned her. She felt nauseous and faint. Her knees buckled as Roy pulled the needle out of her neck, the syringe now empty.

Mimi looked up into the cold, cruel eyes. They gripped her heart with fear. She said a prayer to Jesus, asking him to reach out and help her in her hour of need.

With her eyes focused on Roy, Mimi didn't see the door to the lounge open and Lenny burst into the room. But when Roy turned to face him, she could see Lenny, and she could see he had murder in his eyes.

Roy reached into his lab coat and pulled out a second syringe. He took the cap to the needle between his teeth and pulled it off. The needle was a long and lethal one: a spinal needle. Roy crouched, holding the syringe in front of him in a fighter's stance. Lenny put his hands up in defense, not sure how best to protect himself from the ugly needle.

"Give it up, asshole, the cops are on the way."

"Oh, yeah? I don't see any police. You see any police? You hear any sirens?"

Lenny backed up, but Roy still closed the distance between them. He jabbed with the needle, making Lenny duck and weave.

"You're going to take a nice long nap, my friend. You're going to sleep for eternity."

As Roy raised the syringe preparing to strike, Mimi plunged her nursing scissors deep into his neck. Though she was weak from the drug diffusing into her blood stream circulating to her brain, her anger at Roy and her fear for Lenny's safety had triggered a surge of adrenalin. With the last of her strength she had risen to her feet, pulled the scissors from her pocket and raised it above her head.

Roy looked back at Mimi, shocked by the attack. His plan had been so perfect, how could it go so wrong? He sank to his knees, one hand reaching to his neck to staunch the flow of blood that was pouring from his neck.

"Carotid...artery..." he gasped. "Help me."

"You can suffer like Jesus at Calvary for all I care, you bastard." Mimi sank to her knees. Her vision was growing faint, her muscles becoming like putty. She fell forward just as Lenny reached her. Cradling her in his arms, he yelled at the top of his voice, "I NEED HELP IN THE STAFF LOUNGE! HELP ME, PLEASE!"

Seconds later the nurse flew into the room, followed by a barefoot Dr. Austin.

"He injected her with something," Lenny said.

Austin felt for a pulse, which was rapid and thready. Placing two fingers lightly on Mimi's chest, she saw the woman wasn't breathing. She opened the stricken woman's mouth, pinched her nose and pressed her mouth to hers, blowing in a precious lungful of air.

"Call a code," Austin told the nurse. "And call the OR, tell them to bring up a reversing agent for a paralytic. Tell them STAT, it's for staff."

The nurse rushed out of the room while Austin continued giving mouth-to-mouth resuscitation. Between breaths she instructed Lenny to monitor Mimi's pulse. He gingerly felt at the wrist until he found the pulse.

"Okay, I feel it."

"Good. Let me know if there's a sudden change."

With Lenny feeling the pulse and Austin administering life-saving breaths, they waited together in the little room for the Code Team with the reversing agent to arrive.

50

Louis approached his wife at the kitchen counter and put his arms around her and baby Lilly, snuggled in her papoose. "I can't believe how you can make spaghetti and meatballs with the baby in the wrap."

"Oh, it's not so hard. I'm so used to her curled up on my chest, she doesn't get in the way. I'm gonna miss her when it's time to lay her in the crib."

He kissed her cheek, then pulled the papoose open enough to see the baby. Lilly was sleeping, her head between Catherine's breasts. "I think the lactation nurse was right, hearing your heartbeat and your breathing, it's just like when she was in the womb. It's gotta be a comfort."

"Mmm, yes, I know it is."

Louis set the table. "Glass of wine?" he asked.

"Half."

He poured her drink and set it beside the plate. The wine was a deep burgundy with a nice bouquet. "I was wondering something, babe."

"Oh, what?"

"When you pump your milk, when Lilly's older and all, and I get to feed her with the bottle, do you think I could carry her awhile in the wrap like you do?"

Catherine turned and smiled at her husband. "Sure you can."

***

Mimi raised her glass and gently tapped Lenny's, then everyone at the table shared a clink and a "Cheers!" With food ordered, everyone was ready to unwind in The Cave after too many stress-filled days.

"Would you really have let the bastard bleed to death, Mimi?" Lenny asked. He had worked alongside the nurse for years and never imagined she could be so cold-blooded.

"Sure I would, he tried to kill Doctor Austin! Hells bells, he tried to kill *me*, why should I render first aid to a creep like that?"

"Good for you," said Patience. She poked her husband in the chest. "Seems to me you've administered street justice more than once in your time, Lenny. So why are you surprised Mimi would do the same, 'cause she's a *woman*?"

"No, because she's a nurse. Nurses are compassionate."

"I've got no compassion for that man, he's pure evil," Mimi said.

Moose agreed, letting Roy bleed to death would have been okay with him. But when the doctors and nurses were trying to save Mimi's life, she wasn't breathing from the paralyzing drug, they couldn't ignore the guy bleeding out right in the same room.

Lenny reported that the police had searched Roy's apartment and found his laboratory equipment, complete with incubators and samples of bacteria. There were vials of insulin and other drugs as well. "After going after Mimi he was bound to attack Austin again. She never would have been safe."

When the appetizers arrived, Lenny complained again that Patience had ordered charred brussels sprouts, but the others shouted him down. "They're good for you!" Birdie reminded him. "You can't eat fried chicken and cheesesteaks all the time."

Lenny grumbled and passed on the sprouts, eating some French fries instead. "I hear the Zika outbreak is finally turning around."

"That's what Doctor Auginello says. People listened to the DOH and cleaned up their yards, got rid of the standing water, that made the difference."

"I thought it was all the bug spray Patience sprayed on me and the kids." He told his friends about Carlton's idea about masking a person's breath to stop the mosquitoes from finding their victims. "He's had some goofy ideas in the past, but this one might really pan out. Go figure."

"You should be protected already," said Regis, "That cheap bourbon you drink will scare off all kinds of bugs."

"Har, har." Lenny sipped his drink and didn't comment, although he could have pointed out that Regis never turned down a drink when he was over to their house.

After a few moments of quiet and reflection, Mimi said, "It's a shame about the nurses taking back their pledge cards. I was so sure they would join your union, Lenny."

"Two unions in the house divides us, it's what the bosses want," he said.

"A nursing union's better than no union at all, don't you think?" said Regis. "I mean, we can still work together."

"But they'll have a no strike clause in their contract, so they won't be able to honor our picket lines," Moose reminded him.

"I talked to the UNP organizer," said Mimi. "I told her before I signed a pledge card for their union I wanted to know if they would support the service workers union. She said they would set up a joint committee and find ways to work together, so it might not be a total loss after all."

"You signed with them?" asked Patience.

"Yes. So many nurses called me and asked me to tear up the cards they signed, I knew we didn't have the support." She turned to Lenny. "I guess we lost, didn't we?"

He replied, "We didn't lose, we just didn't win." Raising a glass, Lenny turned to Regis. "Let's raise a glass for Regis Devoe, starting college in the Fall for pathology tech!"

"Right on!" said Moose, raising his glass. "You found the right place to work, that's for sure."

"I know working on cadavers and organs isn't for everybody," said Regis. "But it's not scary, least not for me. Doc Fingers likes my work, and the dead've got nothing to complain about..."

"Let's drink to the living," said Mimi. "And all the workers in the hospital who deserve respect!"

"To the workers!"

ABOUT THE AUTHOR

Veteran nurse Timothy Sheard is a writer, publisher, mentor to writers and union organizer with the National Writers Union, UAW Local 1981. After writing several mystery novels featuring hospital custodian-shop steward Lenny Moss, he launched Hard Ball Press to help working class people write and publish their stories and has published over 200 authors.

Timothy believes that when workers write and tell their stories, they build rank and file solidarity and union power, and they advance the fight for social justice. Their stories help to combat the anti-labor and anti-working class assaults by the One Percent, allowing the reader to walk in the worker's shoes, face the challenges, and find joy in the victories. Hard Ball Press is proud to publish books about working class life.

ACKNOWLEDGEMENTS

The author is deeply grateful to Larry Christensen for his thoughtful and diligent criticism and copy edits, and to Eve Faber for her thoughtful critique of the manuscript.

A special thanks to David "Q" Bass for his patience as I struggled with the novel and finally delivered an edited copy ready to print.

TITLES FROM HARD BALL PRESS

CHILDREN'S BOOKS from HARD BALL PRESS

Joelito's Big Decision, La gran Decisión de Joelito:
Ann Berlak (Author), Daniel Camacho (Illustrator),
José Antonio Galloso (Translator)
Manny and the Mango Tree, Many y el Árbol de Mango:
Alí R. and Valerie Bustamante (Authors), Monica Lunot-Kuker (Illustrator). Mauricio Niebla (Translator)
The Cabbage That Came Back, El Repollo que Volvió
Stephen Pearl & Rafael Pearl (Authors), Rafael Pearl (Illustrator), Sara Pearl (Translator)
Hats Off For Gabbie, ¡Aplausos para Gaby!:
Marivir Montebon (Author), Yana Murashko (Illustrator),
Mauricio Niebla (Translator)
Margarito's Forest/El Bosque de Don Margarito:
Andy Carter (Author), Alison Havens (Illustrator), Sergio
Villatoro (Graphic Design),
Artwork contributions by the children of the Saq Ja' elementary school
K'iche tranlations by Eduardo Elas and Manuel Hernandez
Translated by Omar Mejia
Jimmy's Carwash Adventure, La Aventura de Jaime en el Autolavado:
Victor Narro (Author), Yana Murashko (Illustrator), Madelin
Arroyo (Translator)
Good Guy Jake/Buen Chico Jake,
Mark Torres (author), Yana Murashko (illustrator), Madelin
Arroyo (translator)
Polar Bear Pete's Ice Is Melting!
Timothy Sheard (author), Kayla Fils-Amie (illustrator),
Madelin Arroyo (translator)

HOW TO ORDER BOOKS:
Order books from www.hardballpress.com, Amazon.com,
or independent booksellers everywhere.
Receive a 20% discount for orders of 10 or more, a 40% discount for orders of 50 or more when ordering from www.hardballpress.com.